**Author: Josephine Wrightson**

Cover & formatting by: Sharon Brownlie, www.aspirebookcovers.com

# *Dedication*

My husband…whom loves and supports me always.
Who sits and listens whilst I question him, quietly
offering his opinions.

Love you always.

And the readers too who without you this one
wouldn't have names…

Thank you all.

# *Prologue.*

Are all as we see them? Probably not. Some have hidden secrets and lies. And a darkened heart about them which never leaves.

Is man just that…man? Not in all ways some have nothing more than the dark hearts of beasts. Yet then the beasts! Are they the same? What do you see in them? No, some beasts have the goodness of heart and minds that man could learn from.

Some men are nothing more than mere beasts and some beasts have more than the hearts of man.

# Chapter one

Every ten years or so one was delivered; deliberately sacrificed to the beast left waiting for when he came down from the mountain tops. No one now knew where he had originated; time had blurred everything. It was just something they continued to do; believed that it had to be done. Nor in actual reality knew for sure if he even existed or ever had. If they'd put some thought into it; in all fairness when the sacrifice was given, left drugged in the farthest darkest part of the forest; screams were not easy to forget and none wanted to own what they were party to. It could just have been coincidence and the animals of the forest which took the lives. For no one ever wanted to rush back; they were lucky if anyone returned within the month; death then was a major factor with no food or water and the animals would finish the rest; excitedly having their own little feast; each and every time. The forest had always been a dangerous place.

By then common sense would say that all would be left was bone and sinew. The forest feasted well. It did not care.

It was believed it had begun to keep the village safe stop the beast from walking along their own streets. Screams were hard to un-hear.

But was that it? Or was it just an insatiable need for someone or something to remember what touch was? Or something again, even darker?

For once someone was willing to sacrifice herself; her life was nothing to many. If she wanted to die, then let her. That was what drifted through the village; heartless. Egged on by one; who knew the truth and more. But he was the only one. It was an easy decision for most; but not all… She did have some friends. But for the rest she was a constant reminder of their negligence and inabilities; or thought she was just a pure born liar… Which of course she wasn't, she carried the scars to prove it. Not that they cared.

And her? She only wanted to rest and leave what had become her nightmare. It had become hard to bear; her life. She hated the stares and the guilt weighed upon her head. But for her few constants she would give her life eagerly to save theirs. The only few who had stood by her. The years seemed like so much of an eternity. She felt so much older than her years. They needed what hers couldn't be, a good life.

Within the shadows he waited; the shadows which were his friend and life. For he was the beast that was real. Watching, uncaring of the life he was about to snuff. Not that ever was his intention. But inevitably he could no longer be tender and gentle. Empathy was not his to have any more. Eager just to touch clean female flesh and feel the things he remembered. The rise of his huge erection always inevitable; the beast was not all of him, he had been left just enough to realise what he missed. He was stuck, not entirely all his own fault; but it was his torment for eternity.

The beast was not all of him, and that which was still man could not partake of the other; the rutting of the beasts of the forest it had to be a woman. For that and for his almost forgotten words; he was a beast that talked; not that he had in a very long time. It was usually just gibberish and screaming; he listened too.

Kalista looked at the faces around her, all their indiscretions laid bare. It wasn't these she was willing to sacrifice herself for. She sniffed at them, disgusted. Knowing none of them were worth it and they knew it. None could look her in the eyes. But Kalista did not do it for them, she did it for the ones she loved, the ones who had believed her and helped when it had all inevitably blown up - as bad things always had a way of doing. Serena mostly; there had been many rumours that they would take her; she had little value and no profitable family to keep her from the choosing. Kalista's own treatment at the time by these awful cowards was despicable; and she had never forgotten nor forgiven. *I do not do this for you.*

But now she no longer cared. They were the ones left to live with this and all its horror. She would give them no respite from their torturous behaviour. She would not be forgiving anyone.

A bowl of some disgusting looking liquid was handed to her; thick and smelly. Kalista screwed her face up…

"No I will not be taking that." Shock washed through the keepers…

"You should!" He'd wanted her too. *But what the hell.*

"I said no! What more can be done to me that hasn't already been done?" There was nothing else to be said. Scolded eyes just walked away from her. They did not care at all. *So be it.*

Staring, his blood red eyes missed nothing. He watched as the others walked away; but something about them this time was different. Uncaring, there was no wailing, no weeping. Definitely no sorrow. *Hmm.* He watched, she was the littlest female he'd seen but then he hadn't seen a female in a long time… his body knew. There was no waiting for him this day. It was done. The years came and went so slowly but he knew it could only end in death each time he did this; so limited himself. Empathy; not that he believed in it. He saw the curvy female walk; her dress seemed to be a colour in the night it was hard to distinguish usually they came in the stupid virginal white. This seemed to be some sort of rose pink. Plain with long sleeves and bindings at the chest. Tightly bound. He knew what heaved beneath there. A grumble rattled in his chest driving downwards to settle in his loins. Already eager to finish the intent powerfully ingrained in him. With her little torch held tightly she leaned against a tree to drop herself to the ground; to sit and wait. His furred eyebrows once refined and striking furrowed. *This is different. She does not look drugged.* But he could smell her fear… acrid and buoyant. Hanging around them both. But it wasn't portrayed in her demeanour. She was different. *Very.*

Where he would normally charge out snarling and eager to embed himself in the females flesh. The waiting grown too great. His terrifying erection demanding release; always fully displayed. He had discarded clothes long ago. *What was the point?* He waited years each time for this. His insanity yet sanity, he had to have it. But this beast would not be fulfilled without force biting even shredding all they were. Suddenly something in him shifted… *Do I pity her? No… I will have her.*

He just watched. Unknowing of how long he stood for. Wanting to know what she would do… His heavy breathing was dismissed by the wind rustling through the trees. They had grown so close together hardly any light got through, just the odd ray. Not that it mattered it was always night for this. Dense and dark, the forest was mostly his kin. Within its hidden depths that none would enter gave him some respite and peace away from those that would call him monster; beast, but that was what he had become. Beast. He'd watched as all their torches left disappearing into the distant fog. Just her own little glow left. No noise, nothing. Until, eventually without moving, he spoke with his long unused voice; words barely more than a deep growl. His curiosity rising.

"Why do you just sit girl?" Kalista startled at the noise; almost formed words, but ones she did understand. Spun her head looking for where the voice came from. But it was too dark for her. Words she hadn't been expecting, growled and harsh but still words. Lifting the torch carefully it was her only source of comfort she didn't want to distrust it. Her heart racing in fear she needed to be sure her voice did not waver. She would show her fear to no one again. With defined deliberate effort she finally spoke.

"What else should I do?"

"Be afraid!"

"What makes you think I am not?"

"I know you are! I smell it. I cannot be fooled."

"So? Who said I was trying to fool? Should I do as you expect and wither and wail with fear?" She swallowed. "That I cannot do." He guffed at her, almost a laugh. She not only pulled at his ferocious need but his intelligence too. He had almost forgotten he could converse. This was more than satisfaction and searing flesh.

"You know what is to come?"

"Yes." She seemed to stare harder trying to see him. Death was what she was here for. Whether he would eat her; abuse her, she knew it meant death.

"But you do not run?" He smelled the air loudly; sensing more than her fear now, Kalista heard, his growling breath was noisy. *My God what is he?* Her thoughts did betray her fear. "But you are not drugged!"

"No."

"Why not?" *This will take your breath before you can draw it. You should have...* But did he want just another drugged vessel?

"Because." *Why?* Her answer was long and complicated; mostly because she was sick of living, had suffered more than he knew and maybe just maybe she could welcome death. Not so much the pain and degradation but to keep them all safe who had stood by her they deserved more… Serena had a good life to look forward to with Jack. She wanted to keep them safe. Not all but some that she cared about she would gratefully lay down her life; for what it was worth, too many times she'd been led to believe she was worthless. It had stuck. "That is a long and complicated answer."

"Tell me!" *Why would he want to know? It wasn't going to make any difference!*

"I do not know wether I can." He snarled again.

"Try."

"Because… I.. Pain I would wish to avoid." She thought just to drop that in. This time the air filled with his growled laughter. He had forgotten how to do any of this other than with growls. So he thought. "But death would be a welcome respite." That he truly wasn't expecting; all noise stopped, all Kalista could hear was his heavy breath.

"Yes it would." Taking her scent to him fully. He wanted to know her; know her story. *What had they sent him?* He abruptly stepped from the shadows. Upright stood as a man but not so. His clawed feet thumped into the ground.

Kalista gasped loudly automatically pushing her small frame back against the tree till she could go no further. Escape girl; was all he conscious being told her; screamed at her to do. But she didn't Kalista stayed put. This was her fate now. But words left. She just stared open mouthed.

He stood before her; the huge thing he had become covered in thick black fur; as dark as night. His features impossible to make out in the darkness just a mass of dark fur with sharp white teeth. His eyes flame red; eyes that glared down at her reaction. She studied them; something flashed in them, were there tears in there… *No. There can't be! Could there?* Kalista swallowing down some of her fear looked harder his eyes the depth of anguish. Hiding so much emotion. *Aaa so what is your story? You have one I see it.* She knew what pain; real pain looked like.

Trying to control her fear Kalista lifted the little torch; her only sense of comfort, being so very careful with it she didn't need it extinguished. But having done so what drew her attention and pulled even more fear from her was the huge thing protruding from between his legs. Unclothed; it could have almost been human, apart from its size. Managing to drag her eyes from it she saw a smirk cross his face; white teeth protruding. That was what she was there for! Her stomach lunged; again. *And you want to... Use that thing on me.* She knew why she was there; exactly what this beast wanted. One thing there was though which was a bonus… *At least he is flesh and blood... Not.* Kalista shut her thoughts down fast. They weren't for now. *God no. The last thing I need is a panic attack.*

"You do not fear death but you should fear me." The beast moved his head and smelt the air around her. He knew what that scent meant… *what had they sent him? Who had they sent him?* He glared done at her his eyes burning even brighter. *No matter she would still have the right bits in the right places!*

Kalista tried to put her thoughts back into some sort of order he was getting so close. Fear wasn't her friend right now. Knowing she had to be firm and quick. More wits than feminine wiles. He hissed and bent down to her… intimidatingly.

"You are no virgin!"

"And you were a man once." That erection aiming in her direction was no animals.

The beast stopped short of getting closer; shocked that she saw that. It had been a long time since anyone had thought he was man. Calmly now watching her. Before pulling himself back up to his full height. *Hmm. This isn't going as before.* By now the others had already been stripped and embedded by him. The witches curse making him need before any sense of mortality; or morality. He had never seen them as anything other than empty vessels. But her this one snapping back at him in fear; for it was fear not confidence but fear. Was compelling him to be more than the beast he'd been cursed to be. But the need was still there; he had to get it over and done with other wise he would burst and the burning need he'd been cursed with would override him and the rutting animals of the forest would be his only route and then that would be it for him; his speech his thought everything that made him remember if only a little, would be gone; the curse and the beast would take him in his entirety; and there would be no going back. He would be beast. He had become a killer by way of trying to save himself from that. Unwittingly his beast usually taking over at this point; but the beast would do it so much more, he needed the man in him to reign it in and one each decade to save the many was how he resigned himself to the awfulness which he reigned on them. Just for one end, his own need. Which had been cursed above all else.

His beast began to rage within him. But this time felt so very different and right now conversation was as equal as the act he'd been all set to rage into her. Slowly with as much dignity she could muster Kalista raised herself from the floor still holding onto her torch its glow holding very little light. But did she really want to see all of him? *No.* The dark was more her friend right now than the light.

Breathing heavily Kalista finally found her voice; standing before him she hardly reached his chest. Strong round muscles rippled beneath the fur. *You were a man! Why this?* Curiosity crept into her fear. *Why not?* She could just ask? What had she to lose? Her life! As far as she could see that had already gone.

Should have…

Would have…

Could have… I'm gonna.. Were no longer a configuration in her life at this moment. As far as this beast before her was concerned her life was done about to be snuffed in a none too pleasant way. *Maybe that drug would have been an idea!* But then. *No.* Because she would have lost this ability; the ability to talk. He seemed to be wanting it really.

"Was that a requirement?"

"What?"

"Being a virgin?"

"No."

"So; why even mention it?"

"You gave it away?"

"You're trying to shame me!"

"What would be the point of that?"

"I have no idea…but that is it. What does it matter to you? You are about to take what you want? What difference does it make if I'm not a …" she struggled with the word this time. *It had mattered; before.* "Virgin… And what makes you think that hasn't happened to me before?" Kalista had no idea why she was saying all these things or why fear had driven her to this but one thing she did know was that for once in her life; what was left of it she would be honest if nothing else; her last moments were important and she decided not be brow beat into grovelling like an animal. He was no animal of that she was sure now. He was a man. Or at least had been.

# Chapter two

The beast couldn't believe his ears she was not only talking but actually seemed to be disagreeing with him about her own death. *My God!* What the hell did she think this was? *Am I not clear enough?* A naked beast was hovering over her about to. He stopped and seemed to take a small step backwards not forwards. *They'd sacrificed her for their own ends.* He knew they were ashamed that was why they looked so sick. *But why what would that make a difference? They should be they chose each time.* Every time it was their choice they picked one from the whole to bring to him. Usually young; nubile and virginal; not one that now he looked on her was older than he first thought and although afraid had an air about her even he could admire. His thoughts shocked him. It was almost human again.

"You did not choose."

"No!" Kalista jumped in too quick. It upset her. So much more than this; her own life and its abuse; from the beast she'd always known in the guise of a man. Not this beast that was man. She didn't want to remember.

"Why did they choose you for this?"

"They didn't!"

"What?" He struggled; surely she couldn't be saying she….*No.* "You can't have."

"What? Choose to come? Why not?"

"Because who would choose… This?"

"To be sacrificed for the greater good is not a lesser thing to do." Tilting his large head the beast began to see her as a woman not just a vessel. *Heart... you have heart.*

"No." He growled. Deciding if he thought she was beautiful or not. Some weren't; not that he cared. "But why? You must have had a life to enjoy." *Enjoyment...* Something he now knew very little off. His voice slowly began to gain a tone and became less of a growl.

"Does that matter now? I have come to you as your… sacrifice." He huffed. It did for some damn reason it did.

"I want to know."

"But I may choose not to tell. My end will be the same no matter what." His hands formed fists which he knocked against his thighs. Kalista saw; she didn't understand… *What is it? What goes through your mind? But why? Why would you make me remember my own pain?*

"I… this I have to do."

"Why?"

“Because.”

“See you will not tell me.” His chest heaved. “What difference will it make to tell me?” She felt as if she needed to relent.

“None. It cannot be stopped; nor sated.” There he had already given her more information than he had intended. *Shit. This talking lark is…* Good but he couldn’t admit it. The beast was baying for her but the man he was struggled to withhold, just a little longer. “So we are at stalemate.”

“You are intelligent!”

“What?” The beast couldn’t believe his ears.

“As the beast you have become, the man must have been educated.”

“And you say that why? I haven’t even said I am man.”

“You don’t need to I can see that you were.”

“How?” He gestured with his claws to the rest of him. This was no man… But Kalista lowered her eyes to his still throbbing erection. With a lowered respectful tone she gave him his answer.

“That is man.” *My God.* His eyes nearly popped from his head. That had never been said before. “And your speech although it doesn’t flow is clear and well formed.”

"It is nothing more than a growl."

"It was at the beginning… but not now."

"You are not daft either." Red eyes scrutinised her. She shrugged.

"I think maybe I must be. I'm here aren't I?"

"Tell me why?"

"There will be no time."

"Tell me!" He left her with no illusion that he meant what he said and was insistent on knowing. But still she wasn't content with just that.

"I will make you a deal. I will tell you If you tell me why a man is now a beast?" Trying to lick away the saliva his talking was creating he pondered her question. Could he tell her? *What difference would it make?* It wouldn't but for some reason his heart told him it would.

"Deal!"

"Ok. Shall I start?"

"Yes."

"And you swear to tell me yours too you will not just renege and just finish me." Her courage was expanding.

"I swear." He meant it.

"Where to start? I said it was a long story but I

will try to give you the short version." Kalista swallowed hard attempting not to relive her words too much or it would make what she was about to go through ten times worse than it needed to be. "For me this is painful not just emotionally but physically too; my body remembers." *It would.* He knew. "I was an orphan my parents both died from disease. Too early in my life and I became the town's problem and if you know them compassion is not a feeling that most have. They are mostly out for themselves but the few that aren't tried to help. But weren't in a position to take me in. Famine had been rife, food was rationed and I'm sure you understand what that brings out in people. If you have been here as long as I have been led to believe?" He nodded but did not speak just listened. She sighed. *Ok I will keep going...*

"None like that could take me so I was made a ward of Victoor's He was town's man then."

"Yes. I remember him." Kalista listened to the strange noise he made... intensely deep. Even him the beast did not like this man he could smell his rankness he assumed he knew what was going to be her next words. He never had any care for the lives he sacrificed; nor humility.

Kalista now raised her eyebrows the look in his eyes told her he did and the way his lip curled as he grumbled. *You did not like him either. You the beast, you have goodness.*

"He took me and at first all was good, for years in-fact. I have a vague imagine of him choosing for you. Now I know he did relish it. He enjoyed the power over life and death."

"He would! But you?"

"I flourished as all should but then I grew to womanhood and that was when the problems began. Nothing much at first, just the odd touch and tap." Kalista seemed to stall; he knew she was reliving her memories. But he wanted to know. "It went on for month's maybe years each time picking up a little more attempting a little more. It has all become a blur for me."

"I understand."

"You do?"

"Keep going?" Kalista felt a little unsure; she hoped he asked for the right reasons and not because he got off on it. Not that it mattered either way.

"As I grew, so did his desire for me. I tried to tell but I just couldn't. Not then. To say the words made it too real. I became his own personal plaything." Her eyes shut in pain. He quietly moved a step closer without her even realising. He could be quiet. "It went on for years." Kalista tried to ignore his closeness and continued on. "And years. I was an emotional wreck assault, abuse."

"He raped you?"

"No, yes… Not in the sense you mean… He was unable. He was impotent, had been for years. It made him so angry… That was the only reason he took me in knowing no one would believe me. A vagabond. The only time I was free of him was when he went through this, the choosing." The beast raged. He had always known there was something about the weasel of a man. The way he left the girls; drugged… He remembered the way he; Victoor's had positioned them way too much more touching than there needed to be. He growled loudly. Kalista knew she had to finish her tale and quick before her courage failed her and she was just a weeping wreck. Her voice was already breaking. The beast could hear; sense her agony but he wanted to know all of it… In fact it felt all important to him to know. "Used, he used things on me; tools whatever he got his hands on me. As I got older it got worse and then as I complained and cried he began to beat me too. I think that was as bad… that was what gave him glee seeing me beg for forgiveness and he would even drool." Kalista remembered every single thing; every breath and noise he made, every look, when she'd said it was all a blur she had lied. It wasn't that she just tried always to hide from it. Even to the way he drooled when he was touching her. Not unlike a beast would… "He was a beast!" Unwittingly a sob escaped her. But she quickly swallowed it back.

*You cannot feel this!* He wanted to touch her to try and give her some sort of comfort he knew exactly how all that felt. *But I am a beast.* "He did this for years?"

"Yes." Kalista raised her face to his. Surprised at what she saw there in those red flames eyes. Suddenly a little flash of something that wasn't red; and compassion even in the flames he had compassion. Unlike Victoor's he never held anything other than disdain. For anything or anyone other than himself.

"So how old are you?"

"I'm led to believe about 28. But I have no records; it could be a little more."

"He left scars?"

Kalista frowned she was shocked by that question but knew to answer. His curiosity was driven by something else something buried deep within him. Compassion. *I know you have it.*

"Yes."

"Show me!"

"What?"

"Show me…" Again his voice hit her as too

severe. None of this was making sense.

"I…" He growled.

"Show me!" Shuddering Kalista slowly lifted her hands to the ties at her chest and began to undo the bindings. Everything in her was aware that this was something she needed to do but filled with fear of everything; of him, the beast and everything she was imparting of the beast she had already survived. Her eyes filled with anguish and tears just welled. She sniffed hard trying not to give in to the emotion sweeping its way through her. As she finished loosening the final binding she turned; no longer facing him. Her back to him. She couldn't seem to go any further her hands just froze. Her eyes and nose streamed … wiping her face with the back of her hand. Unable to pull the dress from her shoulders. Her breath came in heavy fitful spasms. This Kalista hadn't done not even to show Serena whom had known some of it; she'd come to a sort of impasse with life. Knowing she didn't need any of them to see and truly know; they were nothing to her just idiots and her own competence was all she'd needed. Or so she'd thought; but Kalista was a long way off from acceptance of herself.

"I…l." He knew she had gone as far as her courage would allow her. Lifting his clawed hand to her and with one single digit; so very carefully and with gentle expertise he thought to no longer own tucked his sharp nail under the material and pulled; pulling it from her, the fine material just slipped down her flesh. And he saw. He groaned. Her back a criss cross of scars some fine some jagged and thicker.

"What did he use?" Weeping now Kalista spoke quieter trying to fight back the sobs.

"A belt; a whip, a paddle what ever was to hand."

"And they run down your front too?" She gaged.

"They are all over me." She sobbed and shook her whole being seemed to be going into shock; not many had believed her even now or so they seemed when they criticised her. For once it was just all truth nothing more and now as she was to be sacrificed. She was crumbling; her legs began to give way. He did not want her to fall nor fail in her courage. *And they allowed you to come to me to suffer further. Bastards.*

"You speak the truth."

"Yes." *Off course I am!* He rolled his head angrily on his shoulders… clicking every bone he could… *Such precious flesh.* His thoughts betrayed his empathy. Moving quickly he carefully and trying his best not to hurt her in any way wrapped his strong arms around her; pulling her to his powerful chest. Being sure to keep his claws from her skin. He held her tight; feeling her ample breasts against his forearms. He refrained from growling as his instinct to became strong. He tried to speak… but nothing came out. He just held her. A gesture unlike any other either had experienced. What made him; neither had any idea but it was done and he was touching without ripping and shredding. Suddenly warm and cosseted Kalista didn't care who it was that was giving her this relief. She wanted it. She wanted him. Even his strong odour didn't make her recoil… Because he did stink. Her senses were only filled with what she remembered each touch smell and sight she'd endured. She began to sob unlike she'd done for many a year she'd fought and fought; it was all she could remember, fighting. Till death became her imagined only chance at peace. Tears ran down his face too; he pulled her as close as he could without harm. His erection still plaguing him but even that felt different. It seemed to want something more than release… a little warmth and pleasure something his beast had never experienced. She was broken. *Broken. You are as broken as I.* He grumbled in her ear. Trying to whisper. Her sweet smell wafting its way through him. Her very essence.

"My turn." She nodded unable to answer. But not letting her go; both man and beast seemed to want to keep a hold of her; her little heart beating through him was a welcome sensation. One he didn't just want to snuff out. Backing up; still holding her he allowed his heavy frame to drop to the floor to sit. Her hair whipping around his face; what once was his mouth now nothing much more than a muzzle. The sensation wasn't unpleasant. It was sticking to his fur… He grumbled trying to stifle the growl which seemed to be gaining momentum. He manoeuvred her a little so she wasn't plagued herself by that which raged to have its way. He fought himself at present too. *Fucking witch…*

Freeing a hand from her he grabbed her legs which were almost astride him by now and pulled them both to the side. He'd given his word to tell his tale and he would. Before all else. Things were unlike any other time for him. What was his destiny seemed to matter not. He pulled her further up his chest so that he could push his heavy erection out the way. His body did not complain. *Unusual… What have you done little one?*

"Comfortable?" She nodded her back pushed into his chest still bare but right now she didn't care she was warm and comfortable. More than she could have imagined. As her sobs quietened the beast spoke in very different tone to what she had heard from him up to now. If she kept her eyes shut he was man; his toned voiced returned.

"You are right I was a man once more years ago than you have been born. And probably even before your own parents." A little gasp escaped her. *True.*

Kalista realised some of the tales must be true.

"The tales say nearly a hundred years." Her voice hoarse from crying.

"Hmm. Maybe so." That he didn't want her to know because if she did then she would be able to work out how many women's lives he had taken. He prayed for them regularly at first but recently it hadn't been something he had partook of they had become nothing more than vessels for his insatiable lusts; until her this one sat like a lover on his chest. He pulled her in closer. "I have never spoken to anyone of this. Listen; do not interrupt." He snarled down her neck; almost eating her essence as he breathed in. *Aaa. What was she doing to him?* Kalista remembered he wasn't all man. He needed to remind her. As a silent gesture Kalista lifted her hands from beneath his arms and hesitantly laid them over his arm, unable to resist twisting her fingertips into the long fur which covered them. It wasn't as course as she had imagined in fact it was soft. Not unpleasant. He felt her touching him. But he wasn't sure about it. He huffed loudly at her… Remembering he was man. Not animal.

"I'm no pet dog." She immediately stopped. Stiffening. Feeling his hot angry huff searing across her still bare shoulders. *That's anger.*

"Sorry. I …" Guilt crept in, he was right, he was a man once. She needed to remember that and nurture that side of him. *He needs it.* But in truth she could not understand.

"No." He was it had actually been nice. But her hands just laid there was enough. "You wouldn't. Listen." Trying to settle her instincts to play with his fur Kalista began to breathe easy and relaxed again. "I was a young man some called me handsome but I have to admit to being arrogant and uncaring of those around me. Women came and went easily; I discarded many and I shouldn't have done. Then one not pretty bit of an ugly bug really but I knew her to be virgin or so I was led to believe." *So that had to be a part of this!* Kalista was listening and taking in all she could. "But it didn't make any difference to me I took her all the same, then like the others just ignored her and moved on to the next. She was less than pleased she had a brother. They were very much alike. I was wealthy and titled I had sufficient funds to do as I pleased but I should have known better. All in this world is not always as it seems. But you understand that." Kalista nodded listening intently. "They were true brother and sister and their looks were similar but there was so much more to them than I realised she wasn't finished with me nor was he. It had been a ploy from the start on their behalf she wanted me because." Now all he was man and beast seemed to stall not unlike she had. He growled low and mean. Anguish just resonating. Making Kalista's heart beat frantically. *He's angry. He's hurt!* She felt it. So did he; her heart skipped a beat.

"I am angry at myself, not you." He tried to comfort her. Which surprised her; not that it should he was already cradling her like a long lost lover. Resting her head finally against his chest she sighed. He could feel her breath running over his chest and blowing into his fur. *Gods. What is this?* "I was a full on stupid idiot… nothing mattered but the chase and… I think you understand."

"Yes."

"But know one thing I never forced myself on them they were all willing; it was just all stupidity I should have showed better judgement. Life didn't revolve around just that. I have to admit I was nothing more than a rutting beast." *Hence the beast!* "She wanted me because he did." Kalista stiffened and her eyes shut there was a horror in his words now too.

"It wasn't just his own perverted sexual desires but the fact that they weren't just man they were… witches!" Kalista pushed her head away from him and stared into his face trying to look into his eyes but he wouldn't let her. He put a clawed finger to her lips and shook his head. *No, do not speak sweetness.* She swallowed and imagined what was to come.

"They worked a spell and she changed her appearance and made herself gorgeous long flowing blonde hair; clean white skin with such blue eyes you could drown in." Kalista suddenly wondered what colour his should be. *Green. Was that not what she glimpsed before?* Running two of his fingers if that's what you could call them into her hair he pushed her head back against his chest he didn't want to look on her as he spoke. He didn't want to see her pity. Kalista let him. Holding her breath as he carried on.

"She conned me; I met her, she took me to a different house or so I thought; it was all a spell and then I touched her and I tell you I drowned in her; it was like nothing I had experienced before; intense enjoyable all the things it should have been… but then something seemed to change. I had been drugged and had words spoken over me which I now know to be incantation; I was useless, what started of pleasant and enjoyable, I thought I had been about to burst became dark and disgusting. And I saw him above me touching me doing all sorts as she laughed." He growled loudly almost a howl and gaged too. Kalista understood and dug her fingers into his fur and flesh hanging on to him trying to ground his pain.

"You do not have to say more… I."

"Listen!" Hanging onto him she did. As more tears ran down her face; tears for them both. "He reined unspeakable acts on my body; but that I know you get. It was excruciating I have no idea how long it went on for. I drifted in and out of consciousness. I could feel my own blood running from me. From my shoulders where he had cut and whipped me." Bile arose in his chest. "And down my legs; where he had…" Kalista could feel his emotional reaction in his chest she could hear his strong heart beat alter and falter.

"Stop, please." Kalista begged sobbing into his chest. Her sobs for him did more damage right at that moment than any pain could. He pushed his muzzle into her hair breathing in as much of her as he could. Her scent, so reassuring.

"I need you to know it all."

"You are not bad… I do not need to know anymore."

"No. Stop… You do. Please listen." Finally he pleaded; he had never imparted this knowledge to anyone… it was time; it was like a gigantic tidal wave which was being forced to run its course. Kalista fell silent and he carried on. His own voice cracking and breaking too. *But you are so big and strong!* She felt his pain with a powerful realisation Kalista knew no matter who; pain could still affect us. No one was infallible. He was as empty as her. "I bled. I was weak it could have been the drugs but the blood loss too. I knew he was going to kill me. I was never brought up to be a weakling but they had made me so. I felt helpless… disgusted in my own being."

He swallowed almost choking on his own spit.

"B." Kalista realised she didn't know his name he had to have had one and she didn't want to call him Beast. He was so much more than the sum of himself. More to the point of what he had become. But his eyes also told her again she was butting in. She chewed nervously on her bottom lip desperate to ask him. He watched her little action. There was something she wanted to ask. He coughed clearing his throat.

"What? Go on you are ok."

"What is your name?"

"Do I have one?"

"You must have had… then. Do you remember it? I do not want to call you Beast."

"That's all I am."

"I do not believe that."

"Maybe not now but later. Do not forget why you are here."

"I will cross that bridge when I get it." She was feeling more than comfortable with him right now. And all his tale was still not told. He was still a monster now.

"Hmm." The beast in him wasn't sure how to take that statement. Remembering. *You came here of your own accord to die. Do I want that? Hmm. Does the beast want it?*

"My name was…" Did he doubt he should tell her. *No tell her.* Even his beast wanted her to call him by name. "Barakan."

"A strong decisive name."

"Hmm a name now which can instil fear."

"I." Kalista shut her mouth quickly. *No you shouldn't go that far.*

Barakan watched her closely but conversation was drifting. *Her name. What was her name. But?...* Should he take his sacrifices name. *Probably not.*

"Do you want to know the rest?"

"Yes."

"All of it?"

"Yes." Kalista tilted her head to try to see him better. His muzzle dark and not too unsightly until he opened his mouth and his viscous teeth could be seen… *wow. They could do some damage. No wonder the women didn't survive. How was she going to?* But then another realisation hit her. Something within her had shifted and death although was still on the cards might not be entirely what she wanted any longer. *Do I still welcome it? If not what do I want?* She tried to see into Barakan's eyes again. Her nightmares were not only hers… Others suffered them too. *Could I possibly be something to you? No... you're a beast. Yet!* Kalista knew there was a pull to him that she had never ever experienced before. So strong it could all either begin or end in one night. *Can we be friends.* She imagined that was what she wanted. Cradling herself once again into his torso she wanted to know what had happened.

"You stare at me!"

"Sorry. Barakan." She spoke his name for the first time. There was definite shock on his face, Kalista knew it hadn't been used in a long time. "I was looking at your teeth. I'm sorry." She quickly went on. "You haven't heard your name in a long time have you?"

"No."

"Does it not sound good?" He grumbled the vibration rumbling through his chest.

"That is of no relevance do you want to know the rest or not?"

"Yes. I will be quiet."

"And I will not raise my teeth so much if you would feel better that way."

"You need to open your mouth…" she stalled at that point it wasn't a mouth any longer… well mostly not.

Barakan rolled his head on his powerful shoulders. This was turning out to be a very long conversation and he just wanted to get it over with. The pained memories were making his beast raw. Control was going to be hard.

"My teeth do not need to be so obvious." Barakan lowered his eyes a little to see her laid against his chest such an angelic sight. Her creamy skin cuddled into his black fur. He shook of the emotion. *I do not feel anything.* But he did.

"Ok." Her nervous fingers had begun to twitch again and both realised she was toying with his fur again. She clenched her hands into little fists attempting to stop her automatic reactions to his softness. Barakan rolled his eyes. Knowing he had been enjoying it. Something else too long missing.

# Chapter three

"I was bleeding heavily; the blood I was passing didn't relent… not even after she had done this to me. But that is overrunning my story. You know what he had done to me."

"Yes."

"It was hard for me to comprehend it wasn't real; I wanted death but my instinct to survive was to great. I had always been taught to fight for life and that was what I did. His final torment was to brand me in death as his and tie me too them for eternity in death too."

"He… Br…" Kalista couldn't bring herself to say the word. "Bran..." she tried again

"Yes. You do realise your questioning only makes this harder."

"I… You spoke to me!"

"Not so much. I let you talk." Kalista coloured embarrassed he was right. She did keep chipping in. She shut her mouth tight shut.

"The branding. That I couldn't stop; but the fire he ran through me from the brand triggered something in me so powerful I couldn't stop it I was enraged and the instinct to survive just took over it had to be instinct because I was too far gone in pain drugged under their spells for it to have been anything else. I began to fight back without strategy just rage. I was like an animal." At that point he stopped letting out a breath. "Hence my beast... but somehow and I cannot tell you how I took the branding iron from him and clobbered him with it. I smashed his head in, hitting him again and again. He hadn't been expecting it. But I left him a bloodied mess and somehow naked managed to crawl away I had just reached the tree line when she appeared." He snarled this time raising his lips over his gums so all his teeth showed an automatic reaction to the hate he felt for her. It took him some seconds to get it under control. Kalista seemed to hang onto him tighter not pulling away in fear. She wanted him to regain control. "I was on my knees naked bleeding like a stuffed pig and had no sense of where I was or which way to go. She screamed filling the air with so much hateful bile it made me puke. Everything left me thought; concentration speech. She took everything from me. Her hate for me was massive I not only had killed her brother but her lover and sole mate…They had an incestuous relationship." Barakan heaved gaging on the bile rising. "And… and I had…. With her … then he." Kalista was desperate to ask him if he was ok but knew she shouldn't. He had to get through this under his own steam like she had. "They were totally and utterly evil and degraded none of which I had known but as a witch what could I have done? She had me in her sights earlier than I knew well for him anyway. And he took from me what he wanted. I will not go into that any further. She laughed and cursed and decided not to kill me when I begged for death and I did beg; believe me I begged… she laid a curse on me instead as I had took her lover from her she would never let me have one I would be the rutting beast as she had seen me as; tied to her for eternity by the brand and that the women I had would only die and she made my sense of need so strong that I wouldn't be able to fight it so that sooner or later I would go to the beasts of the forest for the release I seek unless I became a killer; but in that moment when I decided not to fulfil myself with a woman risking taking her life I would be lost to my humanity for ever. So yes what you saw and said was correct that part of me is still man. But it is filled with a monstrous need which I must fulfil. Otherwise my heart my conscious and all that makes me man will be gone for eternity. And that is a fate worse than death to know what I have lost but never regain it. I will not die." Suddenly Barakan stopped. And it felt to her like he had held his breath. He waited for her reaction. Again tears streamed down her face. *What to say? There is nothing.*

Barakan felt her shivering.

"Why do you weep?"

"Because suffering knows no bounds."

"Hmm." Barakan wasn't so sure. "Your own or mine?"

"Both! That is not a good question." *Are you telling me off.*

"There is nothing good about what we are here for."

"Maybe not but I wasn't talking about that so no, the question was a low one." *You are telling me off.* "I was talking about what had happened not what is about to happen." She was frustrated by his words; in that one sentence. "I came here under my own volition and I am under no illusion about what can happen I think you know that now." *I do.*

"Yes."

"I know what it feels like to be abused…" Her voice pitched at him in her anguish; but still he only listened. "Have something foreign and unnatural shoved into one so hard you do nothing but bleed for days."*How dare he!* Her words spat at him. *By the Gods.* Her words harsh and ungiving were true. He too knew that feeling. She wiggled a little in his arms attempting to be released. *I pitied you.* And right at this moment he was belittling all they had both suffered. But Barakan didn't let her go. He liked her little frame rested against his too much. And as she did her legs moving made her behind wrapped within the material of her dress press against his erection. He moaned loudly.

"Do not do that." Pulling her higher away from it he held her tight. "You will make it impossible for me to stop the need."

"I didn't think you could?" *Wasn't that what he had been telling her?* But it didn't alter the fact she was still angry at him.

"I can't not at this point it has already been too long." She sighed. *But what worth is anger?* There wasn't any.

"So what happens now?" She had to resign herself to her fate. Barakan didn't answer for this once he had no idea. "I would ask one thing of you first Barakan." Emotions up and down; her voice softened.

"What?"

"I have had enough pain to last many lifetimes I would ask that as you have; that…" another sob escaped she was giving in. "What it is you have to do, that you let me die easily. Please. I will not fight you." *She was asking him to kill her during before the pain.* Shock filled every inch of him. His fur rustled and began to stand on end. *No.* A question so far removed from her question… Or was it?

"What is your name?" Now it was her turn to be

indignant. *I'm offering you my life here.*

"Does it matter now? I won't be needing it much longer." Barakan snarled.

"Tell me."

"Kalista… but my friends call me Kal." *Hmm.*

Finally moving Barakan allowed Kalista to gain her feet as he stood. Watching as she scrambled to pull her sleeves back on her properly resting against his chest she'd needed no covering and the material had slipped further. Her breasts were nearly bare. Barakan wanted to watch but turned away abruptly as he howled loudly into the night. It made Kalista's ears hurt. Without fastening her ties she put her hands to her ears. Quieting he turned to her. Something about him drained. *What is your intention?* Kalista had no idea.

"Barakan. I do not understand."

"No! Neither do I but…" His hands fists loudly thrashed into his thighs. His body shaking. "I can't. I cannot; will not take your life."

"But that means losing yours."

"Do you not think I know that."

"But."

"There is no buts. Go! Leave run from me as fast as you can, you have to."

"I will not; I will not... not you. I will not have anyone lose their life because of me." Her voice pitched at him. "If not me then who? They will bring Serena... No I won't have that; you got me and me it has to be. I will not have Serena's suffering nor..." Her words slowed... *Him she wanted to save him.* "Your's. On my conscious. No!" Barakan pounded his heavy feet into the ground frustrated anger about to burst and began to pace... circling her. Dropping to all fours as if to stalk her his beast showed; but still he only circled. Anger rustling through his fur.

"You cannot mean that. I have given you an escape."

"Just mine though not theirs; not yours." He knew she meant the other women. Both lost in their own thoughts... Kalista trying hard to find a way through for all. *I am here now. It has to be me. I'm not entirely afraid of you Barakan.*

"Barakan?" She tried to follow him with her head as he pounded around her she was turning like a top.

"What?"

"Is there no other way?" It was easy to see he scowled his teeth showing...

"What do you mean?" He guffed snarling loudly at her. "No, off course not. Don't you think I have tried over the years?" His tone full of sarcasm and disdain. "Doing it myself does nothing." Kalista flinched that wasn't entirely what she meant. But it also gave her an insight to the fact that he had tried… *You're not so much a killer as a creature of circumstance.* It made her feel even better about him to know he had looked for other routes. He moved a step closer. *If this is what she demanded. Noooo***.** He turned away again howling. Kalista was forced to raise her hands once again to her ears.

"Barakan… I know this is." There was no words to describe how difficult this was. "Painful and horrendous.. but please don't do that you are going to burst my ear drums." He snapped his mouth shut. His teeth clanged together.

"You test my patience."

"As you are doing mine."

"Kalista? It was the first time he had called her by her name and both knew he had done it for a reason he could not take her now…she had a name was real life flesh and blood not just a vessel. He liked saying it. He said it again even louder.

"Kalista."

"Stop it I know what you are doing. Giving me a name makes me real to you… doesn't it?" Barakan did not reply. Just kept his continuous pacing.

"Barakan!" Kalista raised her voice. He turned

on her all teeth and bristles.

“Do not shout at me… I’m offering you your life.”

“And I have already given you mine signed and sealed.” He was astounded by her words. He salivated it ran from his teeth..

“Be careful Kalista my beast may still change his mind.”

“I think he should!”

“What? …. Woman you are infuriating. No. Enough!”

“Barakan is there not a way. There has to be a way.”

“I have tried what I can. So no. There is no way. I cannot carry on like this if beast I am then beast I shall have to be.”

“No!” Barakan just stopped. Even breathing. A sadness sweeping through him.

“There is no salvation for me I have taken too many innocent lives…” Kalista’s heart began to crack. The one and only being she had fully opened up to not even Serena and he was a broken and abused beast and was going commit suicide for her… in all these years; just her. *No, no, no.*

‘‘No, no, no. I’m not having that… No.” she

stamped her little feet. Barakan saw the amusement in that. *So little yet so adamantly angry.* In a soft drawl he gave into his emotions.

"There is no other way forward now Kalista.. This is my end. Or yours." Kalista busy thinking… didn't answer him. Tears streaming down her face her body beginning to shake with frustration. *I will not let any of this happen. So many lives including theirs.*

"Kalista!"

"This thing… This curse, so you're a beast…So what? But; but the curse; this." She swallowed down her embarrassment. "This need you have to fulfil. It is part of the curse?"

"Yes."

"And you cannot stop the need?"

"No." Something jumped to mind she'd been considering it all along.

"But not one you can fulfil without a woman."

"N o o o." The growl was elongated. "As I have said these." He raised once his hands. "Do nothing to release the need. There is no emotion; no pleasure and cuts from these." He referred to his claws.

"Cuts that you inflict on others."

"Kalista!" He did begin to stalk her. Consumed

and confused by his own pain he didn't seem to want to understand. It was all so hard…

"That is not what I am trying to get at Barakan. You don't see what I'm saying." *Not at all.* "What if I." Barakan stared that hard at her it was if his eyes were burning into her soul branding her like he had been. "Oh my God Barakan you know exactly what I'm saying. I'm asking if my touch would be."

"How would that make a difference?" She shrugged her shoulders.

"I do not know but that depends if you can find pleasure in it… coming from me." He gaged at her words. *Did she realise what she was saying? Probably not.* "Barakan please stand… You being on all fours is unnerving."

"Do you not think you should be?"

"At this moment in time I have no idea about anything. But please." He did. Pulling himself back up to his full height he towered over her. Her eyes were drawn to that of him which was man once again bulging and almost red…

"I do not understand the full meaning of your curse."

"It is not that hard. I am forced to take a woman to try to fulfil this need that all feel but in me is no longer normal. I have tried to fight it and do for years but it comes around that it can only be fulfilled by a woman or else… you got that bit?" *Years?* A thought came and went in Kalista mind but did not stick long enough for her to comprehend. Other things were uppermost.

"Yes." She snapped back at him. He wasn't making this easy at all. On either of them. Both their emotions raging penned up and hemmed in for too long. They were both wound tight like a drum and one minute they wanted to scream and shout the next to stop and just halt all breath so it ended. The pain that chased around them both.

"A woman or I will be lost for eternity and know it… but in doing it the women are torn to shreds. Making me a serial killer."

"Barakan… stop it I know. But what I'm trying to ask if it has to be the actual act or if my touching you will be enough?"

"What!?"

"Oooo for Gods sake for an intelligent being you are being dense." Rather her dignity than her life; dignity she lost before she even knew what it was.

"Kalista!" Now she knew she was going to have to spell it out. Time and his need was obviously running against her and she still had no intention of absconding. *You need me.* She truly didn't want to think that he was cursed and condemned for eternity.

Not when her life was… *No Kalista you are not worthless. Not anymore.. this makes you worthwhile.* She threw hands in the air talking so fast he struggled to hear... but he did finally get it.

"It doesn't work when you do it because there is no feeling no emotion. It is just yourself no closeness… But Baraken does it have to be the actually act." She heaved. "Sex. Or can it be just a woman touching you till… Release." There she spat it at him. "Have you tried that."

"Off course not…"

"No… Because they have always been drugged and afraid and never spoken to you."

"No."

"No one like me!"

"Not in the hundred years."

"No." His great size was really intimidating but Kalista was determined right now more than she had ever been.

"Either one of us or both of us are powerless in this thing Barakan. I would try to get through it whole."

"I told you; told you to go."

"I know. But I'm not please let me try. For my friends but mostly Barakan." She sighed so loudly he lowered his head to her level not so much to intimidate this time but to see her expression as she finished her sentence. Her voice wrapping itself around him like she was taking him home.

"For you… Let me try to help you."

"Why?" Kalista tilted her head a little gobsmacked at his reply he really did need to learn a little tact. She knew he'd forgotten.

"Because I'm not the only one who has been torn apart." Barakan just stared. He had no idea what to say or to do, this thing was fast overtaking them both. His eyes welled with tears. She saw them. And something more the flash of colour from before; she had been right they were green.

"Your eyes Barakan they are green."

"What? How do you know that?"

"Because I can see it."

"What? You can't... they are just flames now."

"No they aren't Barakan." Kalista raised her hand to him under her own volition slowly reaching high for his face; gentle laying her hands on what was left of his mouth. "Whatever this is; I think is meant to be; I can see your eyes." Her hand just sat on his face. As it vibrated with the noises he was making. She'd just touched him again. Without fear and it was nice. He began to shake. "I see the man you are." *Did she?* "I know you question my words Barakan but please let us just try. I'm willing." Barakan rubbed his face against her hand. He didn't want her to let go; nodding in acceptance. But if it all went wrong he would never do this again. This was his last however it turned out. Kalista closed her eyes in acceptance of his answer. *Now how?* Her hand gripped his face just a little tighter Barakan knew she was afraid.

"You are not the only one who is afraid." Kalista knew he spoke from his heart. Opening her eyes again she dropped her hand stepping a little closer to him. There was something else she needed to ask of him first though. But as she did Barakan took it for a different action and quickly backed off. Kalista watched him unawares of what he was up to until she saw him move towards the forest… And. *Oh my God.* The beast was always there. Standing with his back to her at least.

"Barakan what are you doing?"

"Is that not obvious." Kalista was really struggling now she couldn't believe what she was hearing running water… He was relieving himself. And in that condition. *How?* Her naivety was fast leaving.

"Barakan. A beast you may have become but I'm not." As if she had slapped him Barakan stopped; looking round at her, her embarrassment more than obvious.

“Oh.” Before her eyes faster than she thought him able to move he was gone moved into the shadows.

“Kalista I am sorry.” He reappeared, huge erection an all. She shook her head at him. Overjoyed that he was apologising.

“Man and beast will have to remember I am neither.”

“No.” He moved towards her.

“But Barakan keeping that in mind I would ask one more thing of you first.” His eyes dropped. *Did she realise how little time there was left?*

“What?” *Again with the what.*

“Is there somewhere where you can wash I’m afraid you stink.” Barakan sort of snarled or was it another form of laugh Kalista couldn’t decide.

“My smell offends you.”

“No… Yes. You do though Barakan you smell and if I’m to.” She stopped; it wasn’t a hard request.

“Washing has not been a requirement.”

“No I understand that but is there?”

“Yes. I will do that for you. But you go sit by your lamp and do not move, the forest is dangerous for you.”

"But not you!"

"No. I won't be long."

"Ok." Kalista did as he asked. And when she turned around he had gone.

Breathing heavily filling her lungs to their full capacity Kalista dropped again to the floor. Staring at the long shadows of the forest around her; more afraid now than she had been with him. He had gone left her. *What if he didn't return? Would the forest then be her end?* "Please Barakan return to me." What she didn't realise was he could hear her. "Sweet Kalista... You are my heart." Leaping from the cliff edge he dropped into the cool pool waters below. She did have a point and he knew it. But as beast what did it matter? But he was not all beast. Kalista dropped her head into her hands gentle weeping; life or death this was it. *But it is my decision this time no one else's.* The control was hers. She didn't know how long she sat weeping.

"What am I doing?" She spoke aloud again. "No tears Kalista... This is your choice."

"You can still back down Kalista I will not hold it against you. Tonight has been." Barakan came into view and had obviously heard.

"You were listening?"

"No I heard there is a difference."

“Ok.” He didn’t need to say more. Kalista raised her head to look at him as he walked nearer. His fur somewhat wet but not totally it was strange. She puzzled him.

“I have washed.. I dry easily. I just.” He shook and the remaining water flung everywhere.

“Barakan; that went over me.” A small, smile crossed her face. Knowing he had done it deliberately; his effort to lighten the mood.

“I meant what I said Kalista.” Everything seemed to drain from him. “I won’t stand in your way if you wish to leave.”

“No Barakan. I’m sticking to what I have said; and.”

“And?”

“I want to do this for you.”

“Why?”

“I’m not so sure which one of us asks so many questions.” He seemed to shrug; a long ago gesture he had forgotten.

“Because Barakan… You are the only person who has listened; believed and showed me compassion.”

“Have I?”

“Yes.” Kalista made to stand. Barakan looked at

her little torch. There wouldn't be much oil left now anyway.

"Extinguish That Kalista." She looked from Barakan to her torch; reluctant but she imagined she knew why. "You will not need it with me and." She turned back to look at him.

"It maybe better if you do not see." She contemplated his words. *But I already have.*

"I think I… Would like to see." Barakan took a step backwards away from her; this was all more intense than either man or beast could contemplate.

"You **cannot**." He couldn't contemplate that she would want to lay her eyes on him in such a state in anyway shape or form. He was ugly tormented and it would show. For her Kalista found that although some of it laid in a very small amount of curiosity; her main aim was control and self preservation. If she saw she could gage his reactions to her and what she was doing or so she hoped anyway. But together was the only way forward now. That was for sure.

"Do not stop me Barakan. I have my own demons as well as yours to comprehend and this is…" She swallowed hard. "Difficult but believe me still when I say I will do this; I know it can only end one of two ways. Do not make me speak the words." With hooded eyes he just nodded abruptly; grumbling.

"You should have run."

"But I didn't."

"No." He turned his back on her looking around into the darkness knowing… he would much prefer that. He saw too much of his own selfishness as it was… "How do you want to do this Kalista."

"Here." She moved to one side where she was stood gesturing to the gap where she had been sat in-between the trees. "If you sit here… sit. Not stand you are too tall for me and maybe if you need something to hang onto." She pointed at his claws. Her words soft and uncertain. But yet still to the point. "You can hold onto them… Rather than me." *Oh my God she means to go through with this.* He was still expecting her to take to heals and run. Kalista watched him a little puzzled at his resistance. *You need this! But Kal… he doesn't want to harm you.* That she knew now for sure. His words when he told her to go were genuine. The damage he'd suffered made worse each time the witches full curse came to boiling point. *You are no killer. That was the curse.* Was she was thinking past tense. But could this work neither had any idea. But right now everything that Barakan had repressed was once again at the point where death was a factor. And this time this once; he would it be his than hers. The death of his humanity what was left of it anyway.

"I know it's those that do most of the damage…

please Barakan. Help me."

# *Chapter four*

Barakan hated the fact that he felt so petulant; not towards her she was only trying to help him. *Help.* Something he had never been offered. But it was so hard he wanted to howl pound his great fists and tear at his own body… if it offends thee… *By the Gods it does.* Offended him so much he just wanted to rip what was man from him and then maybe the curse would no longer plague him, but if death didn't follow how would it stop? *It wouldn't... So we are at this...* Which was all either of them had now. Neither knowing where any of this was heading or going to end. *If she lies dead at my feet but the end of this I will. I will be beast nothing more.* Breathing that loudly it sounded like he was forming a gale. Kalista watched as he hanging his head walked past her and lowered himself to the floor; being careful not to knock over her torch. He sat on the ground; his legs splayed in front of him. A peculiar sight.

"That won't have much oil left."

"I know; it only has to last this little bit longer doesn't it." His muzzle moved and twitched. Moving towards him slowly Kalista knew he was holding back. But she wasn't going to push him any more. She knew. No one had touched him since his terror had begun… he was delaying what had to be. *You not me..* But in that she knew at this very moment in time she was the one with a little of the power she had offered to do this and it was on her terms; but he had to feel helpless against the need and trying desperately to stop it so he didn't hurt her. Because as she was about to take control and touch him she wasn't herself being touched… *Could I allow that?* Probably not. She would be screaming screeching wreck. Kalista stopped the dark thoughts flooding her again as this wasn't that this was her doing the touching not being touched. Believing he would not hurt her. He could so easily already have was what she kept spinning into her thoughts.

Barakan watched as she lowered herself to kneel before him. There was to be no gentle whispers… No love.

*My God how can I allow this she is so good.* Barakan couldn't watch he shut his eyes tight. Lowering the rest of himself to the floor so he laid there. The beast he was submitting to her. Thinking of everything anything which would keep his rage under control.

Slowly and gently not knowing all of what she was doing Kalista knelt between his legs. Seeing him. Man and beast combined. It was a sight to be beheld. She swallowed back her fears. *This has to work.*

"Barakan… I." Kalista wanted something to be said between them before this all happened; if things went wrong and she was unable to speak again she didn't want him to feel she held it against him. "This is a choice. I willingly take… I do not hold it against you." Barakan growled too loudly. Leaving her under no illusion that there were no more words from him. She stopped and very carefully and a little shaky lifted her hands and at first laid them on his furred thighs. She immediately felt them shake under her touch. *Barakan you're afraid.* It immediately struck Kalista he was afraid of not only himself and what he was capable of but her too. He was afraid of her touch. As no one had touched him offered him any sort of kindness at least she had gotten some from Serena and Jack. Some was always better than none. She gentle put a little pressure on and wound her fingers into his fur kneading her fingers into his actual strong muscles. Hanging on to him for them both; he had been forced to become a killer and….. Kalista stopped her thoughts there it was too much she couldn't imagine him the man being that… not that.

Drawing her eyes to that which was man Kalista coached her fingers closer to him. Shaking visibly herself now she gentle caught his soft hanging flesh first with just her finger tips. Pushing her confidence to go further. Warm and not as soft as she had expected they were hard and moved as her fingers touched him. Moving away from her or to her it was hard to decide. But the flesh began to roll under her touch as her touch grew. Barakan felt her tiny little fingers caressing him. He couldn't believe that she was doing this. He breathed in before stifling his breath as the growl which would follow was massive… Man and beast wanted more but in pleasure not in assault… They tried to wait. He knew as she caressed him he flinched and rolled wanting so much more from her it was powerful need to hold onto but hold he would… She was all he wanted. Alive.

Kalista carried on her courage falling and rising with every breath she took. Her heart raced her mind just concentrated on nothing but him; she couldn't afford to falter in any way. Life depended on it; both his and hers. *I will do this.* Then again with hesitation she drew her right hand upwards pulling her fingers to touch his huge erection; engorged and throbbing. But in the light was no more beast than she was. There was no fur nothing unsightly just his size… but then she had nothing to compare. Just a flaccid wizened old man whom caused nothing but pain and still breathed. Kalista shook violently at the thought. But chewing her gums frantically she chased the memory away. This was not him this was Barakan and her all her choice. *Mine.* No one at this very moment was hurting her.

Barakan knew she faltered. Kalista felt him pull away a little as whispered words like breeze wafted past her.

"Kalista… do not…"

"Sch." Was her only answer as courage grew again; Kalista stroked her fingers along him this time Barakan was unable to stop the groan. In that one single moment Kalista realised how the power had swung to her. Her fingers traced their way slowly over him with each second growing in confidence, the heat he emitted scorching which surprised her but it was not unpleasant against her fingers.

"Barakan!" She had a confession to make. "I do not know what to do." She had heard chat and rumour but as no one really talked to her and she only had Victoor's experience for fall back information it wasn't that appropriate. He was never able… This was. Different. Barakan had known; he dropped his head down onto the ground hard. Needing the pain it caused to keep his need in check… he would chew off his own leg at this point. He lifted his head a little to see knowing he couldn't risk catching her with his claws. The image which he'd been avoiding seeing was there burning itself onto his retinas. *My God.* Kalista was sat between his monstrous legs her face flushed eyes spinning with something he wasn't sure about; not fear but something he could only question as apprehension.

Her delicate little hands on him. Stroking and teasing without understanding. There were no words.

Slowly with as much care as he could muster Barakan raised his hand to her extending a single claw to her little hand resting against his huge girth. Desperate to have her touch him but not wanting to harm her either. It was a hard thing to achieve. Barakan touched his claw to the top of her hand and tried to carefully push her fingers to him following it around with his claw as she wrapped her fingers around his hot erection. Kalista allowed him to show her; watching as his claw touched her. *How gentle you are!* She did not raise her eyes to him; she dare not; not yet. She held him fully in her grasp Barakan started to groan it was impossible to stop. As realising her fingers he lay what would have been his palm on her hand and began to move with her… Now the groan became so much more. He suddenly dropped his head back unable to stop the noises now emitting from him. Kalista did not stop once he had pulled his clawed hand away. She gentle moved her hand up and down as her left hand didn't relinquish its hold on the rest of him. She saw his hips begging to move with the movement she was causing. Instinctively she took a tighter grip and a howl escaped him quickly stifled. *You are enjoying that.* She knew. Without knowledge she knew. Leaning into Barakan further Kalista began to move her hand faster. Tickling him with the other. With a snarl

Barakan found impossible to stop he flung both his hands out either side of him and as Kalista had suggested grabbed out at both the trees. He needed something for his hands to grip to other than her. Immediately his claws dug into the bark Kalista heard it crack under the force; grateful for the trees. Kalista knew now she was comfortable in what she was doing. *This is right.* She pumped at him harder and watched as his tip glowed under the light, he was wet now. Kalista was making connections in her mind as to what could be pleasure having known only pain. Slowly again unsure of what was right but feeling she wanted too. Kalista lowered her face towards her hands.

Barakan felt her hot breath before she even reached him… *No. She couldn't be.* But as he felt her warm wet lips… She did. Unable to stop Barakan thrust his own instinct taking over. She kept a grip of him as she found he suddenly filled her mouth but she didn't care. This was it what he needed; sensuality in touch. She allowed it to happen moving her mouth up and down with her hand. Barakan's snarls were infectious.

"Kalista!" His claws gouging at the trees.. again and again. She kept going. Everything in Barakan shook inside and out. His hands wouldn't stop moving. His heart missing beat after beat as he gasped for air… She was doing it giving him pleasure so long missing. He wanted to hold on to her tight and never let go. This little offering was pulling everything from him. As she pulled his orgasm at this very moment. He felt it building; running from his groin up through the whole of his being and back down again settling where it needed to be. Kalista felt Barakan start to stiffen every muscle and sinew tightening in him under her. She let go with her left hand and gripped onto his thigh hanging on as movement for both of them became more; she didn't want him to fling her off. Barakan knew it was happening as did Kalista she could feel it under her fingers building. Barakan new it was tremendous he felt it building like he couldn't remember. He snarled growled and the noises coming from him were feral and loud…

"Kalista." Reaching up to her with one hand… fast; for now it had to be just a hand otherwise he would hurt her. He pushed the palm at the top of her head pushing her abruptly away.

"Stop!" Kalista felt the force he put into the push and didn't fight it. She fell back against his leg away from him as a massive wave of energy moved through him and his orgasm found him. He came. Loud and vibrant.

Kalista sat quietly taking it all in. His reaction to what she had done; Barakan lay stiff unable to move trying to put it all back into place this thing that together they had achieved. Even his breathing wasn't right not yet. But one thing he did feel was.. Relief. She had done it for him. For them both. After some minutes of listening to her constant excited breath. Barakan raised himself up towards her still sat leaning against his leg. Sweet innocent. *Oh God I desire her.* Desire; not need or the curse, she had bypassed that. He tried to speak but Barakan found for the first time ever he was hoarse. Swallowing heavily his teeth showing too much all of him had been involved in that orgasm. He tried to hide them. Kalista watched as he tried to gather himself and seemed to be struggling but she didn't speak just waited.

"Kalista." He noticed all the pieces of wood still stuck in his claws. They both saw. *That could so easily have been flesh.* Without words Barakan couldn't find any quickly shaking the bits of bark from his claws he lifted a hand to her face realising now he did have some control. He carefully laid it on her cheek cradling her face as he gently run what would have been his thumb cross her lips. Such a loving genuine gesture. *What now?* Neither knew. But did either care at this moment. Kalista enjoyed his touch. For the very first time someone was touching her not in lust or hate. Just touching her. It was nice.

Both just stared lost for words. Barakan smelled her very essence mixed with his own but there was something a little different about her from what he'd already smelt. So very faint but still there. He was shocked… *That could be desire.* Sighing. He began to move.

"Kalista.. stay here. By the lamp… I need to wash." *Was he embarrassed? I am not.* She wasn't.

Kalista sat with her own thoughts. Waiting. *That was! Not unpleasant.* She prayed she'd done enough but a knowledge of certainty within her said. ***Yes.*** The lamp began to flicker it wouldn't last much longer. Kalista wasn't keen on the thought of being sat here alone with no light at all. She had no concept of time since she'd been left here and if daylight would even get through the dense trees. She huddled herself up to a tree to lean against it. Pulling her legs up to hug them. It was getting cold with Barakan she hadn't realised how cold it had gotten. Suddenly her lids became so heavy and exhaustion rushed through her. Lowering her head against the tree she tried to get comfy; not that she could.

"Barakan. Hurry." She remembered he'd heard. Then within seconds she was gone. Exhaustion taking her.

Barakan once again dived into the cold waters. Feeling so very different this time. *Wow... Kalista. How?* He had no idea what had actually transpired the only thing he did know for sure was for the first time since this had all began he had the smallest amount of satisfaction crawling its way through him. *All you Kalista.* He ran his hands; for that was what they should have been over himself through his fur. Cleaning. Trying to make himself more man than beast. She deserved that. Yet his mind couldn't help but think. *What now?* She had fulfilled her side of this bargain that others had not even survived. *Will you leave me?* He knew she would have to. What else was there? Yet something was gnawing at him. *I don't want you to.*

Then he heard her…

"Barakan… Hurry." Her words surprised him; she wanted him back? *Why?* Her tone was tinged with just a little fear. *What is wrong?*

The beast he was burst out the water noisily; easily leaping onto the bank. Dropping immediately to all fours he charged through the trees back to her; his heavy hands and feet pounding like drums… His heart panicking. *Kalista?* He worried that something was wrong and words which he didn't even know whispered their way through his being.

*Please God let her be alright.* The forest should not take her now. *Mine mine mine.* The beast was so sure. But his fears were unfounded. He burst into the small clearing his eyes immediately finding her.

"Kal…" His words staled as her steady breath and calm heart beat told him she slept. *Why?* It was then he realised the torch had gone out. "You do not like the dark little one." Relief filled him but besides that he considered her. Soft little woman that she was. *Hmm.* As his eyes covered all she was. He saw her shiver. Knowing she was cold. Standing tall he moved towards her.

"Kalista!" He tried to talk softly something he hadn't needed to do before. So as not to startle her. "Kalista I'm back; you are cold." Kalista heard him but couldn't bring herself to wake up and actually answer. She was fast asleep. Barakan knew that; her steady rhythm told him so. "I can warm you." He didn't want to just take it on himself to sit beside her in sleep and frighten her. But he got his answer by way of just a light groan speaking his name.

"Barakan." A smile crossed his face. What was his smile anyway? He had no idea how it looked only how it felt and that was nice. "Ok little one..." Carefully settling down beside her he easily lifted her little frame to him and foetal position she curled up on his chest. Not waking once. Barakan knew she was comfortable with him. For now anyway. He laid his face against her hair. Smelling her memorising. Sometimes the simplest of things seem so important. She smelt good clean and full of live.

He'd hold her for as long as she needed in sleep.

His own thoughts varied and complicated. *Victoor's the bastard... How dare he spoil someone so perfect.* He wondered if the slug was still breathing.

Kalista felt her body hurt again; it's burning tension flooding her almost splitting her in two; his rankness attacking her consciousness. Suddenly a scream echoed loud and high pitched. Hers…

Barakan's eyes opened wide glaring red. He hadn't been sleeping just relaxing. *What was wrong?* His own conscious realising it was Kalista. It was her screaming like some wild banshee. He couldn't help but growl at her screams of pain as along with the second scream came a great surge of energy and her arms and legs started kicking and flaying about like some great dying insect. Her voice pitched at him…

"Noooo… it hurts." She moved with determination trying to get away from what she saw hurting her. Barakan knew if he was to try and hold her chances were he would do more damage. She needed to wake carefully and see she was no longer in that nightmare. His heart filling itself with her almost burst with her terrible cries…

"Kalista." He tried to whisper her name.. But to no avail moving too wildly she fell from his arms scrambling around on the ground she had no contemplation of where she was. She was deep in her own nightmare.

"Kalista." Barakan moved and staying down on her level tried to reach her again. "Kalista you are safe. He is not here." She screamed again almost howling like he had into the night. Her eyes wide open but not seeing anything other than her too true nightmare. She grabbed at the ground with her little hands; pulling and scratching. Little hands that had done so much for him.

"Kalista you are going to hurt yourself." Now he knew he had to try the stones and bark; sharp like knifes would cut her to pieces. "Kalista it is Barakan. You are safe. Please wake up." He moved a little closer raising his voice some; she had to hear. "Kalista. It's ok." He tried with all in man and beast that was compassion he tried. "Kalista." She blinked and slowly began to stop moving. Looking from Barakan to her hands then back again to his face so near hers. *What had she done? Oh dear. Nightmares.* She looked into his eyes; brimming with emotion. Focused on her. With each single syllable she tried to speak. Knelt on all fours himself.

"B a r a k a n!"

"Yes. You are safe Kalista." Not moving from the floor she dropped her head to look at her hands fingers ground into the floor. *Oh dear.* She moved both hands lifting them from the damp darkness. But unable to see them in the dark; all she knew was they were sore.

"I."

"Was having a nightmare."

"Yes." She swallowed before carrying on. "I do sometimes; when I'm frightened."

"And tonight you were frightened." She held her hands to her chest.

"I was." *Was?*

"And now?"

"I don't know Barakan." Honesty.

"I will not hurt you Kalista."

"I know! I'm sorry I don't have cont…" He jumped in.

"Never apologise to me. Are your hands sore?" He could smell her blood. She had hurt her hands no matter how small.

"A little."

"They will need attention."

"Yes." It suddenly struck her; she was alone. *Alone.* Undecided whether that was a good thing or a bad one. It was something although she had always felt lonely never was; and if you could be both? "What do I do now?"

"What?"

"Now Barakan what happens now?"

"I do not know this is all new to me too." She could feel his hot breath gushing over her and it wasn't unpleasant; she found it reassuring especially after such a bad episode. *It had to happen now! Showing how weak I am Urgh. Idiot.*

Barakan saw the thoughts whizzing around her mind and he knew.

"Never apologise or be shamed because of what others have made you."

"How do you know what I'm feeling?"

"I can sense it in you. You are far from weak Kalista." He knew she had taken him on and if only momentarily; for this one night tamed the beast which watched her as closely as the man. The one and only.

"And I had every intention of saying the same to you."

"Hmm." A little soft growl left him; as he sniffed at her. *Not so sure it counts for me. They may have made me this but I have complied.* "What do you want to happen; you have fulfilled why you were left here for."

"Have I?"

"Yes. I will not hold you; you should go home."

"Home?"

"Yes among your own kind. With your friends."

His words seemed to spike in her causing a wave of annoyance.

"With my own kind! That's a joke."

"Kalista." Confused.

"I have no kind."

"People you should be with people."

"Not those ones."

"You really dislike them all so much? Not just the few?" He understood that but. *The two.*

"I have two people that I care about that is all and my presence only makes their life harder. No one else; none of them even look at me without contempt. I hate it. None believed then and not now, but they still do not allow me to forget. My treatment has been appalling. They walk on the other side of the street they turn their backs on me. How can I have a life like that." Her voice had begun to rise again and she knew it. *It's not your fault Barakan.* Breathing heavily she tried to calm her furious anger at them. "I cannot." She shrugged. "He still manipulates his family to stop me. He would rather me be dead." *He.*

"He!" *Still; does he live?"* "Victoor's still

lives?" Barakan hadn't even considered that he would still live… Her words before he hadn't considered them in respect of him still breathing. *My Gods.*

"Unfortunately…" Kalista physically shook. "Yes."

"Is that why you made this decision? Because of him?"

"Yes… No partly. I know they would have sent Serena to you."

"Your friend."

"Yes. And then Jack he would have been heart broken. I couldn't let that happen to them. They are to be married."

"Your two friends?"

"Yes." Barakan mulled over what she was telling him and a realisation knowing Victoor's too… entered his mind. And now more than before he could see it in her eyes too. She knew.

"This wasn't entirely your decision was it? No matter what you said before. What made you believe they would send Serena?" Kalista hugged her sore hands closer to her chest hanging on to herself.

"I was told so."

"Victoor's he still chooses."

"Yes.. He is old now and no one sees him but he still pulls all the strings. When I ran away I had." She gagged remembering. "I can't Barakan please don't make me. Not now." Barakan leaned into her being careful not to raise his lips over his teeth and rubbed his face against her head. Attempting comfort.

"It is ok little one. I want to understand. I do know now they manipulated you; they knew you had a good heart." He breathed heavily his hot earthy breath running down her neck making her flesh twitch; Kalista realised she found it comforting.

"So Kalista we find you another village!"

"No." In the seconds now when Kalista realised she found comfort in him. She made a different decision. Maybe one he wouldn't like but one she wanted. More than anything. Her mind again raced and she plotted.

"What do you mean … No. You cannot just stay here. The forest will kill you."

"I know and I don't intend to."

"What then Kalista?" He had an inkling of what she was going to say but. *No. She couldn't mean too... could she? How?* "Kalista?" His voice strong now. Daylight was coming and he should have already have left.

"Barakan… Take me with you." Barakan pulled

away from her staring hard. “Where ever you go; you have to live somewhere please let me come with you.”

“Kalista…. I. We. It isn’t possible.”

“Why not?”

“Because Kalista look at me. I’m beast.”

“I do not see just the beast.”

“Anything could happen; the beast could decide to.”

Kalista tilted her head at him shaking it.

“I don’t think you will Barakan.. But whatever I will take what comes and deal with it.”

“Kalista. That may not be possible.”

“Anything is possible Barakan if we want it enough. There is always a way. I have already proved that.”

“But.”

“Is there a but Barakan?” He found himself salivating again. *Off course!*

“Kalista.” He was lost for words. *How can I ?* He grumbled.

“Would you not like me for company Barakan?” She knew he had been starved of it.

“Kalista that is not the point.”

"I think it is. I would do whatever it took and stay wherever I need to feel safe."

"And you feel safe with me?" That seemed to surprise him. She blew heavily.

"Tonight… the answer to that is yes Barakan. Once we talked. Off course before then it was nothing but terror. But now I know I have felt better with you than I can ever remember feeling. Not since I was too young to know what it meant anyway."

"And you think that can continue?"

"Yes. Do you not?" He stopped talking and just stared firstly at her then up into the sky morning was here.

"Kalista…" *what do I say?* "I do not know Kalista. I cannot say yes because I just do not know."

"But Barakan, do you not want to try?" She did with a force which was driving her hard at the moment. *I will not go back there.* "I do."

"Are you sure; I would see you safe where ever you want to go. I will take you."

"Then that is with you Barakan. And yes i am sure; take me with you. Please." There wasn't much more she could say and do to persuade him. It had to be his choice to for it to work. Kalista found her heart was in her mouth whilst she waited for his reply, which didn't seem to be forthcoming.

"Barakan?" She was just unable to wait... nerves now playing a part she really didn't want to watch him walk away from her. "Please." Pulling himself up to full height. Barakan gestured for her to stand no words. Until.

"We need to go. Morning is here. They could come back to." Kalista almost leapt to her feet; more than pleased with what he was saying. *Thank goodness.* Relief filled her. But was that to be short lived. Would she regret her decision? Would Barakan? Very likely. He knew it. But the pull to keep her from any more harm was so strong in him right now. It beat all other sense. Sense which Barakan knew he needed to keep. But which seemed to have left him.

"I understand." Kalista made to move past him her injured hands wrapped tight against her chest.

"You will not walk the distance like that Kalista. Your hands they are hurt." She shrugged.

"I will manage."

"No you won't the distance will be too great and I cannot afford to dawdle." He groaned slow. "I will carry you."

"Oh. Ok." Barakan was quick to step behind her and with ease lifted her once again. Without catching her with his claws. It had become easier he had found there was a knack to it. Kalista didn't wiggle she knew she needed to be careful around his hands; they were what as lethal about him. Other than his teeth which again she found herself very near. He huffed at her.

"You're staring again."

"Sorry."

"Do they worry you?" Barakan took his first step away from the clearing with his prize in arms.

"What?"

"My teeth?"

"Not so much as your claws. "He snorted at her.

"Yet you still want to come with me?"

"Neither will hurt me deliberately Barakan."

"You sound very sure of that!"

"I am. Yes."

"Hmm. I'm glad one of us is."

# *Chapter five.*

Barakan was awash with emotion; he had no idea what he was actually doing or why? Just that he had to do something and couldn't just abandon her to what she had already suffered. *Victoor's.* There had always been a rotten smell about him and now he knew why? He was even worse than him; he didn't do this through choice unlike Victoor's.

But then he did have a choice; his heart and mind were now banging with the pressure of what she had achieved and how many times he had relented to the curse and just taken… The death of so many; could they have been avoided? Now the guilt he'd always felt just seemed to be impacted and made worse. Because she had helped him… *helped! I am a killer what am I doing with her?* But there was no way he could relinquish her now. As he strode through the forest he found his pace getting faster and faster. Wanting to be away with her far far away. But what would she think… Of his. *Home?*

It had been a while since he'd called anything home. It had started off as that; he'd tried to be man, but it hadn't worked. Just a large cavern with separate caves which he'd hidden in at first, high in the mountain range above the forest. Away from prying eyes. The best place for him but over the years; in truth it was more than lonely. Even for the beast. At first he had taken what was his and tried to pretend setting them up in the cave at the farthest side away from the entrance but as year after year had gone by he'd entered that cave less and just had a mattress nearer the entrance where he could see all that was below. He had been more beast than man. But with her he knew now things would have to change. Was he looking forward to that? A curios sensation which wasn't unpleasant filled him; he would have a companion. Someone to talk to. He hoped his stuff would be alright for her; after a good clean anyway. The caves themselves were a secret that he had been lucky to fall upon on his damaged state. Big enough for him to hide in but deep within its bottom was a hot spring; water come up from the ground warmed and then another that ran from the walls excellent clean spring water. Enough for body and soul. But then there would have to be food and cooking. *Urgh.* He knew how to get that. *Roberts.* He didn't know how many Roberts down the line over the years this one was but a family once tied to the manor and him. They had never seen him but he left coin and notes occasionally telling them what he wanted and it was provided. But the notes had gotten harder and harder to write if there had been anything recently it had been more symbols the written word. The occasional thing he fancied. The man still didn't want everything raw. So a long note would probably have to be written. She would need meat and bread and utensils, Barakan realised he actually didn't know what he had any longer. There was probably stuff there he totally forgotten. As beast he would have no call for. Practical thoughts filled him. He hoped she could write. But something in him already knew. *Yes.* She was too intellectual not to have been taught and Victoor's he would have kept up the façade.

Kalista just kept as still as she could; he was still naked. The thought of what she had done burned into her. Unashamed but surprised it hadn't been as wrenching as she'd expected. He had not touched or hurt her in any way. *Could I do it again?* Her thoughts of his very body troubled her. Unsure of what it meant. Barakan moved faster than she would have been able even running. And his stamina. *Wow.* She would have been worn out within the hour. Never mind this length of time. But held against his solid heat listening to his heart thump; again and again it was a calming sensation after her stupid bloody episode. *Nightmares. Aaaa.* Kalista couldn't believe after all that she'd achieved this night for them to have started again. Leaving everything that she knew behind not that; that bothered her particularly life there had been too traumatic and awful, so it could only be a good thing but still the bloody nightmare had took a grip of her. She hated that they made her feel so powerless. If her hands hadn't been so sore she would have laid them on his chest but still cradled them to her own chest. Knowing they would heal once clean it was just that right now they were just so sore.

"Barakan."

"Yes." He slowed a little.

"Where do you live?"

"I." He pondered on how to explain it without making her think she was going to a hovel; it was far from that. "I stay up in the mountains; away from people."

"That isn't a surprise. What?"

"I think you should just wait to see."

"Oh ok." *My goodness is it that bad?*

"It isn't as bad as you think Kalista. You will see."

"Ok. I can walk if you want me to."

"No. Too late. We go up here." Barakan nodded towards what looked like just rock.

"That.. Where? It's solid."

"No it isn't look closer." Barakan slowed to almost a standstill. Kalista squinted to try and see into the shadows. Nothing jumped out at her but there had to be a way for him to mention it.

"I cannot see it Barakan; but from what you have just said there has to be a path."

"There is. Keep still I wouldn't like you to get cut on the rocks."

"Is it that narrow?"

"For me. Yes."

"So let me walk then." Barakan couldn't admit that he had enjoyed having her close.

"I cannot hold you or stop you from falling if I don't carry you. My hands." She knew exactly what he meant.

"I won't fall."

"It is a very uneven path."

"Barakan! I'm not a mountain goat but neither am I incapable." *No you're not.* He relented. Slowly he allowed her feet to gain ground.

"I will go first and you follow do not lag behind and be very careful where you put your feet." He looked at her shoes. "Those slippers aren't the best."

"I wasn't expecting to be doing this."

"No but even so you walked through the forest in them."

"I did…" She shrugged. "Who knew!" *Hmm.*

"Come on." Gruffly he strode passed her and just seemed to immediately disappear. Kalista gasped. He was gone. *Where?* His clawed hand appeared like an illusion from inside the rock…beckoning her.

"Come on then." This was her idea in its entirety. Barakan worried. In a single moment Kalista stepped forward and disappeared herself into the rock. Her life no longer the same as it was before. Everything was changed; for the better? Who knew? But one thing Kalista did know was she glad to be away.

Stepping into the unknown Kalista put one foot in front of the other. Feeling the unevenness and the rocks beneath her feet; he had been right these soles weren't any good for this but who had known this was what she would be doing. As far as she had imagined it was to be a one way journey. Nothing more. But instead Kalista felt that so much more was opening up for her. This man which was beast but then no she couldn't entirely see him as that. She could see the man; more man than Victoor's had ever been he had been the epitome of evil and beast to her. This beast was nothing like that; not to her anyway. Maybe having her life tinged with so much nastiness allowed her to see that little bit more than others.

"Ouch." Having stepped on a particularly hard sharp stone Kalista had tried to stop herself from knocking into the stone wall she was sandwiched between and had laid her hands out to stop her. Catching her fingers in the process. Barakan was immediately besides her. Breathing down on her from his great height. She raised her eyes trying to be sure not to look where she shouldn't.

"Kalista… What have you done? Are you ok?" Looking into his chest; aiming to keep her eyes concentrated; there was hardly enough room for them both.

"I'm ok. I just put my hands out to steady myself.. They are."

"Sore I know I can smell them. I warned you."

"Yes .. Yes you did. But I'm ok. Just keep going before you catch me with your hands and." He snorted at her.

"I thought you said I wouldn't hurt you?"

"I don't believe you will Barakan not deliberately but please." She shoved her forearms into his chest. "Keep going. I would be out of here it is claustrophobic."

"You don't like it?"

"No not really." *What else have you suffered? Victoor's!*

"I will go slower stay with me."

"I was trying." It didn't take many more minutes before the strange couple emerged from the rock. The mornings light now in full swing. Kalista stopped and gasped. *It's beautiful!* What met her eyes wasn't what she had expected. The dark forbidding forest had gone to reveal; a mountain range so beautiful trees and bushes teeming with life swept before her as far as she could see; nothing dark about this side of the rocks.

"Barakan. It is beautiful."

"Yes. I can still appreciate beauty." Kalista stuck him with a stare.

"Did I say anything about you not being able to?" He glared at her. *You are getting awfully brave.*

"We just go up here and that is my… Home." Stalling the words sounded so strange on his lips.

"Ok what is it? A hut?"

"A cave."

"Oh." *Oh dear but oh well!* Barakan heard the tone of her voice. *Not so sure now are you lady.* He let out a noise which made Kalista look at him with curiosity. *Are you laughing?* Momentarily stopping Kalista tilted her head to study him harder. "Are you laughing at me?"

"Maybe! Come on." He shoved her this time

with the back of his hand. Always conscious of his claws. “It is best you just see.”

“Hmm.” Kalista found herself feeling somewhat piqued at him. *Fancy laughing at me. Huh.* She followed.

They seemed to be walking up an incline that over the years the stones had almost become steps. She studied them smooth and large. *Your feet have done this Barakan.* But then her attention was drawn to the very large cave opening in front of them nestled in the mountain. It’s darkness mesmerising. Silence.

“Is that it?”

“Yes!”

“And this is your home?”

“Yes… You wanted to come with me.”

“I did…!” *Hmm. Oh dear.* Barakan’s felt amused another emotion long ago disposed of.

“Come I will show you.”

“What it’s a cave!”

“Kalista!” Barakan seemed to chuckle as once again stepping behind Kalista he picked her up. “Don’t act like a foolish woman now.”

“I. It’s a cave.”

“And I’m a beast so what did you expect?”

"I don't know. But I don't care."

"Liar."

"What?" Barakan moved with ease through the caves entrance slipping down into the unused bit. Passing his own meagre bed. His eyes easily accustomed to seeing in the dark. Kalista not so. But there was something about the place it didn't smell; not damp or stale like she had expected. And if he would slow down she was sure she could see more the walls seemed to be twinkling in bits… it was a lot dryer than she would have thought. An entrance before them seemed to be hi-lighted from above daylight streaming through. Kalista looked at Barakan frowning herself.

"Are you smiling?"

"Maybe! This will be yours Kalista." He strode through the small entrance to show Kalista what was within…

Now she gasped loudly. It was a room full.

Kalista could not imagine what was now before her. Furniture lots of lovely wooden furniture. Obviously it hadn't been used for a long time but it was all there almost set out like a bedroom study. Very manly and nothing feminine but it was beautifully carved and full of character. And she could see them. In the daylight there was some light.

“Put me down Barakan.” Her voice intimately grateful. This was nothing like she had expected this was stunning. *No wonder you teased...* There was even a wash stand adorned by a lovely jug and bowl. Her eyes were filled with the room his nakedness forgotten.

“Barakan! This is … its.”

“For you Kalista.”

“I … I.” She was lost for words. Moving between the furniture she gingerly began to touch the pieces… Running her little finger over them; it was not too sore. Barakan watched her with something akin to pride. He growled. Drawing her attention back to him

“There are things you will need. I will attend to that as soon as I can and a mattress you will need a stuffed mattress. I will get you one of those this day.”

“But how?” It wasn’t as if he could just go down and shop.

“I have my ways. Although it hasn’t been necessary for a while but I can.”

“This; these.” She gestured. “Are all your belongings?” Barakan just nodded. Watching her intently as she stroked what was his. “They are beautiful; very well made."

"Yes." He growled a bit too sharply. "I was lord once." Kalista watched his face.

"I hadn't."

"Why would you? It was long ago now." He seemed to struggle to shake of this emotion. "There will be other things you will need. For starters now. Food! Are you hungry?" As Barakan said the words her stomach seemed to understand and grumble in answer. He heard. "That would be a yes then. Sit accustom yourself with what is in here. Through the day the light is enough for you to see; I have some lamps somewhere which you can have for evening. And I will go get some food. It will be plain."

"Anything Barakan." He grunted at her. "And Barakan."

"Yes."

"Thank you." Watching her through his raw eyes Barakan shook his head. Her sore fingers momentarily forgotten.

"I wouldn't be thanking me just yet." He turned and stomped through the entrance; his voice booming as he left. "It still may not work." But he wanted it to God did he want it to. Everything about her silenced his beast but in the same breath made him jump to rage. He wanted to be near her; around her and… *oh my God in her.* He growled loudly it echoed through the cave. Kalista heard and the annoyed tone but still whispered back at him.

“All the same thank you Barakan.” Becoming practical to try and take his mind of her Barakan ran things through his mind which could be put into place to make it better for her he didn’t need much more than a place to lye and food. Which he realised now she wouldn’t want raw…

The meat wasn’t a problem but lighting a fire could be. Then his mind concentrated on her wanting and needing food every day. There was a delve in the caves entrance which if he managed right could be made to house a fire for cooking a pan and hook and maybe even an oven if he could build it with rocks; making them tight enough to keep the heat. *Hmm. That could work. But now right now she needed cooked meat.* Leaping from the entrance he left her.

Kalista wandered around what was to be her quarters. Not unpleasant so much better than she could have expected; come the winter it could be interesting but right now it was fine… The furniture was just amazing could do with a clean but nothing more it was well kept and dry in here. She was definitely thinking long term not just for now. *Why?* She had no idea; the fact that she didn’t belong here with him just wasn’t in the equation. She pulled out the chair and sat at the desk… unable to stop her curiosity. *He had said to acquaint myself though.* She carefully pulled out the drawers; a little stiff at first from not being used. The first empty. Then the next full with fairly recent paper and an pen. Kalista flicked her hand over them. *Definitely new.* But underneath. *That's not.* Something caught her eye. Leather carved. Beautiful. Pushing the paper to one side she touched it; with her knuckles. Deciding whether she should take it out and look. Caressing the bindings. *That looked like some sort of arms… **No.*** Kalista pushed the draw shut with determination curiosity filling her but it wasn't for her to go digging into him without his say so. She wanted him to tell her. Because she wanted to know everything and all about it but from him.

"Kalista." His voiced washed over her pulling back from her thoughts. She turned to see Barakan filling the doorway; for that's what it effectively was. Still the beast and naked. Kalista wondered if she could get used to that. But he was holding something which she had to admit smelt good. *Food.*

Nestled on some sort of flat stone maybe slate was something small and cooked. *At least that is something.*

"Barakan that smells delicious." His eyebrows seemed to raise doubtful.

"Does it?"

"Yes. Why does it not to you?"

"I suppose so."

"Why suppose?" She made to stand. "Please tell me you don't just eat everything raw!"

"A little."

"Urgh."

"Kalista!"

"I'm sorry; do you have to? Or do you prefer it that way?"

"It has just been easier."

"What? To just eat raw food?"

"Kalista … I am." He moved over to where she was and slid the slate onto the top. "Just eat. No more questions."

"But without questions how am I to get to know you?" *Did she want to?* Everything about this little woman was a surprise to Barakan.

"Do you need to Kalista?"

"What?" She tried to pull at the white meat…

"Ouch…"

"Too hot?"

"No my fingers they are still sore." *Shit I forgot.* Too wrapped up in her well-being he had neglected her wellbeing. He was frustrated with himself. Bending once again to her. He lifted her.

"There is something we can do about them now whilst that cools."

"Ok." Leaning easily against his so strong form she allowed him to take control.

"This cavern is special there are hot spring below us where you will be able to wash which is why your quarters are so dry and fresh running spring water." Kalista liked the sound of that but was surprised at the domesticity she could find in this cave with him.

"And it's all yours." Bending his neck to look at her his words just came out.

"Mine. Now I think maybe ours." Kalista found her heart so frail before now filled with him. With what she did not know but he filled her. She could live.

"Thank you Barakan."

"Hmm." Turning into a narrower part of the cavern he allowed her to slide down him to the floor. Both enjoying the touch too much.. "Here." She smiled as before her trickling form the wall was beautiful clean water splashing on the small rocks at their feet. "It's cold so be careful but clean." Kalista nodded and carefully pushing her fingers forward to test the water.

“Oo.” He was right. It was very cold.

“Make sure they are clean Kalista.”

“Yes.” If he had been looking at her face he would have seen her roll her eyes. *Mother hen.*

“Does that feel better?”

“Yes… Thank you; yes it does.” The cooling clean water was pleasant.

“Come on then.” Barakan quickly grabbed at her. “Back for food.”

“Ok.” Kalista didn’t complain but that was a little to swift; she wasn’t sure if his claws had caught her dress. She hoped not it was the only one she had. Back in her quarters he dropped her back into the seat.

“Stay here there is something else we can do to help the injuries then you can eat.” Before Kalista has time to speak back to him he was gone. Quickly returning with a handful of. *What?* Kalista wasn’t sure what; it looked like leaves. “Here Kalista.” He dropped the pile onto the desk. “Rub them into your hands they have properties which will help…” He searched his memory for the right word. “Natural antiseptic.”

“Ok.” She did as he bid. Immediately feeling the cooling sensation stretching over her fingers. *That’s ok! Not unpleasant.*

"Now eat Kalista before it gets cold. Can you write?"

"Yes." She nodded a well as spoke a little ungainly as she was chewing too. "Sorry." She covered her mouth; as she continued to speak. "Yes I can read and write. Why?"

"We will need to make a list of what you will require."

"Oh ok I can do that. This." She shoved another piece of meat into her mouth. "Is delicious Barakan." But she frowned just studying him. "Are you not eating?"

"No." No explanation or reason. *Hmm.* Kalista looked from his hands to his teeth. *Maybe that is the reason.* Pulling another especially large piece of lean meat from the carcass; she quickly with ease and without too much forethought shoved it at his face and into his mouth.

"See it's so much better cooked." Barakan was forced to take the offering unless he was to catch her with his teeth. Her fingers brushed past his lips as she retreated. "Good isn't it!" She watched as with reluctance he began to chew. The smallest amount of spittle escaping. *So that was the reason. Prat. I'm not in the slightest bothered about manners.* "It is isn't it?"

"What?"

"The food it's better."

"It is food."

"Barakan. I see you enjoyed that piece." Kalista quickly pulled another piece and held it up to his lips. He hadn't had any intention of eating in front of her. His beast didn't have the best of manners.. *But...* He had lived as beast too long. But... Kalista had taken the decision from him. Her hand hovered over his mouth; unflinching. Carefully allowing his tongue to protrude just a little he slowly and gentle took the piece of meat from her fingers and let it fall back into his mouth. Kalista interestingly watched his so sensual movement. *Oh.*

"It is ok." He relented. Enjoying the unexpected attention she was giving him. Together they both dug at the carcass until there was no meat left.

"Kalista the draw besides you is paper and pen. Could you make me a list and put mattress and blankets top of it please and anything else you can think of that you will need. But do not worry there is no rush . The mattress and bedding is the main things for today, I would have you as comfortable as possible."

"That isn't going to be hard Barakan this is all lovely."

"It was once." *But still not as lovely as you? What the Barakan...* His subconscious was playing with him. The rest of the day was busy for Kalista. He was fussing like some old hen which she found amusing. He kept disappearing then reappearing. At one point she had to pin him down to ask where she was to use the bathroom… That was an enlightening conversation. Kalista shook her head picturing his face. Stunned.

"Barakan. Will you just slow down and stop for one minute there is something I need to ask you."

"More questions? Woman."

"This for me is quite an important one."

"What?"

"I need to relieve myself and unlike you I do not intend to just go stand in the corner." He had just stared at her hard, he actually looked embarrassed. The man for that moment overshadowed the Beast. Then she had seen his face change and he again had swept her from her feet and took her to where the water ran.

"Here for now. But till you know the way I will have to bring you." He sighed remembering his manners. "The water flows way down the mountain." It had been a plan and she had managed although she wasn't so keen on the fact that he hovered around the entrance like her own personal shadow. But necessary.

By the end of the day he wasn't even telling Kalista he was off. But for now she knew better than to explore this was still early days. And she didn't want to piss him off. Then he came in carrying a mattress and she immediately knew it was the best stuffed with down. It would be warm and comfortable. Better than what she was used to.

"Barakan you got that for me?"

"Off course. Do you not like?"

"Yes off course I do."

"Thank you" He allowed it to drop to the bed. Large solid very nearly a four poster. Big carved wooden legs at the bottom thicker than the ones at the top. Kalista looked from Barakan to the bed. *What about the curse? Kalista it is still there.* But she pushed her doubts away sure that she could scope. There was a beauty in this that wouldn't be denied. What they were building together.

# Chapter six

Kalista stared at the heavy mattress. It was brand new.

"Barakan where are you getting all these things from?" She had written the note. *Hmm.*

"Does it matter?"

"No. But I wouldn't want you."

"What Kalista?"

"Putting yourself in danger because of me."

*You wouldn't?* She was joining the dots. But if he had help then someone knew… *Surely that means they could hunt you?* Barakan took a single small step closer towards her hovering like a great mountain over her; everything he was on edge the work had made him pumped and sweaty. He had moved through the forest like lightening. The exercise was good but made his blood sing.

"It worries you?"

"Off course." His heavy breath blew past her face mixed with his so earthy smell. She found her heart racing and her mind joining in; as she wondered. *Will I be in that bed alone? God what have I got myself into?* But her face showed none of the doubt suddenly creeping in. She'd been so sure before.

"Because obviously you fetching all this stuff means something is different..."

"Could they not come looking?"

"No." He was adamant. "Roberts; they gain too much from me to repeat what they know."

"They do? You pay them?"

"Off course. Roberts was tied to the manor many years ago he will be long dead but each time they pass it goes down to the next male."

"Never a woman."

"No!"

"Barakan I'm sorry." She could feel his annoyance at the woman comment. "I didn't mean to. I was only concerned." He panted the beast wanted something and he was unsure what. It was going round and round in his soul like it paced. *What? She is concerned? What is that?* Barakan looked down on her so small beneath him. So lovely and delicate. Yet so broken. Forcing himself he backed up.

"Do not worry; nothing will be said. And even if it was I would deal with it. Kalista you are safe"

In a huff he turned and left again. Leaving

Kalista with words still on her lips.

“But I wasn’t…. I was only worried for you.” He heard her last words as a whisper. But night was drawing in again and the forest would be alive. He charged to the entrance and man and beast set of at a pace that would relieve his unspent energies. Or so he hoped. It had started off so well but as her smell was encompassing all he was the beast and man wanted more.

Kalista dropped down onto the mattress bemused what he just happened; that wasn’t how she saw today ending. She sighed.

“Barakan. I am sorry.” She hoped he heard. But did it matter if he didn’t this time she would tell him again. And again if it was necessary. Standing she crossed to the desk where Barakan had left her another torch larger than her own. Making sure it was bright. Stealing herself she had to go to the bathroom. It was somewhat of a necessity.

“Here goes.” Kalista imagined she could find her way.

Holding the torch tight she left her comfortable space. The cavern was a very different space in the dark. But Kalista kept her torch tight; picking her way carefully through. Hoping she remembered the way. It took her a little time and a few about turns but eventually she did. Whilst she was there she cupped the cool water from the spring in her hands and drank it tasted so good. *It could be good here…* She knew it. Given the time and chance. What else would she need. Gathering herself she stepped from this area and tried to find her way back to hers; realising where she was; the entrance was to the right. She stepped towards it. In reality hoping to see some sign of him. The silence was deafening. As she stepped towards the entrance something caught Kalista's eye; what looked like another alcove. She hadn't noticed it before mind you she hadn't been looking. Stepping closer she lifted her torch to see inside. Catching her breath loudly as she did. It was just another cave but in it was just a mattress old and worn and smelly. She stepped inside. Immediately knowing what it was. This was where Barakan slept. Alone.

*Barakan.* Her heart went out to him. It was so sparse; nothing of man. Guilt of intrusion filled her and she turned to go. But again something else caught her eyes something leaning on the floor against the inside wall. Kalista stepped closer holding her torch towards it to see.

"Oh my… Barakan." Her words were clear and filled with grief. Bending she inspected it closer. What she saw was what would have once been portrait; old and darker than it should have been aged beyond recognition but then too he had ripped it to shreds obviously more than once over the years. The only thing that was still recognisable was a pair of green eyes staring at her. Beautiful strong adorable eyes. *No wonder the women flocked to you. Barakan.* Her heart cried out to him. Then something made her shrink back.

A shadow loomed over her the breathing suddenly so heavy it made every hair she had stand on end. *Barakan... Angry.*

He was just beast. Kalista stood attempting to turn. Then everything seemed to alter so very fast. He heard her every unsure breath; the beast smelt her. *Mine, mine, mine.* Snarling that loudly it bounced around the cave. Lunging forward Barakan barrelled into her forcing her back against the wall… the portrait what was left of it banged against the rock and shattered with the force of his legs. Kalista couldn't breathe he held her trapped beneath his powerful chest fast. Her back hit the rock.

"Ouch." She groaned in pain. *No not again. Not pain. Anything else but pain.* Her thoughts betrayed her fears. Lowering his head to hers all teeth and saliva Barakan. Growled at her.

"What are you doing?" He pushed his claws into the rock either side of her, grabbing hard to control them. Kalista could feel him hard hot and sweaty, all of him. His already hard erection pushing at her. She struggled to talk. Barakan breathed her in. *Gods woman.*

"Do you know what I could do to you?" His snarls voicing his emotions.

"Yes."

"Kalista. You shouldn't have come in here."

"I'm. I. Was looking for you." She swallowed. Fear rising. Fear he could smell. Which only fuelled his own anger; he was the one causing her fear. *Barakan!* "I missed you. I wanted to say sorry, I." Tears began to run down her face.

"Barakan. I'm sorry."

"Because you have been caught?"

"No because I have upset you." His grip on her began to lessen but he didn't move.

"I would not have you seen that." Barakan slowly snarling; lowered his head to her and run his lips down her face nuzzling into her neck. She just smelt so very good. His blood raging around his body was not going to be quiet this night. No amount of running or exertion had stilled it. *But you could!* ***No.*** She had been in his space all day now; filling it with her smell, her essence. He had tried to rid himself of it with spent energy; but that hadn't worked.

"Do not play games with me Kalista."

"I wasn't." She could taste her own salty tears.

"I needed to relieve myself I found my way there and."

"You ended up here." His body moved with a will of its own against her.

"Not entirely; my intention was to stand at the entrance and watch for you." She sighed. "But I noticed this alcove and curiosity got the better of me and the smell." He snarled again.

"You do like to tell me I stink." Kalista tried to raise her head a little. As he nuzzled into her further. She whispered unsure what reaction she would get but it was the truth.

"But you do." What was he doing? She had no idea. He had been so angry; but she could feel it slowly dissipating as he nuzzled her flesh. *Did he need more now from her? The curse. But... No.* Then; that before, felt different that was a necessity to stop the burning pain of need the curse caused this in him now felt different.

"Kalista." He whispered her name the red hot emotions cooling... He could taste her tears on his lips. He knew he had handled her roughly... But. *But. She saw.* She'd seen the portrait. Gone now finally; he felt it beneath his feet.

Instinctively without forethought or malice he

allowed his tongue to leave its haven between his teeth and with more than care ran it over her flesh. Tracing a line down her neck. Wanting to taste her. Kalista involuntarily shuddered. A loud and guttural groan escaped him. Although afraid and hurting Kalista didn't find the sensation unpleasant. She panted.

"Barakan." Too quick he suddenly released her. Just staring. His flame red eyes; telling her all she needed to know. "I'm sorry, B…" He chewed at the inside of his mouth.

"So am I. I have hurt you." Kalista could only look at his face knowing that great erection of his pointed directly at her. She shrugged knowing there would be no point lying he would know.

"I will be bruised that is all." He picked up her torch out now. *How do i make this right?* Both suffered from the same doubts.

"Barakan." Kalista's voice was nowhere near as assured as it had been. "I am sorry I had no intention of prying. I. Shouldn't. I." Barakan stopped her from carrying on.

"As I am… I have hurt you. It is not you I am angry at. No matter what know that it is not you." The air between them heavy.

"This is where you sleep?"

"Yes. I told you I am beast; the beast doesn't need anything more." Pulling herself away from the wall Kalista stepped closer to him once again; erection and all.

"I do not see the beast Barakan." Her words although quietly spoken had a massively profound effect. On them both. Silence reigned between them just their breathing could be heard. Barakan needed an escape. *Now.*

"You are right Kalista I do stink… I will wash." Grabbing at her dropped torch Barakan turned to lift her… again. But this time Kalista put her hands up. Effectively stopping him.

"I can walk Barakan. I walked here." He tilted his head deciding. *But I don't want you to.* He enjoyed the closeness when he carried her. "I found my way here."

"But it is darker now."

"Yes..." She stuttered not really knowing how to describe it but she knew in his heightened excited state; touching him could be dangerous for her. *Unless.* She attempted too. Kalista wasn't totally against touching him again; if that was what he needed from her. It suddenly hit her that he could expect her to touch him more… *Do I mind? No.* She knew she didn't, not really. "But." Her eyes lowered finally to his now throbbing erection. Barakan followed her eyes to where they settled on him. *Hmm.* He turned abruptly... "It may be wiser for me to walk Barakan." Suddenly more than aware of his own body Barakan just grunted.

"So be it." And continued his way from the cave. Carefully picking her way over the broken bits of the portrait frame. Kalista couldn't un- see the stunning green eyes she knew still existed; her mind was overwhelmed by how emotive they were for he; Barakan had described himself as more of an emotionless man but what she saw wasn't not now nor then. Those eyes told more than he knew; or was just willing to admit.

Kalista followed Barakan; silently keeping a few paces behind him. His head snapped back at her his voice loud.

"You are not my servant!"

"What?"

"I don't expect you to walk two steps behind me."

"I. Oh… No; but…" She raised her hands in a gesture of frustrated helplessness. "I give up." Taking her life in her hands Kalista quickly stepped past him. "Please yourself." Imagining she knew where she went Kalista stormed off. Or attempted to. But she found herself growled at loudly…

"Wrong way you need to turn right." Stopping momentarily Kalista nearly swore but restrained herself. Before taking the correct corridor. "How the bloody hell was I supposed to know. Aaa." Barakan could hear her every grumble even as she reached her quarters and realised it was too dark.

"Woman!" He still held her torch. Barakan strode after her. "Do not move or you will fall over something. I will light you torch again." Talking as he entered. Ignoring the fact that she refused to turn to him; all he saw was her back. *Bloody woman.* How he had managed to light the torch before was a feat in itself. But again he managed. Lit it threw a little light out giving the room a warm glow. Still she didn't look at him.

"I will bring you more light after I have washed. I have candles and matches too."

"Thank you!" Barakan stared at her; but didn't say anything he turned and growling left. Kalista knew he had gone. Immediately she missed him. Everything about him filled the room and her. To try and keep herself busy the blankets that he had left earlier she threw onto the mattress and tried to make the bed. *Bed... Nightime ... Bed. Alone or... Oh my goodness.* She had absolutely no idea of what was to come next. So consumed with just getting away and escaping her life she had no consideration of what was to happen. Not that she had cared and even this had to be better than what she had before. Victoor's would have made sure she was dead one way or another sooner or later. She had no home. Sitting down heavily on the end of the bed she dropped her head into her hands. Running them into her hair, untidy unruly and definitely a mess. *Home.*

It hadn't taken Barakan long to make his way to the hot springs. Not deep enough for him to swim in but plenty deep enough to wash. Today he had sweated much for one reason or another; the hard heavy work had created more heat in him than it had used and then even the run hadn't dispersed the feelings running through him. And he knew they were feelings nothing to do with the curse and need this was so different it was frightening. Hence the anger again. And he had turned on her, Kalista. *Kalista.* But despite what the beast wanted they had both reigned it in man and beast. She was so fragile and needed to be cosseted not stalked and brutally taken. No matter how willing she was to die. He sat in the warm water for a while.. hoping his erection would lessen. It didn't. Groaning. He hated this but her touching him and giving him so much pleasure only made it worse now. His own hands. *Claws.* Where useless but he needed to do something before he returned to her. Carefully wrapping his fingers around himself making a fist he began to slide them up and down his length. An immediate growl escaping him. "Kalista." He groaned and thoughts of her filled him. Nothing else mattered any longer she was all he wanted man and beast alike. It didn't take long before he found himself rising to orgasm with only images of her; her smell reaching him. He snarled loudly as he reached orgasm. Snarling her name . "Kalista."

Kalista didn't know how long she sat contemplating her life; before then and now. There was so much difference and one thing she knew for sure was she didn't want to go back. No matter what. She moved realising how much her back hurt. Then she heard him. Growling so loudly it filled the cavern. She sat bolt upright. Listening harder. He sounded like he was in pain. *Maybe he was.* Her little hands resting on her knees made fists Kalista heard him snarling her name.

"Kalista…!" *Did he need her?* He was shouting for her. She had no idea what to do stay put or go to him? But having no idea which way he had gone the hot springs where near the cool spring waters but she didn't dare delve deeper into the cavern alone. Knowing no matter how much she felt the pull to go to him she shouldn't best to just wait to see. If he didn't return soon. Then maybe she would try to go look for him but until then staying put was the best idea.

"Barakan." She knew he heard her more than

she realised so she tried speaking to him instead. “Barakan I hear you; are you ok? You sound… in pain.” There was nothing more she could do now just wait. For a while anyway.

Raising himself from the water Barakan heard her words they swept over him. *Kalista you are concerned about me... This cannot be, I.* Shaking himself free of the water. He realised, maybe she would like to wash. Especially after he had bruised her. They would welcome the warm healing waters here. He had gotten her some soaps from Roberts they were still stashed near the entrance with a crate of wine and foods. Things he himself couldn’t forage for. “Kalista.” He moved quickly along the corridor returning to her. Barakan hadn’t expected to find her sat on the end of the bed watching for him. Her eyes just trained in the doorway. He stalled in the entrance staring at her as she stared at him.

“Kalista!”

“Barakan.” Her tone full of concern. “Are you ok?” He snorted not wanting to tell her what the noise was about.

“Yes.” He finally stepped into her space for it was her space now it stopped being his long long ago. “I’m sorry Kalista. This is … I’m…” He was struggling for words.

“It’s alright Barakan. As long as you are good.”

“Kalista it is not but I will try; I hurt you. For that I’m sorry would you like to bathe too. It will help with the bruising.” Kalista looked at him her own emotions easing. *Yes.*

“Thank you Barakan. Yes I would appreciate that.”

“Good I will take you now.” Barakan moved towards her with the expectation to lift her to him again. But as Kalista made to stand herself he stopped.

“I. You should know we will take the torch but it is dark down there it could be difficult to walk right now till you know it better. It would be better if I carry you.” Kalista had already noticed he was not in such a state of excitement like before.

“Is that ok with you?” She needed to be sure.

“Why would it not be?”

“Before … you. Were. It wasn’t advisable.” He understood. Picking up the torch he handed it to her. Before answering.

“You are safe with me Kalista.” He bent to fold his arms around her. “Always.” Kalista felt the strain in him as he slowly spoke the words. Before it had just been her that believed he wouldn’t now it was him too. It eased her tension. She allowed him to lift her to him. Whispering as he did so.

"Thank you." He momentarily held her tight against him. *Mine.* Before he made his way out her quarters and back along the corridors. Kalista knew where he was headed as they went towards the cool spring but then as he entered they carried on a little further and as Barakan squeezed them both through a smaller gap she felt the warmer air hit her as they entered. It was beautiful again nothing like she was expecting. Nor as dark. The walls seemed to be stuck with crystal which catching the light from her torch caused many prisms sending lovely rays of light darting all around.

"Barakan it is perfect."

"It is and the torch I hadn't contemplated the crystals would give us more light. I don't need it."

"No." Carefully he once again let her drop to her feet. Kalista saw the water. In the corner oval shaped disappearing into the rock. Clear and clean.

"Where does it come from?"

"Below it bubbles up through the rocks. It doesn't get stagnant it runs off and refills constantly. I used to use it more at first. When I offended myself but now I don't normally bother. It has been just me." Barakan put the torch on the floor.

"But." Kalista turned to him. "You will now?"

"Yes." He seemed to smile. "As my stink seems

to offend you; yes, I will."

"Good." Kalista watched him expectantly as did

Barakan her. Kalista coughed. He didn't seem to be doing anything or going anywhere. *Oh my. Are you… oh dear I don't think so.* Kalista realised she would probably have to tell him to leave her be.

"Barakan I can bathe by myself." He knew but he would check her bruises first.

"Yes. Turn around."

"What?"

"Woman do as I ask and turn around." She did as he bid unsure of what he wanted from her. "Undo the bindings."

"What?"

"Just do it. I will not hurt you I just want to see what harm I have done."

"Barakan it is…"

"Do not argue with me Kalista just do it." Slowly turning and putting her hands up she loosened the bindings on her dress. Allowing the sleeves to hang loose from her shoulders. Barakan saw her so perfect flesh come into view; never mind the scars he already knew where there. *If only I could touch you.*

"Kalista I am sorry." He saw the blue bruising

already apparent by tomorrow she would be black too. “I did that to you.”

“It is ok. It is just bruising, it is nothing in comparison to what I have inflicted on me before and against what you could have done it is nothing.”

“It is still pain which I had no intention of causing you. I am sorry; it will not happen again.”

“And for my part Barakan; I hadn’t intended to snoop but I did and for that I am sorry.”

“I will have to remember you are not built like me.”

“No.”

“Get in the water and I will go get you something to wrap yourself in when you have done.” He was gone,

Grateful of his disappearance Kalista quickly stripped and striding to the water; stepped in….

“Wow this is fantastic.” Talking to herself she allowed her body to slip into the water. Laying out totally it felt so nice, it’s warmth enveloped her. The twinkling crystal around her was special. She shut her eyes enjoying the peace. In the cave and in her. It was magical. *This had been worth sacrificing for.* Barakan filled her thoughts, her body seemed to come alive, his beautiful eyes all she wanted to see.

She ran her hands over her body; cleaning enjoying. But something else was happening something so keen she didn't know what to do with the sensation of emotion building.

Dipping her head underwater; she did not hear anything. Finally needing breath she lifted her head and breathing opened her eyes. Jumping immediately to try to cover herself.

"Barakan." He was there looming over her. Barakan saw her full for the first time, the water hid nothing. *God she was so perfect.* His mind shut to the scars and welt's his eyes took in. *Victoor's.* In that one single moment Barakan made a concious decision that he would see Victoor's for this. Her smooth flesh not spoilt in his eyes; full round breasts tipped with tight pink nipples right at this moment showing more excitement than he had expected. He tried to stifle a low grumble as his eyes burning red hot slyly lowered across her heaving chest to the neat little triangle which he could smell all around him. This time not mistaken. *Desire...*

"Kalista. Here." He put something down beside the pool. "For you." Before abruptly turning. Knowing he would shortly have yet another full on erection his desire for her too great. *Control Barakan you twat get control.* He almost ran for the cave. "I will wait outside." As he turned his back on her Kalista moved to see what he had brought.

"Soap." She lifted it to smell it; perfumed soap. Sat atop a drying sheet. "Thank you Barakan." She knew he would hear.

"You are welcome Kalista." He made himself heard too. Kalista knew this day she had been spoilt.

Barakan let his heavy frame drop to the floor to sit and wait. Listening to her splashing about in the water. It all sounded so normal. So every day. But it wasn't. He wondered how long could they keep up the pretence, yet he didn't care he stared down on his growing shaft…

"Urgh." Lightly groaning hoping it would settle before she saw… Again. But knew one thing for certain he wanted her here with him. No matter how difficult it became.

Kalista soaked her bruised body and battered soul; knowing he waited watching over her; it wasn't an unpleasant thought. *If only my sweet beast there was a way through!* Kalista mulled over her surprising thought. *Where had that come from? Did it matter what he looked like? He was man and beast.* One thing she did know was that he was trying and that was all she could ask. But then another ask came to mind. *Maybe I should say? It may be safer for both of us. Especially me. Hmm.* Kalista pondered the question and practised in her mind; how to put it without sounding offensive…

Kalista was finished. Clean and relaxed feeling much better; she climbed from the water and grabbed the sheet to cover herself soft and warm from where he had left it laid on the rock the heat graduating through them to it. She; wrapping it around her, it was lovely to be clean warm and fragrant. Even Barakan could smell the perfume now; on her it was illuminating.

Kalista dressed quickly hearing him sighing. She knew she had taken some time; he must be fed up of waiting. She lay the sheet back down it would dry for further use if she left it there.

"Barakan! I am done." He appeared in the door; his appearance hard for her to describe, he looked uncomfortable almost disheveled and his face, seemed pain. "Barakan are you alright?" He studied her; her hair wet now dripping down her face and neck.. An erotic effect he would wipe those drops from her. *Urgh... No stop.*

"Yes." His booming voice soft and not a little lost. She titled her head to study him closer in the light. *You're not.* But she knew if he wanted her to know then he would say. She questioned him no more. But then her eyes once again drifted to his groin. *Oh maybe that was it.* Her question seemed to be more than appropriate at this moment. She opened her mouth to speak as he bent to pick up the torch. Holding it out to her. But the way he held his shoulders his eyes. *No not now Kalista.* She resigned herself to leaving it till later. *I would not offend you again Barakan.* She didn't want to spoil the evening now. Breathing heavily almost a pant. Barakan bent again to her. Lifting her like a tiny feather to him. Aiming not to drag her over his shaft; once again wanting. He lifted her high. Cradling her there she smelt so good so clean. Unlike him. In a single moment of peace between them Kalista lifted her hand free of the torch to lay it on his chest. Feeling his heart racing beneath; she gentle moved her fingers.

"Thank you Barakan." He didn't answer nor look at her just strode out the cave. The image of her naked melted all he was.

They quickly returned to her quarters. Kalista saw immediately it was different. Candles lit and strategically place two torches too; the whole too was illuminated. He had been busy when he'd left her.

"You did this?"

"Off course who else?"

"That wasn't what I meant! When you haven't been away from me long enough."

"Kalista haven't you realised yet I move different to you; faster."

"Oh ok I did know but still. Thank you it's stunning."

“And there are matches and a torch tap to light any that go out.”

“Thank you I do not like the dark.”

“I know.” She sighed. Not wanting to visit the reasons why. Barakan seemed to hug her before he allowed her feet to gain ground again. “There on the bed is something else for you.”

# Chapter seven

Kalista quickly moved towards the bed. There sat on it was more food… Some fruit; cheese and a large loaf of bread; a bottle of something and a normal wine glass. One large wooden goblet too. *Did he intend to take a glass with her?* But that was it all beside them were a silver hair brush set and a small hand mirror. Kalista let her fingers touch them.

"These are for me?"

"Yes. We can't have you looking as dishevelled as me." Barakan smiled or what Kalista knew now to be a smile; she was learning his expressions.

"They are stunning." But not feminine; and very old. "Where they yours?"

"Yes. I haven't needed them since."

"No. Thank you Barakan. The food it looks delicious." Kalista climbed onto the bed and got comfortable. "Would you like me to pour?" She picked up the wooden goblet. His. Had to be.

"It is port."

"Yes. Will you join me Barakan?" He nodded.

"I will try." He moved his hands across his face. "It is sometimes messy." Kalista beamed at him as she poured his.

"That is ok." Holding his goblet tight she did not hand it to him. "Barakan sit with me too please." Barakan wasn't convinced that was an entirely good idea. But slowly moving around the bed he with care eased himself down; the mattress dipped with his great weight causing Kalista to move slightly. He tried to manoeuvre himself so his shaft was disguised and not entirely pointing at her. She understood. When he was still Kalista handed him his goblet. With care he took it. Kalista quickly poured hers.

Lifting her glass Kalista gestured to Barakan.

"Thank you Barakan."

"I think it is I who should be thanking you Kalista." Her name sounded so good on his lips.

"It is all just what it is Barakan. Your treatment of me is." She quickly took a sip of her drink. Sweet and heady. It wasn't like him unpleasant. "Something I cannot be grateful enough for."

"It is just one day Kalista. Things alter but know one thing man nor beast that I am would not hurt you deliberately."

"I am already assured of that Barakan." She quickly drank her drink. Before resting the glass down on the bed and pulling at the bread. "Would you like some?"

"Yes." Kalista pulled a large piece off and like before fed him. He watched as her fingers stretched to his face. *Touch me please touch me.* Kalista watched him eat. This was so natural now between them. Putting a small piece of cheese to her lips Barakan watched as Kalista wrapped her lips around it and pulled it in. *Lovely.* She ate.

Stretching her fingers to the brush; Kalista picked it up. She needed to brush her hair whilst it was still wet otherwise it would be knotted. She gripped it and lifted it to her head and pulled her hair forward enough to enable her to run the bristles through it. Watched closely by Barakan. His own bristles rustling. *My God Kalista.* Her movements where so sensual. *Do you realise? No. You do not know what you do to me.* He began to fidget. His whole being suddenly becoming all hot and bothered. His heart beat so fast. *Again.* Kalista heard Barakan snort and let h her eyes fall on him. They were both caught in a stare so intense. Barakan could stand it no longer and stood growling. His huge shaft slapping against his stomach as he did so. He suddenly looked more feral than man even shocked and embarrassed. Shaking his head he tried to leave. But found himself stopped by her soft voice.

"Barakan." Kalista put the brush down breathing deeply carried on. "Barakan. Do you need… do you need anything from me?" A simple question but he would make her no whore. He snarled loudly.

“No. Nothing.” Kalista didn’t believe him.

“That is not what it looks like.”

“Kalista.” Her name bounced of all the walls he spoke so loudly. “No! That is not why I brought you here. Eat sleep and I will see tomorrow. You are safe.” As he said the last words he was already gone.

“I know Barakan. I.” Did he not actually realise that she may actually want to. Kalista poured herself another glass of port; and quickly sipped at it.

“Barakan. Do not leave me.” Standing tall at the entrance Barakan knew he wouldn’t; he couldn’t not now after such a short time everything was changed. He was changed. Raising his large head to the night sky he let out an almighty roared howl. Rattling from the very base of him through all he was. Even within the confines of her quarters Kalista heard. So much anguish. She finished the drink. Whispering …

“Barakan.” She would have much rather he stayed with her. She shivered. Moving she quickly cleared the bed and extinguished some of the candles and the two main torches before returning to the bed sliding her dress from her body she couldn’t sleep in it being the only one she owned. It was left hanging evenly on the chair by the desk Finally Kalista climbed on and in to bed covering herself; wrapping the blanket tight around her hugging herself into it.

Needing comfort.

“Barakan… I. Good night my sweet beast.” Shutting her eyes sleep took her easily. Barakan listened to her every word and breath. He knew she settled into sleep.

“Sleep little one. I will watch over you.”

Exhaustion took her true sleep no nightmares no thoughts. Her breaths came in even rhythm; all pleased Barakan.

Like a night stalker he crept around her bed. Needing to know she was real; she was. Huddled fast asleep. Withdrawing from the urge to crawl on the bed besides her Barakan finally forced himself to leave. To draw his eyes away from the naked form which was so perfect laid beneath the blankets. He needed rest too. In the last 48 hours he hadn’t had much. He quietly left her quarters and went to his own. Dropping his heavy frame down on his own stinky mattress. *She was right! It does stink in here.* Barakan knew he had to remedy that too. *Tomorrow.*

*Kalista.* His thoughts his dreams his body were all her. She had crawled into his very soul, man and beast alike, and would ever erased. Not now. He had wanted form her but much much more than she would be able to give. He wanted it all from her.

Kalista slept like she hadn’t in a long time. Warm comfortable and most of all safe. Not even the nightmares plagued her this time. She knew she was safe. But how long that would last neither of them had any way of knowing. They could stay hidden for months years even yet then something could so easily go wrong and Barakans emotions get the better of him in some way or form and if he hurt her he would not forgive himself and then for him that would be it. His life would be even less than what it had been. His redemption and passion could very easily be his destruction.

The days were beginning to merge in to one. Barakan had provided Kalista with everything she needed including another dress so she had one to wash and one to wear. Similar to hers but more expensive better made with a little patterning at the bodice and it had fit perfectly; how he had managed it she didn't know nor cared. But he seemed to be getting more and more distant with every passing day. She had managed to broach the subject of him wearing breeches around her. In all fairness it could be the best for them both. At first she had thought he was going to get angry again but the immediate reaction to her statement had soon settled and he had seen some merit in what she was saying the beast in him just didn't control desire at all. For it was desire; desire which the beast in him craved with a furious urgency.

They had fallen into a daily routine but as the days drew into weeks. He spent less and less time with her. Barakan had found that even in the restraints of breeches which he knew he looked ridiculous in she still aroused him and it was only getting worse. She seemed oblivious to her own sexuality. But then given what she had survived there was no surprise there. Over the last days Barakan had been questioned her further about Victoor's. Sometimes Kalista was able to open up and talk others she just shut him down unable to even consider her life before. She knew her way around the cavern now without him. Which also meant she no longer needed him to help; he hadn't carried or held her in days and that was killing him. His beast seemed to be baying to be close to her and the man was desperate to keep his distance. It all made for a desperate mix within him. Wanting and volatile.

Kalista had spent another day going through the motions of what was her life. Wishing Barakan would come to her and talk. Conversation between them had been getting more and more difficult he seemed to be shutting down. And it was hard for her to be as relaxed as she was. She craved his company. It was so different now to how it had been that first week she had even managed to hear him laugh and what was their relationship had bloomed or so she had believed now it was all different again and she didn't really know why apart from she knew he had urges which he was struggling with. Desires which both man and beast shared but he refused to even let her ask if there was anything that she could do to help. He was distant. Too much so and it worried her. For Barakan's part he was struggling with his desires for her and nothing shifted them. They were just constant. Didn't fade… He did have episodes like this over the years which always had been hard but eventually he worked his way through them they were more so at first but as the years had gone by they drifted to not so many but this time this one seemed to be dragging him down like never before. He wanted… He wanted her and he wanted something resembling a life with her. *Not this... Never this.* It wasn't supposed to happen like this she had come into his life as sacrifice and for all intent and purpose she had sacrificed herself to him and had made him feel… Which now suddenly had only made things worse for him it had reminded him what he missed… *Kalista.* He knew what these feeling were for her. In their entirety. But he could not nor would not voice them not even in his thoughts…

Kalista crawled naked into her bed. Alone. Her heart ached to speak with him tell him how he actually made her feel. Comfortable and safe but there was something else there too something which made her want to touch him. She felt hot and achy in her own skin. Pulling on her hair so it didn't get trapped underneath her; it had grown even in the short time she had been here. She toyed with it twiddling it between her fingers wanting it to be him Barakan doing it. She felt herself moisten again it had took years in developing; this thing which she knew to be desire. She never expected to experience it. *Never.* But for him she knew she felt it. *If only he would let me touch him. I'm no longer afraid.* Even if he couldn't touch her she wanted to touch him and it was fast becoming a raging need in her to do just that. She knew he wanted her she'd seen it and it hadn't relented in fact she knew he felt it every single day. Presuming that was why he was keeping his distance; for fear he would hurt her. But she had every confidence in him even after that incident in his cave. Then it was all still new and his portrait those eyes must haunt him like they did her. She should have known better maybe he would have shown her eventually. She avoided it now and allowed him his space in there. She never ventured near.

Kalista shut her eyes and tried to sleep; but her mind whizzing with thoughts and hopes just wouldn't let her rest. Hopes which surprised and yet still terrified her. She wanted him to come to her to let her touch him help him through his own darkness.. She whispered into the darkness words which she never expected to ever say to anyone least of all him.

“Barakan… Come to me let me help you please.”

But no shadow appeared not that she thought he would. She tossed and turned on the bed dragging the blanket with her till it was wrapped around her and she fought it; unravelling herself. Then flinging her arms and legs; spread out trying to find comfort. But there was none. She had no idea how long she laid in the big bed like this. Trying to relax.

When a sudden and awful pained noise attacked her ears. So loud she knew it could only be him. A howl a cry and yet a bemused pained shout.

“Barakan.” *My God.* She sat bolt upright in bed the blanket falling away from her. Something was wrong that was a noise she didn’t know; couldn’t understand; and she had heard some of his noises recently. That was painful it made her heart leap and jump in fear. Knowing he was in pain. “Barakan what is wrong?” She knew he would hear her he always did, but the noise did not fade. He kept howling and howling. With words in between too.

“Nooo!”

“Barakan I’m coming…” She leapt from the bed and grabbing at her dress sliding it over her legs;

taking no time to fasten the binding she grabbed her small torch always lit and charged from the room. Pulling her skirts high so she didn't fall over them in her haste. She knew now where she was heading. The noise got louder as she neared his cave. But she couldn't stop to consider what she was doing. He was in pain.

"Barakan." As gently as she could Kalista spoke not wanting to make matters worse by just charging in without forethought. Anything could be happening in there. But with her own demons to contend with Kalista thought she understood what was happening. *Nightmares... flashbacks. Terrors.* He was reliving them all. Standing before his cave entrance Kalista swallowed loudly and tried to reach him again before she stepped in. Then putting one foot in front of the other she did just that stepped into his space. What met her eyes made her heart crack for him. Laid on his scruffy mattress which he'd still neglected to replace. He was laid thrashing and flaying about like something demented. The noises he emitted hurting her ears. He was lost to his demons; and at this moment in time they were all powerful. So much filled her; love hate pain, she loved him, hated the way they had both been made to endure atrocities and couldn't stand to see the pain he was now suffering. Not when she was there and more than willing to help. He should have let her in sooner then maybe this could have been avoided. She knew what this felt like. Being so lost in one's own nightmarish life that one no longer saw what was real. Sighing heavily knowing this could end badly for her but seeing Barakan was hurting and could easily hurt himself with those terrible claws that seemed to be gouging at air. *I have to do something. Make him know he is not alone.* Bending carefully to the floor. She put the lamp down needing the light but not wanting it to be knocked over or extinguished. She bent to the floor; deciding to keep low, away from his claws. Set about carefully making her way on all fours across to him. His noise tremendous. Her voice would be nothing against his; but she still tried. Her dress pulling and snagging as she did but uncaring Kalista carried on. Pulling it up with her hands so that it didn't tangle in her legs. *Bloody thing.*

"Barakan… it's Kalista I am here." She neared but still just out of reach. He knew peace would always just be out of reach. He yelled loudly.

"No!" His whole body stiffened as if in pain and began to shake uncontrollably but at least his hands stilled, grabbed onto the mattress… hanging on for dear life. Kalista saw her opportunity as his claws were embedded in the mattress. She quickly closed the distance between them reached his shoulders instinctively putting her own little hands on him. Resting them on his strong biceps as she whispered again. Keeping to his top half.

"Barakan. Please I am with you; you are not alone. Please come back to me." *But I haven't gone anywhere.* His body shook as he felt the pain inflicted yet again. His body feeling like it was being torn apart; on fire as his very flesh split… Kalista tried again. Leaning further into him. Her smell washing over him. "Barakan… please my darling… wake up. Rak!" *Darling? Rak?* His chest heaved as he roared again forcing Kalista to bury her head into his neck trying to muffle the noise from her ears. She sobbed. Trying desperately to get closer to him any further and she would either be inside his skin or skewered by his claws. But right now she didn't care. Her breasts falling from her dress the bindings too loose rested against him; her legs way too near his claws one wrong move and she would be cut. The dress just hanging; there wasn't going to be much left of it after this.

"Barakan." Now her voice started to climb. "Come back to me. It's not real." She felt his teeth grinding vibrating from him to her. She sobbed tears streaming. "Barakan." His tremors so violent it was as if he was fitting. Then his hands moved flicking upwards fighting the invisible assailant. A single claw just catching her as it did. Slicing into her leg. "Sccchhh." She knew what he had done it smarted. Barakan pushed at his invisible assailant again as Kalista reached up to his face and with a sudden burst of her own energy and grief; grabbed at his face and tilting into him teeth and all trying desperately to avoid his claws leaned all the way into him as if they were lovers. And breathing on his face; immediately his nose twitched and snorted. Kalista knew he sensed her now. “Barakan. My love stop. It is me it’s Kalista.” Dropping her lips to his she kissed him constantly whispering. “Barakan. Please, see me, it is me.” He gagged; her tears salty fell into his mouth. *She kisses me… she’s touching me. I. Oh my God.*

Barakan knew he had to control himself. But it was hard. His terror screamed louder than she could speak. Still shaking he opened his mouth and breathing back spoke her name.

“Kalista!”

“Yes darling it is me. Please open your eyes and see me it is me. Don’t let this consume you.”

“I.” He growled and Kalista felt the change in him as he attempted to regain himself; still he shook. Kalista could feel the fever built in him. His episode was tremendous. Slowly he opened his eyes. Beautiful green eyes she saw them. Not for the first but they were there looking back at her as she was face to face with him. Her lips barely away from his. He dare not speak just looked at her. The shaking just wouldn’t stop. She was laying on him like they were lovers and she’d said … *My love.* His eyes told her more than words.

"Barakan."

"Kalista." She knew he was back. She let her lips again touch his. Barakan did not move he dare not; his body was tight and strained from his nightmare but she was there his adorable Kalista laying on him; kissing him. He never wanted to forget this moment. Slowly Kalista pulled her lips from his; stroking his face with her hand. Her tear stained face and red eyes told him all he needed to know.

"Kalista." He whispered her name. Desperate to take what comfort she had to offer. He didn't want to be consumed by this pain. He wanted to be consumed by her. "You could have been hurt."

"I know. "She began to relax against him letting her weight fall against him. "But you were in pain."

"Hmm. It happens."

"I know; and why?" She wondered if he had heard all she said.

"You kissed me."

"Yes. Would you like me to do it again." Her eyes twinkled mischievously at him. He grunted at her.

"I think you know the answer to that." She chewed on her bottom lip seductively.

"Barakan why did you not come to me; this

might have been avoided." His nose twitched there was something else in the air. *Desire; blood. Hers.* His lips raised so his teeth showed. Kalista knew that as an annoyed twitch.

"You are bleeding!"

"Yes." No point not telling him.

"I hurt you."

"Just a little you caught me with a claw."

"Where?" He attempted to move. Concerned. But Kalista pulled herself further over him; attempting to stop him. Her naked breasts moved; her nipples crushed across his. He trembled unwittingly realising.

"Kalista!"

"No Barakan that can wait. It is not much." She stroked his face. "Talk to me." He studied her knowing it wasn't talking she wanted. He could smell the desire on her. *By all the Gods ... What does she want from me. We cannot. She cannot know what she considers! Can she? There is no one like you Kalista!*

Kalista felt him relent and couldn't resist she had no idea why but she wanted him or as much of him as she could get. She lowered her lips once again to his and kissed him. All very one sided as he didn't move but that didn't bother her one bit; she wanted to show him. He could have a life; where passion could find a way. Barakan could not move he dare not move his teeth would split her lips from her face. Not that she seemed bothered. He groaned nearly a growl.

"Kalista stop." His heart just filled for her. His body stressed and strained from pain one minute had changed and began to want. A different fear filled him. But Kalista she didn't care she was set on her own course; her lips moved on his. Barakan just could not stop her. She felt so good. Slowly he lifted his hands to her and with every ounce of care he could muster he wrapped them around her. Holding her close. Kalista raised her head loving the fact that he was responding to her.

"Your nightmares…"

"Yes."

"You are never alone. I am here. Let me help."

"There is no help for me."

"I do not believe that; there is always hope. But besides that I am here Barakan you have me."

"Do I?" Kalista hung her head to one side just enough to enable her to see all of him.

"Yes." She watched his eyes still green. Loving emotion filled eyes. "Do not avoid me Barakan. Please I missed you so much."

"I. Kalista my beast I'm."

"Sch. We are different but." She needed to say more but something in his eyes told her once said it could never be unsaid. Would it do more damage? But then his green eyes glistened at her lovingly. *You know! You heard.* "You heard me didn't you Barakan."

"Yes."

"Do I need to repeat it? "He pulled her in closer squashing her to him.

"No. please God no." He couldn't cope with that it felt like her words would cripple him. Kalista Let her fingers play with his face.

"Barakan you should know your eyes … They are green they are your own eyes. I see them." He blinked surprised. *You do this all for me Kalista.* He wanted to touch her like never before. He found his shaft growing now needed her. Kalista moved but was pushed away by Barakan.

"No." She looked hurt. "We will go back to your quarters now Kalista. It is not fit for you in here." But Kalista didn't move. Snorting at her stubbornness Barakan moved her against him and easily stood. Shifting her weight as he held her so she was cradled in his arms. He made to leave his cave but bending first to retrieve her torch. He looked on her so sweet little form. The dress hardly covering anything. The bindings remaining undone, her ample breasts moving as she breathed. Kalista knew he looked at her. *You want me...* That she found made things worse for her. It turned her desire onto full. Within seconds they were in her quarters.

Barakan edged them both to the bed. Her bed in a total disarray. Holding her still Barakan looked at her then to the bed.

"You couldn't sleep?"

"No. I. I could only think of you." Honesty.

"Why?"

"Because my strong Barakan I wanted you to come to me."

"Kalista that is not possible."

"So you keep telling me. But I can touch you."

"What?" *What are you suggesting Kalista. She is choosing this!* Barakan found it hard to believe that she would want him in any way shape or form. Kalista was sure she felt him shake.

"Stay with me Barakan."

"You cannot know what you are saying."

"Off course I do." Barakan dropped her down on the bed as if she had scolded him. It was then he noticed the thin slice in her thigh; her dress all scrunched up almost around her waist. Her long limb; pale and slender the cut shone at him. *I did that.* Yet stopped bleeding it was already drying and would soon heal. She had been lucky. He growled deeply at her.

"See that is the reason I cannot. You were lucky this time." Shame screwed him up. He forgot himself and showed his teeth. Kalista raised herself up on her knees her pink nipples peeking out over the top of her dress. Barakan stared. So sensual a sight, he ached for her his shaft twitching with a mind of its own.

"And yet I survived and am still in one piece." She moved towards him. "And I can see you need." She lowered her eyes to feast on him. "Your stress; your need to be touched, let me touch you let me help you. There has to be release for you."

"Kalista!"

"I know it isn't the curse Barakan I know it is your desire to be touched." She was almost at the end of the bed. If she stretched her hands out she could grab him.

"Kalista you ask too much off me."

"I don't ask anything from you; I ask you to let me give to you. Barakan." She did she stretched her hands out and touched his solid stomach. The muscles rippling and rolling under her fingers. *You are so strong my sweet.* She liked his muscles; in fact she was growing to like everything about him. His gruffness; his sweetness when it came to providing for her. Then there was his stiff sense of morality that she would never have imagined to have been there in one so able to kill and had killed. The curse ruled him then. *Would it now? Can I; little broken me defeat a witches curse.* She prayed there had to be a way. He wasn't born a killer nor wanted to be. If it came round again she knew for sure if there was no way to keep it like now under control then he would deny it and be lost. To himself to her and that she was going to have none of. She would bleed for him first. He needed passion he needed love. *Did she love him whole?*

"K a l i s t a! Please I would not forgive myself if I…"

"I know." She wound her fingers around and around teasing him. Stretching that little bit further each time she moved them towards his now throbbing erection. *God do I want to touch you.* She did. Kalista stopped and turned to the top of her bed. "Sit down Barakan. Sit at the head of the bed." Her orders came easily.

# *Chapter eight*

Barakan just stared at her the words she spoke so assured. *You order me.* It was infectious.

"Kalista; you order me?" Was that a glint in his eyes she saw.

"Yes. My sweet." *Had he ever been called sweet?* Kalista tired of waiting for him; decided and unsure if he would run grabbed at his forearms with both her hands and pulled. Momentarily he held his ground she would not shift him but then as her heavy breasts moved with her; voluptuous and so stunning he could rest his eyes on them for eternity. He began to relent and allowed her more of the power. "In this Barakan I am the lord." He couldn't help but guff at her almost a laugh. Kalista knew she had won and got him. *You are mine.*

Barakan knew what she wanted from him; he leaned his heavy frame against the top of the bed resting against the solid head board. The large thick posts either side of him. He positioned himself not unlike in the forest between the posts. They both knew he had to do something with his hands. His hard throbbing erection pointing at her again. He groaned; a large heavy sigh. His soul seemed to be emptying from him. *What am I allowing to happen? I shouldn't.* But too late Kalista climbed over him and pushed his massive legs to one side so she could crawl up between them.

“Kalista. You should not do this. This is not why I brought you here.” Not that her touch wouldn’t be so special to him. She was special.

“I know.” Crawling higher up him this time she was almost straddling him. Barakan held his breath that she cannot attempt. ***No.*** He would throw her off first. She saw the sudden fear in his eyes and the beautiful green change to flames. But that wasn’t her intention. Not this time.

“Sch… Barakan. Relax.” Kalista laid her hands on his chest rubbing; feeling getting to know every dip and delve in him. Her little fingers finding his nipples they buttoned immediately not unlike her own just peaking at him from her dress bindings. He growled low and deep. As he dropped his head back against the wooden frame. He was thrilled with the way she touched him. Leaning forward she dropped a gentle kiss on his chest. But she was so gorgeous. *If only I could see you and touch you.*

“My sweet beast.” Kalista cooed at both man and beast; as she gentle pushed herself away from his chest and worked her way down. Not wanting to rush it this time it was all about touching and sharing. She got lower reaching his so powerful thighs; his erection jutting from between them. Kalista breathed on him but only that; her hot breath sweeping across him. Her hands easing their way over his muscled thighs. Kneading holding onto him as she lowered her head and nipped at first one thigh then the other.

Barakan raised his head; astounded at her wanton behaviour. But seeing her again lowered to him made his chest heave and his breath alter. His breathing came fast and furious. *What a sight you make Kalista.* He snarled as her fingers began their journey towards him. She tickled at his flesh.

"Kalista… Did you just bite me?" She raised her head grinning seductively.

"Yes." Before returning to her ministrations. Barakan groaned so loud. Kalista ran her fingers gently hardly touching over his full length. She watched as he physically moved trying to gain her touch. *No it will be on my terms only.* She needed this as much as him. Her own bodies heat growing. Finally after what seemed like painful ages to Barakan Kalista took a strong hold of him and like before she began to so very slowly pump at him. Pulling her little fist holding tight; the full length and back down again so slowly. He cried out… Kalista liked the noises he was making she would have more. Laying her head against his thigh she just watched feeling his groans vibrating through him to her… It was tremendous and glorious. Leaning just a little further to him she nipped at his base; sucking the flesh there into her mouth. Barakan's growled gasps filled the room. As she spun her tongue on him as her fist still moved. Then she traced a line upwards with her tongue reaching his tip and lapped at him. His hips had begun to move with her. She smiled; enjoying the sensations driving through them both. For she felt it too. Passion. And it was so good. Nice and slow was her route to her own power of passion. She was enjoying it. Barakan could take the sensation no longer he flayed his hands out looking for the posts as in her judgement it was time; Kalista lowered her mouth to him and as her tongue toyed with his tip; tasting him she allowed her lips to once again take him whole. Barakan felt himself enveloped between her hot wet lips. It was more than man or beast could stand the great growl he emitted vibrated through them both. His grip on the posts tightened.

"My God Kalista. What are you doing to me." Kalista just spoke before she thought…

"Making you mine." That was it she had shocked them both. Her movements became more as Barakan found himself unable to stop the thrusting his hips were intent on doing. His chest heaved with every loud growl she drew from him. As Kalista herself found her own body needing more; moving her own hips slightly she wrapped her legs over one of his. Barakan snarling.

"What?" He felt her settled over his leg. Her

core burning. “Kalista… I.” He so wanted to take her heat but withheld all he was. Kalista seemed to growl back at him.

“Sch…” Her mouth moved on him taking all she could. Barakan thrust losing himself as his hands and claws hung on so hard to the posts his muscles straining against the force he was fighting. Kalista moved with tender speed she wanted him and all he could give; grinding herself against his leg. Barakan was shocked but enticed by all she was doing. *My God woman.* Her desire felt as rampant as his. Her lips took him again and again to the height where he thought to burst. Barakan like before with much thought took a hand scratching at the post away and slowly with intent of care pushed at her head. Letting her know she should move. But this time was different Kalista knew she could feel the energies built in him as they were in her, his throbbing moving up through her fingers. She pushed back and did not relinquish her grasp on him with either fingers or lips. She pulled on him till his flesh would take no more and in that instant as he realised her intent. Her own need flooding from her in a wave which took her breath as suddenly without warning for either of them he came. His hips left the bed and the loudness of his growls made her shudder. Kalista realised whilst he released so did she… her body shuddered with the noise he made as well as her own orgasm which raged from the pleasure that she was creating for him. It took some minutes for either to overcome and understand what had happened and was happening between them. Kalista slowly finally relinquished her hold on him and raised her head to see him staring down on her. In awe. *Kalista... what have you done? Again.*

Barakan saw her; his beautiful little angel full of so much love and desire it burned in her eyes. Bright… So very bright. She looked dishevelled her hair worse than his bristles her face not just flushed but red. Her lips swollen and wet. She ran her tongue over them seductively. She knew he watched her. Shaking his head Barakan once again tried to put his hands on her; he laid his palm on the side of her face. Kalista without hesitation rubbed her cheek against him.

"Better?" He didn't stop shaking his head.

"You are…"

"What?" He breathed heavy it washed over her. "Barakan." Her eyes brows furrowed. "I was trying to make you feel better not worse."

"You could never make me feel worse but Kalista that; this was not why I let you come back with me.",

"I know." Her gaze travelled the full length of him.

"I wanted to Barakan… I wanted to touch you. Still do. Do not try to deny me." Pointing his claws away from her Barakan tried to grab at her hair and pulled her to him. Kalista allowed it she let her body fall over his. Hugging him as he tried to her. He could smell his own essence on her.

"If I could kiss you I would devour your lips my sweet." Kalista acting quickly took his cue.

"But I can you." *What?* Before he had time to stop her or complain Kalista once again dropped her lips to his. Barakan stiffened trying not to move. Kalista moved on his lips braver now. Her instinct to have him as hers growing. She drew her tongue slowly over his. He could taste himself on her a heady mixture. Desperate to calm her he pulled her away.

"Kalista stop now." She pouted at him. "Enough." He tried to roll her away from him aiming to move.

"What are you doing?"

"Going to wash! You should too."

"No."

"What?" She smiled at him enjoying his smell on her. She felt good right now.

"There is no rush. Just stay with me."

"What?"

"Again with the what Barakan. Stay here with me. We can wash in the morning."

"You want me to stay in your bed with you?"

"Yes. Maybe then we will both get some rest. It is big enough is it not?"

"Kalista it is just not advisable." She put all her weight on him. Effectively attempting to pin him to the bed.

"I don't care what is advisable I want you to stay with me. In fact I don't expect to be sleeping alone here again."

"What?" That did it. His little spitfire was ordering him about and meaning it. He laughed, hard and long. Pulling her into him again. She lay against his chest. He was forced to admit he felt better.

"Ok you win. We will try it and see how it goes." Kalista nestled into him trying desperately to get in his skin. Something in her told her it was all about to change again and she wasn't so sure whether it would be for the better or not and this; this thing between them felt so good right now. She shut all other thoughts and feelings from her. Barakan too he felt the difference; for him it was massive. She had taken him again this time to her as much as she could but would it be enough to sate the curse. He hoped he prayed so. *Please by all the Gods please.* He knew he needed her for always she was his to keep and God did he want her. Within seconds she was asleep. Warm and cosseted against him. It felt so good. Barakan wasn't long behind her his steady heavy breathing keeping in rhythm with hers. Peacefully he slept. A beginning.

Barakan came bursting into their quarters. His bristles stood that high it looked like he had long hair and his eyes so deep a red they looked like they could burn through anything. *Idiot fucking idiot. You should have checked. Known better. Aaaa* He'd refrained from the distressed howl which was formed it would alert all and that would be no good only stealth would help them right now. Kalista sat up in the bed staring at him knowing immediately something was wrong.

Barakan couldn't help but take a moment to comprehend and the way she looked his adorable Kalista. Dress still on her being naked with him was just impossible but hanging that loose it hardly covered her. Those glorious full breasts of hers shoving their way out the loose binding her nipples just cresting the tops. *I want to touch them.* Her legs akimbo. Moving now as she pulled them to her. Her desire still lingering he could sense it. He pondered the way she shook whilst he came; knowing she did too. She had taken pleasure from moving herself on him. His beast wanted to make her shiver and cry for more. But that wasn't possible. And right now there was other things more pressing to be dealt with. Kalista would not thank him if they hurt her friend. He'd heard the angry words and her cries as they were dragging her to the clearing. This could be a very bad day.

"Barakan what is it?"

"There is trouble. You need to get dressed properly now!" Not that he knew exactly what to do but something had to be done and man as well as beast would see Victoor's and pull his head from his shoulders. He would see what to do as they left. *Should I tell you?* He had pondered the fact on whether to just deal with the situation or to tell Kalista. But he knew if he didn't she would never forgive him and the fact that her take on what was to happen maybe different to his but… *Shit I'm here now. Tell her.* This was going to be something that could end what they had achieved so far, and Barakan knew he didn't want it to end. But whatever it would have to be her choice. Kalista's. He knew he loved and wanted her. With her so imperfect perfect being.

"Why what is happening?" Fear filled her and she knew the feelings of the night before were real. It was happening right now whatever ominous thing fate was going to through at them. She looked at herself. Her dress a mess crumpled and dirty from rolling around with him the skirt even had blood on.

It would need soaking and washing well. Without thinking she began to pull the sleeves from her shoulders… Barakan growled loudly…

“No… Change I will go get you some fresh washing water for you to wash with.” He tried to pick the wash jug up gingerly but he managed it. Kalista turned her back on him pulling the dress the rest of the way. Barakan couldn’t help but turn to see as she let it fall from her hips. Her peach round bottom came into view but not unlike the rest of her marked and tiny little scars running over the soft flesh. He growled loudly. But Kalista understood she knew he looked. The reminders of her suffering as apparent as his.

When he returned she had the new dress on; this was cream; and he liked it. She’d just finished fastening the bindings and was about to brush her hair.

Taking the jug from him Kalista poured it into the wash basin.

“Thank you Rak.” He was stunned with her use of his name. *When did it become that?* But he didn’t mind. He did remember her calling it when he was in the midst of his nightmare. *Rak Rak. My darling wake up.* Her words still swimming around in his mind same as what she had done to him and her own desire it made his nose twitch. Kalista looked at him. *No breeches.* Not that she cared now. She liked to look upon him it gave her a buzz. She should never have made him wear them anyway. This was who he was man and beast alike both that could be tamed. Kalista poured the warm water into the bowl and set about splashing it on her face, Barakan stood over her. Smelling her.

"Maybe we should have bathed last night." She shrugged at his words.

"We didn't know there would be a problem this morning. What is it Rak? What is wrong?" He twiddled with her hair with a single claw.

"I need you to understand that I will not let any harm come to you and yours before." She turned sharply to face him her voice demanding.

"Tell me Rak. Now!"

"I should have thought on I was remiss. They went back; there was no blood nothing no sign of you." Kalista raised her eyebrows not fully understanding at first.

"There wouldn't be."

"No. Victoor's has claimed you witch and they have believed him. They are bringing your friend Serena." Kalista gasped loudly.

"No. They can't… you can't… You don't need to. Barakan I don't understand. We can just let her go. How do you know this?

"We could if that was their only intention but I'm afraid that is not all. I would say they have already questioned Serena about you. And I know Kalista because I can hear them. All of them…" Kalista grabbed out at the top. Nearly toppling her basin. Barakan stopped her with his palm. Steadying it and her he put his so strong body against hers. His strong heart thundering through her as hers began to race terrified of what was to come.

"Victoor's Serena!"

"It seems that since your removal no matter how short a time has brought about a remarkable recovery in him. He is with them and they bring Serena." Barakan gave Kalista a minute to digest the information. "Apparently from what I have heard they have her man this jack in the cell to keep him from fighting for her."

"Oh my God Rak." Barakan lowered his head to hers and breathing over her he whispered into her ear. *What was happening? Why would they bring another?* The same thoughts were whizzing around both. But there was something distinctly rotten in this. Kalista could see Victoor's sneering face before her eyes; touching her. His pleasure. A single simple thought hit her. *No. He couldn't. She was the only one! Wasn't she?*

"We will make it right together you and I my sweet; no more blood will be spread in my name.

Ever. I won't have Victoor's use me. Nor hurt you in any way ever again." Kalista couldn't help but sob. "I can just stop them."

"Barakan we have to stop him… but the rest. How? We can't just kill them all."

"No?" Kalista wasn't sure how to take that. Statement or question. She knew as well as Barakan once they had seen him then he himself would always be in danger they would hunt him. Her heart just sank.

"It could be the easiest solution Kalista.",

"Rak they are not all bad. Just misguided." She was fighting the shock and being sensible.

"But you know what it means if I am truly seen. Legend no more." She sighed lowering her eyes to look at his feet before raising them to his face.

"Yes." He saw the hurt in her eyes. Both knew to save her friend a life they had little choice Victoor's would make sure she was sacrificed even if it meant doing it himself. Barakan did not have to spell out what he had heard.

"Get ready then Kalista they are not waiting till night this time they are on their way already we should go."

Kalista pulled the small boots on Barakan had provided for her. Pulling her hair into two ties making sure it was tight. Kalista walked towards him bit as she spoke she turned to look around her. *No ours.* Their room. Memorising it. She didn't know where today would end.

"Barakan… Rak."

"What?"

"Thank you" Before she had chance to say anything else he wrapped his powerful arms around hers.

"No Kalista. Do not thank me. If it weren't for me none of this would be happening. We will be quicker if I carry you." Kalista nodded.

"But Rak; if this hadn't have happened, I would still have Victoor's at me." Barakan snarled very loudly it filled the air. Kalista's mind was working overtime.

"Rak what would have made them think you hadn't been appeased?"

"Victoor's; him, he uses it, me for his own ends but in all fairness…" Barakan seemed embarrassed. "I have made a lot more noise than usual. Since meeting you." He sort of coughed. Which melted Kalista. "For one reason or another; the forest or I haven't been quiet, he Victoor's listens; especially when he thinks he is going to get something out of it."

"But the forest noise is normal Rak?"

"But Victoor's isn't."

"No. is Serena badly hurt Rak?"

"I cannot fully tell Kalista but if you are asking if she is hurt then the answer to that is yes."

"Oh hurry Rak before he hurts her more." Barakan pulled her closer.

"I know my sweet Kalista I know." He nuzzled her hair as he made his way quickly through the rocks hidden path. "Kalista what makes you call me Rak?"

"Because… We are more than friends and I want you to know that." He did. He was pleased with her answer.

"Do you want me to deal with them immediately or?"

"No Rak not straight away. Let me try if they don't see you then it is all good."

"But they… He may hurt you."

"I'm not worried about him anymore." Kalista pressed her fingers into Barakan's chest. "I have you now."

"Always my sweet." She did and he knew it; she was his love and lover. Her love for him was blind to that which was unsightly. Yet he thought wrong

Kalista did not think his beast was unsightly; different but far from unsightly she loved everything about him now man and beast. Both had their own speciality.

Rak once free of the rocks. Looked down on Kalista.

"I will move faster now Victoor's is with your Serena alone the others have left."

"That doesn't bode well for her."

"No; he intends to use this situation to its fullest for his own ends Kalista; none of which are good for your friends, he will hurt anyone that believes you. He won't leave her for me."

"Oh my God Rak hurry, please hurry. Do not let him."

"We won't my sweet.", Barakan moved swifter than she realised he could, his heart pumping fast through his chest. His muscles began to sweat; he was panting himself.

"Rak… Barakan?"

"Sch it is ok sweet one. Not long now. I am good. I will let you walk into the clearing alone but know I am with you and never far away. But I will turn the others around and send them back to you to see. Is that what you want?"

"Yes. They need to know what Victoor's is too."

"But they could see you!"

"They won't… I can make them turn around do not concern yourself with that." Kalista just nodded. Already considering what she needed today or wondering if it would just come out as rubbish. But. *Serena.*

"Kalista." Barakan brought her back to their reality. "We are nearly there. You do whatever you have to. I am with you whatever. Just speak my name and I will be by your side. Always." Kalista rubbed her face against his chest in gratitude. Laying a tender kiss on his chest. Barakan grumbled low at her. Letting her know how much he enjoyed it and needed her.

Kalista couldn't see much the trees here were just too thick but she trusted Barakan's word. He whispered.

"The clearing is just through there. You can walk I will watch. Do not worry about him my sweet he will get his; one way or another scum always do. Do what you need try what you might but if you need me just say my name." Kalista just nodded words weren't hers at this moment in time. She worried her nerves raged. But she knew this had to be done. Putting one foot in front of the other she found herself walking once again into the clearing she appeared between the trees seeing Victoor's bending over Serena; her dress already split as he held a knife to her chest. He had no intention of just leaving her for the beast... Kalista's mind started to somersault. It was easy to see that Serena had been beaten. *So who actually killed them? Barakan or you?* Doubts raced through her mind. Barakan thought it was him but there could be another killer among them. *What did Victoor's do before Barakan even got there. My God. Barakan.* Kalista didn't immediately make her prescience known, she could see them both Victoor's and Serena who wasn't drugged, they'd dragged her in the morning light to get it done before anyone else could object. That had been contrived. She was full of bruises her eye black her nose bleeding. Her long blonde hair falling in knotted locks down her back and over her face. Her skin so pale. She was terrified. *Off course. Bastard.* Kalista listened. Her knees trembling beneath her; she forced her knees straight to take her weight. *No Kalista; you cannot fail.*

"Well my beauty you should have known where the truth lied and kept your mouth shut and not listened to her. Look where it has got you." He sneered and slobbered. But Serena managed to croak.

"But it was the truth wasn't it?" Now he began to laugh thinking he had gotten away with it all and his reign of terror on the women could continue. *Who have you already hurt?* Kalista stifled a gag her throat filled with bile. *God that burns.* If he had the opportunity to hurt and use the women before he brought them up here was their deaths anything to do with Barakan? *Barakan.* But Kalista knew there was still the curse to contend with. But the women must have known as she did that they were being brought for that one reason to appease him… Her mind was working overtime. She would have taken what he had to give to save her village and then what? Would she have survived? *Barakan you are man too. But Victoor's. You... you.* Kalista knew he was impotent so tools were his choice that would do more damage than Barakan. There was a possibility that this; all these deaths for a lot of years anyway, where nothing to do with Barakan. *Stop it Kalista what was is done... Now. Serena.* Kalista watched as Victoor's walloped Serena again. His vicious words echoing around.

"It is of no concern now you will not be breathing long enough for it to make a difference. And the beast he will take the blame again…" Victoor's laughed so hard. Every hair on Kalista's body stood on end. *It wasn't all you Barakan. My Rak. I love you.* Angry now for so many reasons Kalista found years of it spilling over and her frame just seemed to stretch and grow. *I will have you by the end of this.*

"It might not be hers but it is mine!" Kalista

stepped from the shadows. Staring directly at him. Not ignoring Serena but to keep composure she concentrated only on him. "Victoor's." He spun on his heels and stared at her.

"Bitch." Barakan heard and snarled loudly. The others walking away heard. Looked at one another.

"Shit what was that?"

"What has that dirty old twat got us into now?" They glared into the shadows. Barakan deliberately moved about in front of them. Forcing them back to whence they came. Back to Victoor's. Just thinking about him and what he was about made Barakan fume… His bristles began to rise.

"And you think calling me names is going to help you now." Kalista took a step forward. Trying not to wither even though she was cringing inside. Serena stared. This she hadn't been expecting… None of it. And he was hurting her so much she; felt sick. But that was. Serena hardly able to speak.

"Kalista."

"You bitch you should have run!"

"How would I have run you left me for the monster?" At that Victoor's just seemed to laugh even more. But Barakan was not pleased with that laughter it was cunning and hideous. *Why do you laugh at me old man?* He made more noise forcing the others faster. He wanted to be back to Kalista. *Now.*

"And you like them all believe in him." Victoor's just couldn't stop his laughter.

"And you do not?"

"It's the forest it finishes them off if I leave them long enough."

"So all this is your doing?"

"Who else's?" His laughter just made Kalista sick. "There is no monster girl. You are my proof of that."

"So what did you think would happen to me?" Victoor's even as old as he was seemed powerful to her. This was not the man as she'd been led to believe who was frail and dying. He stalked towards her even more terrifying than Barakan. He didn't pretend to be something he was not.

"Well I was hoping with your…" He pointed to her head. "Issues; that the forest would just tear you apart." Barakan sensed Kalista's fear he heard every word Victoor's was saying trying to join the dots. How he had been with the women. *How did they not believe it was him? The beast? But how many women did he bring? My God...* Barakan made one last drive to make the others go back, they did they started to run. Enabling him to track his way back to her.

“But it didn’t Victoor’s. Why do this to Serena?”

“Because she is like you a trouble maker.” He’d almost reached her. But Kalista side stepped making her way towards Serena.

# Chapter nine

Kalista now snapped back.

"Bastard."

"Language dear."

"Don't dear me you are despicable: you deliberately hurt them all; me." Kalista knew first-hand what he was capable of and for them the others. Her mind and heart exploded for them; they must have suffered so much knowing they were drugged and gona end up dead anyway he wouldn't have cared. He'd manipulated the whole thing for so many years. *So what did that make Barakan? Shit shit shit.. Had he known? No.* And him Victoor's still didn't think Barakan excised; he thought it was all his doing. *Oh my God so many years.* Kalista knew the drugs weren't for their own; the women's piece of mind but to make them compliant. *My God.* "You did all this; you are a sick son of a bitch."

"But boy do I have a good time. This day will be a good day for me. I may as well finish the job this time and slit both you throats; let the animals do the rest." He slobbered. Kalista physically gagged. It was getting too hard to hide. Serena sobbed finding it hard to believe everything that was happening. Just looked from Victoor's to Kalista. She had never doubted Kalista but this this was more than mind and soul could accept. She was struggling to take in all the spoken words she could hear. But they were real and now she knew this was all him. Well since he'd been old enough to. Before then who knew but him he used this situation for his own ends.

"You bastard have been doing this all your life."

"Off course. I was never stupid enough to think that the women were killed by anything other than fear and the forest, so as I grew I thought what the hell."

"But the curse."

"What curse there is no Beast." He chuckled as he stepped to be in front of Kalista. She could smell his rankness. *So many years and lives. Barakan it wasn't all you. They died because of him not you.*

"How many years do you think I have been doing this?" He breathed his foul breath on her. "Before then they sacrificed maybe one every ten years. Foolish people that they were. But this was all me; how many do you think I have brought up here. It has been one every two years or so hasn't it." Kalista was gobsmacked and horrified. Barakan had no idea she knew for fact and her she had neglected to say to him; if only she had said something. He would have known there was more to it. *Barakan.* Kalista's thoughts jumbled she needed to concentrate. Victoor's cared not that these two knew within the hour they would both be dead. Witch and friend. He remembered the first he'd took a women and how this all developed for him. *The beast bollocks.*

*Wow the stupidity of people never fails to amaze me. What do they think this is all about?* An old tale had given him the idea at first. Although he did have a distant memory of women being taken to the forest and rumours that they would never return. Must have happened once when he was too young to bother. But this; this would enable him to do what he pleased and get away with it. Maybe one every few years rather than every ten. With his influence it would be easy to organise. *Brilliant.* Never mind the truth of the matter.

*Oh my God.* Kalista knew Barakan suffered and felt every life he'd extinguished. But those the same as them all Victoor's victims were dead anyway. Victoor's had always made sure of that. He had engineered the whole thing for his own ends and allowed Barakan to take the blame; far from innocent in any death but not the serial killer the people thought. *Does that make the curse mute?* She suddenly hoped; so much hope found its way into her guts. Spreading.

"You should never have done this Victoor's. You should have found yourself a wife it would have been so much better for you." Now angry Kalista couldn't help herself as she threatened him.

"And you my stupid pretty always did have too much mouth. I might have let you live if you hadn't tried to tell; not that anyone believed you." Now Serena spoke finally.

"I did." Victoor's glanced round at Serena.

"Yes and look where it got you. I am infallible. I own everything and you two included."

"No you don't." Kalista snapped back at him.

Victoor's never did like being answered back. Swinging wide to get as much force as he could he walloped Kalista in the face hard. Hitting her high in the cheek her head snapped back on her shoulders.

Barakan heard every single word Victoor's uttered. His whole being already filled with loathing for this man became so much more. He had taken lives allowing him to take the blame; if what he himself had done wasn't bad enough but to kill for pleasure in his name. *My God.* Barakan let out a loud noise so much more than the snarks Kalista had already heard from him. It reverberated through the trees settling in the clearing all heard. Then Barakan heard the slap of a fist hitting flesh and he knew. *Kalista.* He heard her cry as the fist had taken her unawares. He was laying his rotten filthy hands on her again. *No, no, no. You will not.* Barakan's noise made the others; five men in total start running back to the clearing. They didn't like the sound of that and each in turn running, almost dropping the torches they carried. Weapons hadn't been brought. Never needing them before now but for the first time they wished they had... Hating the fact that they had been put in this position there was always something which felt off about this but so many young lives now had been sacrificed and none actually knew why. Apart from Victoor's. The four looked hard at the fifth; his nephew, Thomas as one big guy pitched at him.

"Oi Thomas; what the fuck have you got us into? I told you it was a bad idea. He is an idiot. He gets too much enjoyment out of this." Finally now their own life's where in jeopardy did they have the courage to speak out against him. Barakan missed nothing; he too turned and charged back through the trees to her. *Kalista.*

Kalista with all her might instinctively fighting back slapped out at him. But Victoor's even though much the older found agility in the thrill of all this and grabbed at her hand as she pushed it towards him. He held on too tight that tight she would be left with burns. He began to twist. Watching for the pain on her face. He squeezed and twisted harder..

"Ssssch." Kalista hissed at him but tried hard not to cry out knowing full well that was what he wanted. Determined she would not let him get off on her pain. But it was a fight she was loosing. He twisted more; beginning to twist her whole arm.. Serena tried to move. To drag her pained body from the floor where he was forcing her.

"Stop it! Leave her be Kalista." Serena's voice pitched into the air and Victoor's unflinching; but it was as if he didn't hear Serena at all he just kept on twisting… His focus only on Kalista.

"Kneel bitch." He was determined he would have her at his feet begging first. Then he would slice her pretty little neck and watch her blood and breath leave her. He sneered all before he finished with the other one. Serena managed to gain her feet. Pushing her feet to work. She came up behind Victoor's and grabbed at his arms but her strength had already been sapped. He flung her off easily launching a heavy boot at her as she fell; crumpling to the floor she was no help to Kalista.

"Serena!" Kalista shouted her name. As the men came gambolling into the clearing one then another till all five were there. All stalling to an abrupt halt there boots digging into the ground to stop as they saw what was happening. This was no beast this was him Victoor's. With one girl Serena splayed obviously hurt at his feet as he tried to bring the other Kalista to her knees. But it was easy to see she wasn't going easily. Thomas was the first to speak. Finally finding his mouth.

"What the hell?" Believing he was an old pervert was one thing but seeing it with their own eyes was something else. Victoor's sneered allowing his spit to fall on Kalista's face.

"What the fuck are you doing back here?" But he was beyond caring, they were all his. Under his control the men as well.

Barakan too came to a sudden halt breathing so heavily his hot breath was just vapour which floated around in front of his face. *Kalista.* But he also knew she hadn't called for him; not yet. But that rat bastard was hurting her. The others came into view now too. Barakan snarled. Kalista knew Barakan would be watching and although she prayed for him to just scoop her up and take her away from all this hatefulness searing them all; she knew there had to be a way through for Serena. The others she cared less about. They were all sheep; idiots following a sadistic bastard. She stretched her fingers and gestured them from side to side hoping he understood it as a no. *No not yet.* Then she heard him her ears could pick his snarl out from the forest. But she also saw the looks on the men's faces. They were seeing Victoor's as if for the first time but they could hear Barakan too.

"Stay out of this. **Or** else." He didn't care what they thought anymore he was high on having both women whom he assumed would be his to slice and dice. Kalista struggled against him as she managed to yell.

"See I warned you all of you. Watch your women he will be wanting them next. There is no beast just this dog you see now." Victoor's brought his knee up and caught Kalista in the chest with it. She gaged unable to breathe he had winded her. Serena tried now too. Pulling herself more upright.

"It was him. He did this to me." She knew she had to say and quick. If they didn't believe Kalista they may believe them both. "She is no witch he did this to get rid of her." Victoor's swiped out at her with the back of his hand knocking Serena back to the floor.

"Oi." One of the other men now shouted back. Kalista couldn't see who.

"If any of you try and stop me I will finish you all and you know I can." He leaned back over Kalista pulling his knife from his boot as he did so. "Let's see how mouthy you are with your throat slit." Kalista could stand against him no longer. He twisted her arm violently her knees began to give way and she found herself being driven to the floor. The flash of the metal moving towards her was all she could see. *I love you Barakan.*

Barakan; watching jumping from foot to foot couldn't stand what was before his eyes any longer the loathing he felt towards this being had grown and was now a detesting abhorrence. He wanted this man's blood; more even than the witches which had done this to him. He growled and snarled that loud all heard him and without Kalista asking he barrelled through the trees into the clearing. Branches and leaves coming with him. All teeth claws and bristles nothing of the man she knew but grateful for the beast. He swung round knocking the men over and about like skittles. A few were caught with his claws and were bleeding. They didn't react being so stunned not only by Barakan but Victoors too *And she had just said there was no beast.*

"What the fuck."

All hell just broke out and the noise coming from Barakan and the screams from the men were tremendous. There was no other sounds bar terror and rage the forest was full of it. Even Kalista couldn't see him; his huge form was just a mass of bristles and snot. Kalista felt Victoor's blade just touch the skin on her arms as he in bewildered shock was startled and moved. Pushing the blade at her in the process.

Barakan moved faster than any of them could actually focus on but he barrelled into Victoor's with great force and shoved him away from Kalista;

piercing Victoor's flesh with his claws as he did. Barakan laid him out and shoving his foot over his throat pinned him to the floor. Easily; none of them were a match for him.

Victoor's couldn't breathe; just stared up at this great monster of a beast with his foot on his throat and chest threatening to crush the life from him. Barakan leaned down into him. Shoving his muzzle into Victoor's face. Slobbering all over him deliberately; this man definitely brought the beast out in him. Victoor's could just stare into Barakan's so sharp teeth. As surprisingly to them all Barakan spoke.

"And you said **I** didn't exist… The only beast here is you." He curled his lips up high over his teeth as if he was going to bite into Victoor's face. Victoor's whimpered and cried like a mewling baby.

Kalista didn't know how she felt about this she wanted Victoor's punished and dead would be so much better but knowing Barakan and seeing the awful regret he suffered at the women's death. She didn't want him to suffer even only a little especially not on her behalf. But she just couldn't bring herself to stop him. Victoor's was the beast in all of this. No one else not Barakan no matter what he looked like. But Barakan turning his nose up smelt at Victoor's. Something was off he knew always had been. *But.*

"Big brave man aren't you when it comes to

women but now." Barakan snorted. "You just piss yourself." Barakan finally turned his face to look at Kalista his flame red eyes full of so much emotion. She looked back at him finding so much reassurance in the flames. She whispered his name seemingly pulling herself from her trance. Her nose bloody she wiped it with back of her hand.

"Barakan" It was then that Kalista realised Serena was sobbing and screaming. An angry Barakan was a terrifying sight. Pulling herself up slowly from her own knees; Kalista dragged herself towards Serena. As Barakan boomed at the others.

"Do not even think about it. Unless you want to give your lives for this sorry sack of shit." The screaming voices seemed to freeze. All just watched. Kalista reached Serena and carefully wrapped her pained arms around her.

"Sch my sweet Serena you are alright. No one is going to hurt you." Kalista held her tight willing her to register her words and quieten if only a little she wanted her to come back to her to prove that sense was still hers. "Serena." Serena dug her fingers into Kalista hoping she was real. Flesh soft and warm moved under her fingers.

"Kalista?"

"Yes honey it is me."

"What?"

"Sch. Now is not the time. Maybe it never will be I am good and the beast you see is not all as he looks. Believe me when I say there is only one sadistic beast here."Now Serena found her voice and her being showed.

"I know." Kalista held her tight and kissed the top of her head lovingly. *What now?* Kalista looked from Barakan to the men stood like ice frozen hardly even breathing then back to Barakan. Who saw her struggle.

"It is up to you Kalista." She nodded at him and opened her mouth to speak to the others.

"Now do you believe me?" Thomas hung his head and couldn't answer and the others just stared. Until Barakan still toying with the idea of killing Victoor's raised his head and snarled.

"The lady asked you a question." Thomas finally found his balls and answered.

"Yes." Kalista struggled her breathing started to quicken and she started to cough. She never expected to hear those words. It had a profound effect on her. Barakan hissed her way.

"Kalista." He hated to see her brought down. Lifting her hand to him in a calming gesture she hugged Serena who in turn hugged her back. It was an odd sight. *Barakan how do you expect to keep her?*

"I'm ok Barakan." She started to get a handle on herself. "There is only one beast here and it isn't the one with bristles and teeth. You have seen now what he is capable of." Thomas finally raised his eyes to look at her shame filling him

"Kalista." Her name coming from him sounded so odd. "You; I, we believed what he said he was so convincing."

"Not entirely true Thomas what you mean is he had you all by the purse strings. Grow a pair of balls and admit the truth. You have all harboured a killer. Would you have it known?" Now they not only looked afraid but worried too; all's minds speeding with thought and ideas seeing how they could get out of this. Serena coughed.

"Kalista… I'm so sorry."

"Sch honey none of this is your doing you were the only one. The only one who stood by me. I am no longer angry." She found she wasn't she had all she could ever want in him Barakan. "Thomas. Will you deny me now."

**"No."** It wasn't Thomas that spoke but The Smith.

"Kalista I for one am sorry. I never thought… He. Not to this extent."

"No I suppose you didn't. I never lied he did."

She pointed to Victoor's still under Barakan's foot looking none too healthy. Not that she had an ounce of mercy for him.

"What do you want to happen now?" Kalista aimed her question at Thomas. Finally he found his voice.

"To get home in one piece." Kalista knew. *Should I let you off that easy?*

"If we let you go what will happen?"

"What do you want from us Kalista?" The Smith asked in a shamed tone. The ball was in her court. Their lives were in her hands as hers was once in theirs. She looked from them to Barakan. *What about him? Would he be ok? And safe!* He blinked then nodded telling her it was all her choice.

"To never speak of this and what you have seen today and for it never to happen again." All five nodded easily. "I don't just want nods I want your words each and every one of you swear." Each in turn did. They would sell their soul to the devil right at this moment though Kalista knew it was all done under duress but it was the best she could get from them.

"And something else. You look after Serena… you make him pay for her doctoring. She will need it and whatever she wants and needs you do it. You never nor allow anyone else to treat her like you treated me." Again she got yes's.

"Barakan." Her voice washed over him she was finding her strength and it was good. But how could he pin her to him after all this? "The beast was never the killer?" He knew what she was about and he agreed whole heartedly; he would loose himself to her. She was his heart.

"The beast was only ever." She lied a little. "Victoor's and it stops all of it. No more women are to be sacrificed not to him; nor to the forest. There has been enough death and pain." That they agreed to easily; it had never been an easy task for any of them they were not Victoor's. Barakan growled at them.

"Never again and believe me when I say I will know and if you do I will hunt each and every one of you. You will not be able to run far enough." They were unsure of talking to him but Kalista made them

"Answer him."

"Yes." Each in turn agreed. "We swear."

"And now for you." Barakan scratched his teeth along Victoor's face. "You stink of rottenness." He forced his foot down just a little harder keeping it there several seconds before releasing him and kicking him towards the others he was out cold. But Barakan knew what he was doing much to Kalista' surprise. "Take the piece of shit with you I never want to see or hear him in my forest again." He looked at Kalista huddled with Serena. She needed a little time but for him he needed to go. "You all take care of him do with him what you will; but remember what has been agreed this day." Kalista was pleased Barakan was proving himself not to be a killer. "And never let him near a woman again nor rule you grow a set of balls. I will know." Barakan with his last words stepped to and past Kalista waiting just in the shadows at the tree line. Kalista knew he waited and could hear every word she said.

"Serena my sweet." Not that either of them were that at the moment bleeding dirty and sat in Serena's own filth.

"Do not be ashamed you are alive and jack waits for you. Be brave and live enjoy your life." Tears streaming down both their faces but this time for other reasons.

"Kalista it is ok now please come home." Kalista took a moment to contemplate Serena's words. Barakan held his breath anticipating her answer. *I would miss you so much; but the choice is yours.* Then she spoke.

"It was never my home yours maybe but not mine. Never." A low grumble vibrated her way. Kalista knew he would allow her to leave but also that she didn't want to.

"Kalista." Barakan's heart did not know what to do… it skipped and jumped; and was happy. Momentarily. *But I am still beast.* So much filled him it was hard to pick out the strongest emotion. *My God Kalista.*

Serena looked heart broken.

"But?"

"There is no but Serena not for me. You go home be with jack and have babies. You will you know; get over this." She gestured to the now groaning Victoor's. "He is finished." With her last word she looked at the others waiting for recognition of her words. Thomas nodded; scowling.

"He has done enough damage." Thomas had always secretly liked Kalista and it hurt him now to think this thing which he called uncle had hurt her so. Knowing now; he should have stood his ground not weakened under him. So much guilt drove through him. Kalista nodded at Thomas in response. She had no more words for any of them that part of her was done. And it wasn't something after this day that she would revisit.

"Kalista! Where will you go? Where have you been?"

"Serena all you need to know is that I have been safe and I think I have if I'm honest I have found my home." She glanced up at Barakan. He seemed to be buckling under her words. *Where they not what you expect my sweet beast.*

"Kalista you can't say you have been with… with… That!"

"Serena, do not react like that. It is not all it seems." Kalista considered her words. She didn't want them to know too much Barakan's story wasn't hers to tell. And again Kalista saw the change in his features he was hurt by the fact that Serena was about to call him beast; especially when it came to her; Kalista.

"You just concentrate on your life Serena; I am good, I have been safe and that is all you need to know for now. Maybe eventually when all is settled." Kalista threw Victoor's a scowl as he made even more noise and started to actually come round she didn't want to be here when he did. Kalista didn't want to see his shouting or snivelling. She would be too tempted to finish it for him then, there was so much hate welling in her for him. More than she had expected to feel; she'd been unawares of how much hate she could hold now against him being free from it for a while. Before it had become second nature to feel it every day and swallow it back now with Barakan she hadn't had too. It had been nice. Relief filled here. *Barakan!*

"They will call you witch."

"I do not care what they call me but maybe not if none of this is mentioned. You just remember all of you who the beast here really is… Who kills?" She aimed the words at them all. All stared down at Victoor's. Kalista hoped she had done enough to shift all the blame and not just some of it to Victoor's. "It should stop you do what you want with him hang him as the killer if you need to; I do not care. And neither should any of you but remember this the sacrificing has to stop." Barakan chipped in now snarling.

"I know all of you now you cannot hide from me. You will do this and never sacrifice anyone again. Otherwise.." Thomas jumped in now wanting to be back. Enough discussion had gone by. All he wanted like the others was to be home and lock this weasel in his room away from the village whilst they decided what to do with him. Plans were being formed. Kalista looked directly at him.

"Thank you." She made to stand. His words of contrition would mean little now.

"Take Serena and go. She needs attending to." Thomas leaned over Victoor's. Words he never expected to be saying flowing from him.

"I know you are coming round and can hear me. You rotten old bastard. It is done, you are done." Kalista in that moment realised it was. She looked down on Serena and blew her a kiss.

"Watch for me one day I will come and see you and explain when all this is settled." Tears streamed down Serena's face.

"I miss you Kalista."

"No you won't not when you and jack get wed. Have a happy life Serena." Kalista just turned her back on the few and proudly even though she was injured and felt emotional battered and bruised; walked away. Walking toward him and her new life Barakan watched her with pride. He growled just to be sure they knew he meant every word as the scene behind her changed and they all started shifting about.

Kalista did not turn back. Knowing she would miss Serena  but this what she had achieved with Barakan was so much more. *You are what I want Barakan.*

Kalista reached Barakan. Her breathing laboured and her face full of pain. Allowing her to walk past him he took a last look. Making sure they were doing as expected and not following her. They weren't; Serena was being hauled into one's arms as two unceremoniously lifted Victoor's between them and if he wasn't mistaken gave him a swift kick in the guts for good measure and they did so. He tried to complain; but they were no longer listening to him.

"Shut up. We know what you are."

Both Kalista and Barakan quickly shifted into the shadows and were gone.

Serena tried to look for Kalista but very much like she had appeared she just disappeared.

"Love you Kalista… be happy too." As the men picked her up Serena passed out she could take it no longer.

# Chapter ten

Kalista walked past Barakan feeling his overwhelming power as she did and so grateful of it. Her whole body seemed to hurt. Her wrist sore and burning Victoor's grip had been that tight it had pulled and stretched her skin to its limit; there would be burns. Her shoulder where it had been wrenched would take some days to heal it really hurt right now. And her ribs breathing as she walked was getting more and more difficult but she would not disgrace herself until she was out of sight. The small puncture and swift slice of the blade stinging. Kalista found her head was beginning to swim and an awful nausea was beginning to take a hold the bile that quickly rose into her throat. Kalista wobbled and suddenly fell to her knees heaving tremendously unable to stop it she was violently sick. Again and again her stomach emptied itself of all it's contents. Barakan dropped to his knees besides her feeling inadequate. He couldn't do anything his rotten stupid clawed hands wouldn't let him. But his very presence was a comfort. His hot earthy breath gushing over her.

"Kalista!" He waited for her to be able to speak watching as wave after wave of nausea ravaged her already pained body. Finally weakened and pale it subsided. “Kalista.” She managed to raise her head to look at him. Her skin so pale her face looked terrible the bruising already beginning to show; blood still leaking from her nose her mouth and lips soaked now. Barakan tried to wipe her face with his palm. But Kalista flinched; not wanting him to. She croaked. Her throat was on fire right now.

“I wouldn’t… I stink.” Her comment drew a smile from him.

“That would make two of us tonight then. Come.” He moved closer to her. “I think I had better carry you.”

“But Barakan. I’m unpleasant.”

“Not for long my sweet. We will get you back washed and tended too. You’re hurt?” But he stalled a little; feeling he should say more. “Kalista?” Now she knew that tone there was a question on that mind of his.

“Yes?”

“I. You are not tied to me! You could have gone back with them I wouldn’t have held it against you.”

“Barakan!” Now she had attitude. “If I’d have wanted to I would have; but no Barakan I do not; not then nor now would I want to go back. I thought you understood that!” She groaned as putting too much effort into speaking and breathing too heavily took its toll.

"Kalista your hurt.."

"Yes Barakan. But I will heal. What I won't get over is you being a prat." He pulled her in closer.

"I'm sorry. But yes you will." He had every intention of making sure of that.

"Barakan!"

"What?"

"it wasn't all you; you heard Victoor's words."

"I did but let's forget that for now and get you sorted. I am still beast cursed by a witch that is definate and real." Kalista laid her hands on his chest. Loving him.

"Barakan; Thank you." He looked down at her now settled once again on his arms; where she belonged.

"You Kalista are most welcome." There was a lot to contemplate in his mind but for now his only concern was her.

They moved quickly through the forest Kalista groaning a little as Barakan moved with her but he couldn't make her any more comfortable even though he wanted to. Even his beast worried for her; kept hassling him. *Get back; get back quick, make her well.* Barakan at last squashed them both through the rocks once again.

"Kalista we are nearly there just the pass to the entrance to navigate now." Her eyes shut she just groaned. But he understood.

"Home."

"Yes my sweet we are home." *God.* Barakan even surprised himself how long was it since he'd voiced such words. Charging faster on the solid ground Barakan quickly climbed with her to the entrance then deciding she needed the warm waters of the pool first. He headed straight there.

"Kalista; Kalista we are home." He whispered. "Open your eyes we are at the pool; the waters will help and you will feel better being clean. Kalista." His answer was her groan. As slowly she opened her eyes.

"I hurt. I'm tired."

"Yes I know. Kalista how do you want to do this? Are you up to it?" Looking through red eyes the left side of her face was swollen she could feel it. *Yes.* He was right the waters would help.

"Just put me in Barakan."

"As you are?"

"Yes please." She was beginning to come round a little. "This." She pulled at the skirts of her dress. "Is filthy anyway. I will get out of it in the water."

He nodded and with her held tight against him stepped into the waters. She felt it's warmth rising as he dipped them further and further into the waters till she was immersed.

"Are you ok Kalista?"

"Yes. It is helping." *Thank goodness.* Barakan reluctantly relinquished his hold on her and put her against the farthest side propped against the small ledge.

"I will wash then if you are ok alone I will go find you something to eat and drink." Kalista nodded as Barakan moved away from her dropping his heavy frame lower in the water. She watched as turning his back on her he reached for the soap he had provided for her: he splashed water into his face and run his hands through his fur and over himself making sure he was clean. Using the soap. It hadn't occurred to her that he did. *You are man my beast!* Her thoughts weren't entirely pure even with the pain; she shocked herself. Lifting her hand she began to pull on the bindings not so easy now they were wet. *Shit.*

"Oh my." *Not so much of a good idea.* She looked at Barakan. "I can't undo these." She groaned her chest hurting as she tried to move to enable her to pull at them.

"Kalista!" His lips seemed to chew against themselves. Nerves. *You are nervous!* She knew he worried about his reaction to her but she didn't care. "I c.."

"Barakan you will have to help me. Please." He groaned loudly as he took a step back towards her. Shaking his head. Leaning over her.

"How do you want me to do this?" Kalista found herself glued to his eyes the glorious green she liked but she found herself drawn to the flames too.

"Here." She pulled at his hand lifting it from the water as she carefully wrapped the first tie around his claw. "Pull that careful please while I try to free the other. Carefully Barakan. Remember I only have the two and the other is already torn." He pulled carefully as she twisted her fingers into the other attempting to free the knot.

"I think I had better resolve that situation."

"What situation."

"Get you some more clothes."

"Oh. I don't want you to keep buying me things Barakan."

"How else will you get things?"

"I don't know but maybe eventually I could get some of my own things. Serena she will have kept them."

"You want to go back?" She could here the

shock in his voice.

“No. Maybe later when everything has settled down just to make sure Serena is good. They are a few belongings I would keep. But Barakan there isn’t anything I couldn’t live without. I am home here with you; that is all I want.” She winced as he pulled a bit too hard but it worked the knot free and the bindings were loose her gorgeous globes of flesh came into view as the bodice started to move with the water.

“Kalista please tell me you can manage the rest.” Kalista understood she felt his low grumble. She needed to let him go though she was too hurt for any funny business today. But she found herself considering what she could do with him next as his healthy form muscles an all climbed from the pool. She found herself studying his ass. Like the rest of him muscled and well formed. She was definitely getting braver.

“If you need me Kalista just speak I can hear you.”

“I know Barakan.” Kalista grunted unexpectedly as she tried to pull the bodice from her shoulders. Barakan looked back concern oozing from every pore he owned. But he saw her; her breasts pushing out the water. Growling he spun on his heals and was gone. Leaving Kalista although hurting with a smile.

Barakan placed food on the plata and pulling the blankets on the bed quickly straight it was difficult for him but he managed with a little bit of pulling and pushing. He could smell the bed; it smelt of them both his mind drifted back to what had happened the previous night. His body reacted. *Oh no not now.* But he had no control over his desire. But things were so different now he hadn't yet contemplated all that had transpired that night and all of Victoor's confessions. That would come though as the penny dropped and all he'd heard sank in.

Leaving the food where it was he quickly lit the torches they weren't necessary but Barakan knew she liked them. He desperately wanted to make Kalista feel better. He'd mixed the wine with something he knew would make her sleep and that was the best medicine for her; rest.

Barakan made his way back to her. Standing outside the cavern entrance he spoke quietly to her; she wasn't making lots of noise, but he could hear her.

"Kalista are you ok? Would you like to go back to your quarters?" Kalista had managed to get out her dress with difficultly and she had scrubbed it as best she could but that wasn't much. She was beginning to feel worse again she knew she needed to eat and just rest. Everything just hurt.

"In a minute Barakan. I'm just." She tried to move to get out; but couldn't manage it. *Oh dear.* Barakan could hear the strain in her voice.

"Kalista?"

"Barakan. I can't do it; my ribs my shoulder I can't take my weight to get out." He growled loudly he was hoping to avoid this.

"You need me to help?"

"Yes." Breathing heavily and stealing himself for the task. Trying to control both man and beast. He entered. Seeing her still sat in the water.

"You will be all wrinkly." He tried to lighten the moment and take his mind from the fact that she was naked. *Naked.* Kalista tried to smile but it was too painful.

"You're teasing me Barakan." She saw him smile in his own unmistakable way.

"Yes." She could hear his heavy breathing; grabbing the clean drying sheet he flung it over his shoulder ready for her as he quickly and with ease lifted her from the water. He needed to be quick putting too much thought into her nakedness was not a good idea. Kalista pulled the cloth over herself. But she knew he looked at her. She could feel his heart pounding in his chest as was hers.. Barakan thought she was beautiful despite the bruising already beginning to show. Come the following day she would be black and blue but he was in the belief there was no broken bones.

"Barakan I hurt."

"I know. Come let's go get you sorted and then you can rest." She laid her head against him her wet hair sticking to his bristles. *God I am holding her and she is naked.* He could feel her peach behind resting against him; her breasts. A growl escaped one he was unable to control.

"Barakan?"

"It is fine Kalista; you are safe!"

"I know that." Her voice drifted as she was unable to stay conscious.

Laying her on the bed Barakan pulled the sheet over her more; whispering.

"Kalista my sweet finish drying yourself; you don't want to lay there still wet."

"Ok." Barakan turned as he heard her trying to do just that. With the occasional moan. "Done." Barakan turned to see her attempting to pull the blanket up over herself. He did it for her. Hardly feeling safe himself around her; he kept telling himself she was still hurt but this was another first for him. *She is naked.* His beast just kept repeating the words. *Naked Naked Naked.* Barakan pulled the plata of food up towards her.

"Kalista please eat a little you have had nothing and being so sick; and here drink this."

"What is it?"

"A spirit but I have sweetened it; eat some bread first and it won't burn quite so much."

"What have you put in it Barakan?" She knew.

"Something to help you sleep. You need to rest."

"I do." She tried to reach for some food. But winching she couldn't do it. Barakan knew now this time it was his turn to feed her. Sticking a single claw into a piece of bread he pulled and tore some off.

"Let me help." He held it for her to take. But Kalista didn't do what he expected grabbing at his outstretched hand she held just below the claws and eased his hand towards her mouth. Barakan seemed to hold his breath; praying he didn't flinch and catch her, hurting her further. She held his clawed finger to her lips and with care not only for his benefit but hers too her face was hurting. She took it between her teeth and pulled it free. Barakan caught his breath; as he pierced her a piece of cheese. And they repeated the process. When she had eaten a little Barakan pushed the goblet towards her.

"I cannot hold that for you." She smirked.

"I bet you could if you tried; there is more possible than you know."

"Kalista!" He was surprised by the connotations of what she was suggesting. "Drink it." She did. Her eyes were already getting heavy. "All of it."

"I'm trying." Slowly she did drink it all. Barakan moved the plata and helped her get comfortable.

"You will hurt for a few days but all will heal Kalista. You have no broken bones."

"No just my mind."

"Kalista why say that?" She tried to shrug which hurt and brought tears to her eyes. Barakan knew. *Here it is.* The awful truth was finally out and her emotions needed letting out. "Ouch." A sob escaped her followed closely by another and another. She cried loud and raucously. But it was what Barakan had expected.

"He he tried to do it Serena… He oh my God Barakan all those women he killed; allowing you to take the blame. He." She gaged on the words. "Oh my God he left them hurt already for you."

"But not all of them Kalista the amount he took to the clearing was so much more. I did not take so many lives. I." Barakan now he was actually voicing the words felt bewildered. Was this worse than him?

He had taken life too. Not in such frequency but still. *The curse?* An inkling of doubt or was it fear crept into Barakan's heart. *Does it still exist? What am I to do now?* "You must have thought me just the devil incarnate. Yet you still sacrificed."

"For my friend but it wasn't was it; it was him my luck came when you were actually there. It could have been so different." Her sobs didn't dissipate but so much was falling from her lips. "You were and are so much more than him. He is the only true killer." Her tears just kept coming, her words faltering at times. She hugged onto the blanket pulling it further up to her face and ringing it between her fingers. "He could have killed me so many times… I would have been better off dead." She almost screamed; her voice pitching. Making Barakan think she was swallowing broken glass. Excruciating. It coursed through him too like pain; pain he would take for her. Her screams broke his heart never mind what blame he carried in all this none of it was hers. "I wanted death so many times. Barakan." She shook. Barakan moved closer aiming to hold her but she was so hurt he couldn't just pull her to him. She looked at him trying to get close to her. She had survived and he Barakan was attempting to comfort her. *God do I need you; please be mine.* Comfort which she was desperate for.

"Barakan do not leave me please do not leave

me." He shook his head his own emotions getting the better of him.

"Kalista." He opened his arms. "Come here." With difficulty Kalista did; rolling to his open arms. Once there Barakan was able to pull her in closer and manoeuvre her so she was comfortable and once confined within his solid arms, Kalista began to calm.

"Barakan?" She seemed to pull at his fur hanging on. "Why did you not kill him?"

"Did you want me to Kalista did you want to see him draw his last breath?"

"I thought I did but… No. you are better than him." Barakan nuzzled into her hair. Pulling her scent to him.

"There was no point."

"I don't understand." Concentrating on his words her sobs steadied and she was becoming quieter.

"He is dying anyway. I smelt the rankness in him. He has a sickness which is eating him inside out he will have a painful undignified death." Kalista listened and considered Barakan's words.

"Painfully?"

"Yes very he will be reduced to nothing but skin and bone that lives in its own filth."

"How long?"

"A year if we're lucky."

"And he will suffer?"

"Definitely. Lots." Digging her fingers into Barakan's chest hanging on so hard. She thought about what he had just told her.

"That will do." Barakan leaned his muzzle into her neck feeling her skin against him. She smelt so good and Kalista had to admit so did he. Whispering

"I thought so. Now rest little one. You need all the rest you can get." The concoction Barakan had given her beginning to work she felt herself drifting off her eyes began to shut. *But there is something I must say.* There was something so important to her. As sleep engulfed her she managed to whisper back to him.

"I love you Barakan." She was gone. Barakan heard her words and they hit him like a great swinging sledge hammer. His guts knitted up a thousand times over and over. *How could you? No it is just the emotion of the day? The concoction I have given you.* He was making every excuse he could not believing anyone could. Not her not anyone ever. But one thing he did know as she slept within his powerful frame once again.

"But I love you my little one with everything I

am." Man and beast alike. Holding her close Barakan finally shut his eyes too and slept. *God I love you.*

Kalista awoke alone.

"Barakan." She called his name. *You have a habit of doing this.* She realised she was still naked. Pulling the blanket further around her Kalista realised how stiff everything was. "Urgh." Movement was difficult. "How am I to get dressed?" She frowned. *That hurts too.* Lifting her hands to her face she felt it. Swollen but it didn't feel as swollen as she expected. "God I'm going to be black and blue." Swinging her legs toward the side of the bed dragging the blanket with her she realised how much her ribs hurt too.

"I'm afraid there isn't much we can do about that." Barakan stood in the doorway her dress in hand. "It is mostly dry I did what I could with it." Kalista smiled back at him as best she could anyway.

"Thank you Barakan." Her chest seemed to move. Barakan couldn't decide if she was laughing or not.

"Are you laughing at me?" Kalista again attempted to move groaning as she did.

"Maybe just a little. You've washed my dress."

"I have tried…Yes."

"My great big beast is now a domestic." Shaking his head Barakan walked over to her.

"You could regret saying that."

"I think if I was going to regret anything I would have already done it."

"Hmm." His soft growl told her he saw the funny side of it too. Slowly Kalista put her feet to the floor.

"Barakan I'm not sure I can manage to put that on by myself." He studied her face. She was definitely bruised and if her blue face was anything to go by the rest of her would be worse but he wasn't so sure that this wasn't a little more ruse than incapability. There was something embedded in her eyes which told him she had ideas for him. He growled this time a different tone. Kalista heard and watched him too. He was forcing distance between them; controlling himself. Which was a good thing. *If you control it Barakan then maybe...* Her mind was working over time. *You wait till I'm better.*

"You don't have to get dressed."

"That's not what you have said before."

"Kalista!" Sometimes she did annoy him. "You know full well why that was a necessity."

"I do… but."

"But?"

"Rak It is all different now." She changed back from his full name.

"What makes you think that?"

"Because I know you are not a killer." Dropping to his knees before her Barakan looked hurt. It puzzled her. Till he spoke.

"Maybe not as prolific a killer as you thought; but it's not something that I haven't had a hand in Kalista. You see that don't you?" She titled her head towards him.

"They were dead before you even touched them."

"Kalista there is still before."

"Barakan." She put her hands on his face loosing a hold on her blanket it immediately slipped a little. She rested her face against his muzzle. "Victoor's has been doing this in your name for near on 60 years; not you him. The rat bastard is the only one who is a serial killer you are cursed it is different. But what ever you think." She paused. "You are the one who has stopped it. You. And only you my sweet. Please let's just take the small mercy's and only look forward not backward he will get his just rewards in hell." Barakan felt her conviction he remembered her words of love; right now what she was saying and how… He knew she meant them.

"Kalista." He sniffed at her. The blanket pulling from her chest; her adorable globes coming into view one pink nipple tipping the top alone. "Cover yourself." losing his face she grabbed at the blanket and pulled it up. "Shall I help you with this?" She nodded.

"Yes. I don't want to lie abed all day." He laid it at her feet bodice first.

"Put your feet in and i will pull it so far for you." He swallowed and struggled. "But you will have to do the rest yourself."

"Okay."

Kalista stood dressed and managed to walk over to the dresser where her brush set was. She wanted to look in the small mirror Barakan had given her. She wanted to look at her face she knew what the rest looked like. It wouldn't be the first time she'd seen herself injured and bruise but it would be the last. *Oh dear.* It wasn't such a pretty sight. *But I am free. Everyone is free.*

"It is done." Standing at the entrance getting some air Barakan was pleased for her. Her nightmares would never go but with time they would lessen; she had beaten what had brought her down. Pride for her filled him. *But what about you Barakan? What?* One thing he did know for sure was that him man and beast wanted her with a ferocious need which was hard to control but control it he would. She was his angel. If he said it enough it would be his reality.

He heard her talking and moving about slowly. Chuntering to herself.

"Kalista." He whispered her name knowing she wouldn't hear; he'd been doing that a lot since meeting her. He howled into the day. Kalista did hear that though. And slowly leaving her quarters she made her way to the cavern entrance. She wanted to be around him and to talk to him.

She enjoyed talking to him.

The time seemed to go slowly like her. Movement each day getting a little easier. But Kalista wasn't fully happy with Barakan after the first twenty hours there was something seemingly on his mind he seemed to be getting distant and extremley thoughtful but then she knew a lot had happened. And Victoor's confession; had to have affected him too. None of it had been as either had been duped into believing. But the nights were the best when she could finally cuddle up to him and hang on. She loved the way he felt. Solid grounded and if not even a little sexy. He had discarded breeches entirely now, which was better still. She wasn't afraid of anything about him anymore. Barakan often found her watching him; making him a little uneasy at times. Not knowing entirely what was going on in that mind of hers. Her eyes would flash at him and then he would see it. Desire and that terrified him. It had been a year since something in reality frightened him.

Kalista no longer saw either man, nor beast he was just Barakan; hers. She found as the days wore on and her body healed she wanted to get back to enjoying him. In whatever form it took. His strong heavy body with muscles that rippled was like nothing she'd ever seen. Not that she'd seen many. But his powerful thighs that could run for miles; she found herself imagining; wrapping around her whilst he was buried deep in her. She found herself dreaming about how it could work. She knew he looked at her and was just as desperate to have her for his. His self-willed erection made that much very clear. Which she lustfully enjoyed watching much to his chagrin. He was getting grumpier about it… till it came to bed time then she found him trying to keep himself in check and enjoyed her toying with his bristles but he hadn't allowed her to touch him since the night his own nightmares showed their ugly face. He growled loudly if she let her hands stray. Insisting she was still too bruised and not fully healed. Even threatening to leave her bed for her to sleep alone if she continued on this course. Telling her he was just happy being around her; as he was. But in that she knew he lied. There was nothing content in him as his erection throbbed and looked painful. She knew he must at least try to rid himself of it, it made her desire him more; to think she was causing it and she felt a strong desire to watch him. Between them this thing which was theirs was very visual. *Barakan.* Kalista set herself on a course of action; one which she could enjoy too. Delving ever more into her own desire for him, wether he liked it or not. Planning and with no small amount of plotting; Kalista began to set things up. A shared meal; plenty to drink and then she would touch him… He could disagree all he liked but she was prepared for that and a very determined woman. She went over different scenarios in her mind and they all ended up with her getting her way. And hearing his enjoyment too. She was ready and more than willing. *I love you Rak.*

# Chapter eleven

The days and time moved on; Kalista healing in both body and mind. As the initial shock at what had happened had calmed; Kalista realised that Victoor's confession and the fact that it was seen by the others as truth had vindicated her. And that in itself; to be believed had just helped, the truth was out and they knew she was no longer a liar. She was never a liar and the truth of that had never sat well with her and had always compounded the situation to make it worse. The side long glances and the dislike she saw and felt from them had always just made things worse and her life miserable.

Realisation of how many times Victoor's could have actually killed her; had hit her too. It had all focussed in on her and although there were things that would always be constant reminders; her scars for a start. But Kalista did think they were beginning to look better and fade maybe the fact that she was relaxed and wanting a life, was helping. But overall she felt better and was heading towards the good. She could genuinely smile now and everything just seemed so much easier. Even sleep; but that was him Barakan being with her that made sleep easy and no longer traumatic. She hoped he felt the same. He twitched and groaned but not the full on episode of terror like she had seen him suffer. Even after Victoor's confession and bringing things to the surface; she'd expected him to have so much running through his mins and the possibility it could cause an episode would have been high but it didn't seem to be happening. But he was thinking that much was obvious.

Kalista was determined to help him relax and feel good… and she was sure she knew how. It was time to push this thing between them just a little more. Her heart raced and she knew her desire grew. She felt like a pot boiling.

The day had started off like many others; eat wash talk. Until Kalista and suggested something a little different.

"Barakan do you think we could go for a walk?"

"What?"

"A walk some fresh air the forest is stunning at this time in the morning. Is it not safe for you?"

"The forest is always safe for me Kalista." His lip curled a little. *What are you up to my sweet?* He knew she was cooking something up; he could smell it on her. His curiosity was intrigued.

"I will go leave a note for Roberts today; there are things we need. So we could walk there if you wish?"

"Yes. That sounds great. Do I get to meet him?"

"Kalista! I do not talk to him; but maybe you could. I'm not so sure about it though."

"Is it going to cause you an issue?"

"I would doubt it."

"So I get to meet the famous Roberts."

"There is nothing famous about them."

"Barakan I was joking." Barakan leaned his muzzle down towards her face. His lips so near hers. Kalista found his nearness exhilarating. His earthy breath making her shudder. *This is going to be an exciting day.*

"Kalista; I'm not sure what is happening in that mind of yours but no funny business." Kalista just winked at him and grinned.

"Off course not."

"Hmm." His growl made her skin fill with goosebumps. "Are you ready now?"

"Yes i will just swap my slippers for my boots. But yes I'm nearly ready."

"Ok go get them." Barakan watched Kalista as she sashayed away from him. Her so touchable behind moving so delectable. He grumbled a little it vibrating through him. Low and tender. *You are doing that deliberately you little minx.*

Disappointed right at this moment his feelings charged. *Where do you think that is going to get you?*

The forest and the walk was fascinating; it was pleasant. They felt almost a normal couple whatever that word meant… Kalista's life had been far from that.

"Hey." Kalista almost ran tone besides Barakan. "You've speeded up. You know I can't keep up with you when you do." He looked down on her.

"Roberts I can hear him. I need to put the note out for him; before he gets there."

"Has he never seen you Barakan?"

"No."

"But surely they know."

"The original one yes. But not these."

"Do not rush Barakan. I will hand him the note." Barakan stopped for a moment not sure if he wanted that he didn't want to share her. It was so much better when it was just the two of them.

"You sure about that?"

"Yes why wouldn't I be?"

"He could question you on who you are? It could be difficult to answer?"

"I don't think so. We are friends."

"Hmm."

"As long as he doesn't think you are my captive.."

"Why would he think that? And no; on that I can put anyone straight even you Barakan." She eyed him strongly.

"I'm a captive no more."

Kalista held the note in her fingers and walked towards the man in front of her. Middle aged a little portly but entirely what she was expecting; he would have been good looking if she wasn't so enamoured by Barakan. She spoke first as he just stared.

"Hello!"

"Hello. I." Gobsmacked he didn't know where to look. Who was this beauty walking towards him. Long flowing dark hair whipped by the breeze. *Oh my!* Barakan watched the interaction with discontent; sniffing the air he could smell the subtle change in Roberts. A low threatening grumble built within in guts.

"I'm Kalista and if I'm not mistaken you must be one of the Roberts."

"Yes. Charles." He nodded his head finally in the correct manner of a greeting. "Kalista. Can I help you are you lost?"

"No thank you I am good and know exactly where I am." Charles looked even more confused. Kalista jumped straight back in. "I believe you have come to retrieve this." She handed him the note.

"Oh right… ok" The confusion changed to out and out shock. *She's with it.*

"I."

"It is ok Charles I think I would be shocked too."

"Are you ok?" Charles felt compelled to ask. Kalista smiled. But Barakan was far from pleased by this interaction of hers with Roberts. *I should not of allowed it.* The growl built just came out in a prolonged low threatening grumble. Both Kalista and Charles looked in his direction; hearing. Kalista knew where he stood in the shadows watching. And knew what that grumble sounded like. *You are jealous my love.* She smiled; turning back to Roberts. She winked whispering.

"Take no notice of him." Barakan was really struggling.

"Kalista!" His voice boomed at them both. "Oh Barakan behave. I am good Roberts thank you and all is marvellous. Don't suppose you could add something to that list and bring me some chocolate next time." Charles watched Kalista; she hadn't the demeanour of a woman frightened by her situation.

*Maybe you are ok.*

"I can do that for you."

"Great. And I wouldn't take any notice of him. His bark is far worse than his bite."

"Kalista…" They both heard his temper and his claws as they clanked together. Kalista turned and blew him a kiss.

"Damned woman." Charles took a single step backwards.

"I think I will take your word for that."

"Do. I can assure you I am good and safer now than I have ever been."

"Ok. I should go."

"Alright Charles but don't let him chase you away. I have enjoyed this short chat maybe next time we will get longer."

"Maybe. My father would like to say hello I'm sure."

"Would he?" Kalista puzzled his words. *Why? But who cares?* "I think I would like that."

"Maybe if he can manage it when I bring the things back; he will accompany me."

"Ok yes that would be fine. So I will accompany old grumpy guts here." Barakan's noise grew. *She's making dates with other men.* And they were men this made him so very angry. He tried to stop it.

"I think I had better go now." Charles backed up to leave.

"Thank you for all you do for him Charles he appreciates it as do I." Charles threw her a side long glance nodding and quickly left. *You might say that my lady but he doesn't sound like it.* And within seconds Charles was gone eaten by the forest. Barakan quickly came out the shadows stalking directly towards her.

"What was all that about?" Kalista watched his every move and studied his flames eyes, so very red. She smiled. Bathing in his look.

"You my glorious Barakan are jealous." That stopped him in his tracks. *Was he?* He hadn't considered. ***Yes.*** *Yes yes.* Both man and beast were. He could easily rip that man limb from limb right now. He snarled curling his lip.

"And you try my patience." Kalista moved to him where he stood; laying her hands on his heaving chest. His strength and masculinity just oozed from him. She loved it. Her hands scolded him. He was tense; both knew it.

"You have no need to be jealous I only have eyes for you." Kalista lowered her eyes to look at his uncovered genitals; Barakan could smell her arousal.

"Woman. Stop it." She had been getting more and more blatant in her teasing of him the last few days. "You wanted a walk today."

"I did."

"Come on then; Where now?" Barakan turned trying to get her eyes off him. She was making his erection grow.

"Urgh." Kalista knew. But there was something else she wanted to know.

"Barakan your home?"

"You are living there!"

"No; not the cavern. Your home the lands you owned."

"Still do. They are mine always no one dare take them."

"You go back?"

"Sometimes mostly to keep anyone else from falling for her."

"The witch?"

"Yes."

"She lives; near."

"Yes and No; she creeps around and has no home but she is always there."

"Oh."

“Why do you ask?”

“Because I thought if it wasn’t too far away you could show me.”

“It is too far for you to walk.” He seemed to be considering her words. “And may not be advisable.”

“Ok.” *Yet.* Barakan was excited that she was interested.

“Unless. Are you truly interested Kalista?”

“Yes Barakan otherwise I wouldn’t have asked.”

He considered her request. “If I carry you we could make it. But we shouldn’t stay long. Would you still like to see?”

“Yes. Barakan I would like to see it.” Kalista knew the routine and stood still for him to turn back to her. Barakan sighed unable to hide his growing erection. Kalista smiled as he turned back to her. *I see you Barakan I see what you want from me.* Her grin told Barakan all he needed to know too. *Woman.* He lowered his frame to pick her up; he blew down her neck and she felt it right down to her nipples. They pebbled in anticipation. Today was not done yet. He lifted her and Kalista made sure this time he could not avoid dragging her over his genitals and that growing part of him she wanted to know better.

“Kalista you need to behave or the only place you will be going is back to the cavern.” She tickled at his chest and winked.

"Ok I promise; for now."*Oh my God woman what has come over you?* But he knew now her ghosts had been laid to rest she was free and able to explore her sexuality. And it was tearing him up.

Comfortable in his arms Kalista didn't notice how much time went by as he ran through the forest with her. She watched his face as they did. Unsure of his feelings about taking her to see where it had all began. His features were hard to read right at this moment. He started to slow and Kalista couldn't resist but lay a gentle kiss on his chest. Barakan breathed in and held it.

"What was that for?"

"Reassurance I think?"

"For who?"

"You; but maybe a little for me too. This is where it all began barakan."

"Yes." Barakan slowed to a stop as he carefully lowered her to the floor. "Kalista we are here." She turned and all around her was luscious beautiful trees.

"Forest?" *But ye off course it would have grown in all these years.*

"No Kalista this is my lands but it is not all forest. Follow me." She did. Weaving between the gorgeous green trees. Obviously all old; strong and large they'd been there a long time. She ran her fingers over an old oak as she followed him.

"I used to climb that one as a child."

"You did?"

"Yes. My childhood was no different to many others maybe more privileged but my father he was a good man and believed in hard work and learning. It was only after he died when I was a teenager and all this." They moved between two trees and there inside a clearing much overgrown and not kept at all was a stone house. Still very much in one piece which surprised Kalista. She was expecting a ruin. The shock showed.

"Became mine was where the problems arose."

"This is yours still Barakan?"

"Yes. It surprises you?"

"Only That it still looks whole even after so many years."

"It is kept that way."

"You sort its upkeep. You didn't say."

"No I don't Roberts he sorts it. And why would I; I can no longer live here." Kalista strode through the long meadow grass towards it.

“No maybe not… Can I look closer?” Barakan gave her a quick curt nod no one else was there he would sense them. But it didn’t bother him it would only make things worse; he would never be able to take residence again.

“You will have to go alone but do not go out of sight Kalista.”

“You will not come with me?”

“No.” he didn’t elaborate further. Kalista felt the pull to go strong.

“Ok I won’t be long.” Kalista quickly skipped towards the house. Barakan watching intent on his own thoughts. *You would suit the place so well my sweet.* She quickly reached the property and now it was here in front of her she realised how very big it was. *Wow.* She put her finger to the solid brick and carried on walking quickly over the once stoned walk way now grass all over grown and full of life. She came to the large wooden front door. It was stunning. Solid and so very well made she refrained from banging the large knocker. A gargoyle watching her from way up high. She grinned.

“Hello there sir you guard a beautiful place.” There was a window to her right curiosity filling her she walked over to it. And cupping her hands on the glass she peered in.

"Barakan this is absolutely stunning." He snarled …

"I know." But at that one time as he listened to her; something else struck him, not quite a smell more of a sense but he knew what it was. Snarling loudly he set off at a fast pace on all fours and came to a sliding halt besides her.

"Kalista come we have to go now." Kalista did not understand but saw the unease in him. She nodded.

"Ok." Sliding his arms round her he lifted her easily as he took a glance at what she had been looking at. His study.

"Urgh." He knew what she saw as rows and rows of books which wouldn't be that anymore but just rows of compacted dust. When you touched them they would disintegrate. But right now there was no time. They had to be away. He had caught a whiff of her stench. She was about. And there was no way on this earth he would have Kalista subjected to her. Holding her as if he was hanging on to her for his very life he set of at a great speed. Faster than Kalista knew he could go; again. She caught her breath.

"Barakan! What is it?"

"Sch. Not now." Kalista saw his lips curling in hate she knew in that moment that he had sensed something or someone that made him hate. *The witch!* It had to be. Kalista lay in his arms quiet, and waited. When she felt him begin to slow. She spoke.

"Barakan I am sorry."

"What for?"

"Because it was my curiosity which took us there."

Slowed to his normal pace he seemed to hug her close.

"Do not worry."

"But I do. What happened Barakan?" There was no point trying to bluff his way out of answering.

"I could sense her and didn't want to hang about; that was all."

"That was **all**! My goodness Barakan. I am so sorry."

"Kalista don't be. She wasn't that near it was only the mildest or senses; she was miles away, too far to bother us. I just didn't want to take the risk." Kalista pondered on wether he was telling her the entire truth or not.

"Okay. Can we go home now?"

"Off course. It is ok Kalista you are not in any danger."

"I wasn't worried for me Barakan but I know.

Let's get back I will cook dinner for us."

"You will?"

"I can cook you know."

"Ok well we will see if you are as good as me then won't we." In jest Kalista slapped at his chest.

"Hey…" But she knew he was the one who had been doing the majority.

"Barakan?"

"What?"

"You had and have a beautiful home. The cavern is terrific but so is your house. And I was surprised it was all so well kept."

"Ye." He didn't want to talk about the house she found conversation for the moment shutdown.

Reaching the cavern Kalista found herself dropped to the floor quickly and muttering something almost inaudible Barakan disappeared again. But being here alone didn't bother her. He would be back soon sometimes he too needed privacy. Kalista quickly set about putting things in place she put the lovely piece of beef that Roberts had provided before for them this night. She had eaten lots of white meat and rabbit Barakan needed no help in providing that. But this was to be something special for them. With red wine it would go down easily. Then once pushed into the stone oven and the fire lit that Barakan himself had built she quickly lit a torch and took herself off to wash. She wanted to be clean and smelling good for him.

Barakan charged the boundaries around the mountain. He hadn't been quite as truthful with Kalista than he should have been. He needed to be sure that the rotten smell wasn't permeating here. He would feel better knowing that she hadn't been so close. Thoughts and feeling whirling around him like a great raging hurricane. *You will not take her from me. I will not.* He had vision of Kalista battered and bruised body just red; blood red and it scared him. *I will not. I will fling myself from the mountain top first.*

But death was never his option otherwise he would have welcomed it long before now.

Kalista carried on fervently putting her plans into place. Tidying their quarters, making the bed.. then she looked at herself washed and clean she knew she smelt good but would she look good. She'd been that carried away with herself she hadn't stopped to consider what she looked like. *What will he think of me?* Doubt crept in. Her body was always to carry the scars. But her body wanted him and she knew it. Would he allow her this; she knew he would complain but when he actually saw her; what he was getting out of this bargain they seemed to have built. *Will you still want me.* Naked; his desire could turn to just the need. *I want you to desire me Barakan. Like I do you.* She felt the solid need to make him proud of her and desire her fully; to find her attractive not just the need of the curse. Always there in the back ground.

Barakan did not rush back to the cavern; but he heard all Kalista's rustling and bustling about, her grunts and grumbles at herself. *What on earth are you up to woman? Is cooking that hard.* He was intrigued to find out what she was up to? Slowly he made his way back. The food smelled good he smelt it a long time before he was back. But as he neared there was a subtle scent of other things too. Perfumed soap and maybe just a touch of perfume too. It was a heady mixture. He found himself growling without control. *Kalista.* She smelt so good. By the time he got back Kalista was just a carrying the plata of meat to their quarters. He came up behind her; grunting so he didn't make her jump and drop the food she'd put so much effort into preparing.

"Hm hm… Kalista." She turned to him and looked at him. He had run a long way.

"This is about ready." Her nose twitched. "But do us both a favour Rak before we do eat. Go for a bathe." He grinned at her.

"And she's telling me I stink again."

"I am." She winked back at him. "Go wash quick."shaking his head. Barakan liked the teasing between them and quickly headed towards the hot spring.

Walking back into their quarters Barakan was struck by the little amount of light; no torch's lit just candles and the plata's of food spread out on the bed all tended with much care. And Kalista dressed but there was something different about her; her hair brushed and left loose to fall about her face and shoulders. He liked it that way. *Kalista.* He would love to be able to run his hands through it. Her dress the same one he'd seen time and time again; but he now saw that the bindings weren't fastened all the way. They were fastened not just left loose but only half way. She had done that deliberately her healthy cleavage on display. *Kalista.* A groan escaped him. Kalista knew she watched his eyes draw over her. She quickly pushed him towards the bed.

"Come let's eat." She didn't want him to try and escape. "Sit. I have left enough room for you." She forced him to sit at the head of the bed. As she climbed on after him. Both looking at one another the plata's in between them. Quickly handing him his own goblet full to the top before she sipped at her own. Barakan looked at his wine almost to the brim.

*What are you trying to do? Get me drunk?* His beast thought it comical but the man in him saw the trouble ahead.

"I hope this is to your liking Rak." Barakan's eyebrows furrowed. *What are you saying Kalista?* He sniffed at the air; her perfume stronger now but something else to something that made him twitch. *Desire.* Again.

Kalista held a piece of the hot meat up to his lips… "Try it and tell me if you like it." Carefully opening his mouth they had this perfected between them now. He allowed her to slip the meat into his mouth. The taste alighting his taste buds and his memory but not as much as her right now. Kalista took a hot piece of potato and fed him that too.

"I prefer the meat Kalista."

"I thought you would." She tried to pull a much larger piece apart for herself.

"Here let me." Barakan quickly pierced it with his claw and split it. Pushing the tip of his claw into it before doing the same as Kalista and offering it to her. He put it so very carefully to her lips. Kalista knew exactly what she was about. Barakan was playing right into her hands. She took it all between her teeth meat and claw too; wondering if they would have any sensation or be like nails with none; not that she cared the whole thing was so sensual. She flicked her tongue so very carefully over the tip being steady not to cut herself. She was away in a world of her own. A world where she had a lover. Barakan groaned loud and deep. Pulling his hand away. Grabbing more meat for himself trying to distract them both. But that wasn't going to work; not tonight. Kalista leaned over. Her cleavage on display for him; her flesh moving as she breathed. His eyes couldn't stop looking. She finished her wine.

"Rak would you like more?"

"No I'm good." He stopped and snorted in her direction. "But Kalista… What are you up to?"

"Why do I need to be up to something?"

"Because you are." She shrugged.

"Maybe I am; just a little bit I'm enjoying spending time with you." The wine taking affect making her braver in voicing what she wanted from him.

Barakan titled his head so he wasn't so much taller than her watching her every move. Sensing her every subtle change.

"Do you?"

"What?"

"Enjoy spending time with me." Kalista was quick to see her opportunity and placed the plata's on top of one another removing them from the bed. Standing turning to Barakan she gave him his answer.

# Chapter twelve

"Off course I do."

"But Kalista!" Taking a step closer to him. She carried on. *Not this again. You doubt me so much Rak.*

"Rak this is not the first time we have had this conversation. Look at me do I look afraid?"

"I suppose not."

"There is no suppose about it Rak. I thought we had sorted this."

"I am still what you see Kalista no matter what."

"Yes. Do you know what I see?" Barakan shook his head. "I see a being with heart and soul that has been as broken as me."

"But I am."

"If you call yourself a beast one more time Rak I'm gona. Ooooo. The only beast I know was the rat bastard who has manipulated us all." In that Barakan knew she was right. Up to a point. Her face flushed and her eyes flared. Everything in her heightened. Neither mentioned the L word Kalista wondered if she had actually said it or dreamed it. *Gona have to do it again girl I think.*

"Rak." Kalista moved in further. Just as he raised himself from the bed. *Oh no you don't.* She could see his intention to cut and run. "Don't you dare leave this room."

"You should not get so aggressive with me Kalista."

"Well… You should not doubt me." He towered over her.

"Do I doubt you?"

"You keep questioning my motives."

"Only for your benefit. I am as you see me."

"Oh ye and don't I know that."

"What do you mean by that?"

"A dirty great big silly male."

"Kalista!" He sighed at her. "What do you want from me?"

"I would like to say nothing Rak. But there is something I want. I want something I have never had before; and it seems only you can fill the gap. She hissed at him oozing sensuality. "Intimacy." Barakan leaned towards her trying to sense what she was going to say and do next. But watched instead as raising her hands to her bindings on the dress bodice pulled to undo them. This shocked him. *No no no.* Yet his beast said the opposite. *Yes yes yes.*

“Kalista! What? No. Stop…” she pulled them so they were that loose and only just hanging in her one tug and her breasts would be free. “Please!”

“No Rak I have no intention of stopping do not try and stop me.” He moved to try and walk past her. “Rak do not leave. Stay.” She grabbed on to his arm. “I have no intention of stopping so if not now than another night. Stay. Please.”

“I do not know what you want from me Kalista.”

“Then let me show you.”

“I.. God Kalista this is an impossibility.”

“No I don’t think it is… I believe I have already proved where there is a will there is a way.” She started to pull at her bodice. Barakan snarled loudly and put a hand towards her to try and stop her.

“You stop me Rak?”

“Yes.”

“Why do you not want to see me?” He rolled his head dramatically on his neck stifling the howl which was developing.

“That from you is a stupid statement. You know I do.” He hovered over her. All the male he was. “Just see what you do to me.” She did. *Good.*

“And do you not think I have the same sort of feelings too Rak.”

"Kalista there is no way."

"I will be the one who decides that." Barakan took a step back from her. *Domineering!* That was so adamant.

"I would have you look on me. Do you want to Rak."

"With everything I am yes. But." *Cracked it.* Kalista finished pulling her bodice from her and allowed the dress to fall the rest of the way: it pooled at her feet. She was naked.

Barakan couldn't stop the almighty growl come pained groan as he looked at her; dipping his head immediately. It was too much.

"Kalista." His voice breaking not unlike hers had been in pain as if he had now eaten broken glass; so much fear filled him. "you shouldn't. I. Can't. It's too much." She moved a small single step closer. Tears filling her eyes this was so important to her; to love him and be loved. It was all she wanted man and beast.

"Rak. There is always a way. Raise your head look at me." Slowly as if every movement hurt he did.

"Do you see me?"

"Off course." He smelt the air around her. "I can smell you too."

“And what does it tell you Rak.” *Desire*

“Desire.” She sidled up to him .

“And I see yours.”

“Oh Kalista.”

“It is desire you feel isn’t it Rak? Not the curse! My scars do they not disgust you?” Now that stung as if she’d stabbed him.

“Kalista. How dare you say that to me. **No.** Nothing about you disgusts me. And no this is not the curse but it is the curse which stops me.”

“Then we won’t let it.” Edging her finger tips towards him she stroked at his thighs. “We will find a way.”

“Oh my God Kalista you are killing me.”

“That is not my intention Rak.”

“No but you want to risk me killing you.”

“You won’t.”

“Won’t I? You have no idea what this feels like my beast right now wants everything about you.”

“And Rak my darling do you not know I want everything about you too.” Barakan just stared his eyes switching from flame red to sparkling green and back again. Both man and beast out their minds with confusion. No one had ever wanted him like this. She pulled at the bristles on his thighs. Intoxicating;

edging her little digits towards his pulsating erection.

"Kalista!" Barakans voice was almost a sob.

The heat coming from both of them scolding; the distance between them not great enough for either not to feel it.

"My sweet Rak. Do you want to touch me?"

He gaged loudly. His body beginning to shake.

"Of course I do." He lifted his hands to her; just to remind her. "But how can I with these?"

"Then we won't use them." His look was just pure confusion. *What was she suggesting?*

"Kalista I have been alone so long. My life has been nothing but broken without you. Don't be my illusion don't make me loose you. Not now." Kalista held her breath was he going to say it. She wanted him to. *Yes yes please my darling.*

"Rak. I have waited in the shadows for you too my darling do you not know. How much … I love you." He snarled and howled all all in equal measure.

"Kalista." He wanted to hold her to wrap his arms around her but stopped she was naked. He snarled…

"I love you. I want to die in your arms." Tears ran down her face.

"No one is going to die not yet. Not me and

definitely not you my darling." She stepped that close her nipples were almost touching his chest. "You can touch me Rak.. I need you to touch me."

"I. How?"

"Lick me."

"What?" Kalista put her fingers to his lips and run them along his. As she stood on tip toe and like before laid her lips against his. Barakan froze. *What was she suggesting?*

"Touch me my sweet… lick me. I want you too." Kalista had put much thought into this over the last days and it seemed a solution to their problem and would be as intimate and enjoyable for both. She needed him to touch her somehow. It was a powerful thing which had been growing in her. She was burning with desire which had never happened to her before and not unlike Barakan she didn't know what to do with it. They were both on new ground.

"Kalista. You can't mean it..I..you."

"I do." She pulled away from Barakan's face… pushing him back towards their bed. He couldn't stop looking at her body as it moved. Everything about her was just so perfect. Her full round breasts with nipples that just wanted to be touched. Down her flat stomach to her neat little nest of desire which he could smell so acutely. He growled so loudly. *God I do want you.* Man and beast needed to do this for her; for sanity. The scars all there but he didn't care she looked on him with desire and he was far from perfect. He was hardly man any more. This was something that suddenly struck him as being meant. Destiny had been playing with them both. "Do this for me Rak. I need you to do this."

"You have no idea what you ask."

"I do I'm asking you to share with me. I know you want to."

"Can't we just." He was trying to find a way other than him loosing control. But Kalista wasn't having any of it, they needed to at least try to share.

"Try Rak… if it doesn't work or it is too much then we will stop and I will touch you. But please Rak for me try." *How can I not. You're killing me Kalista.*

Barakan seemed to relent and sat back down on the mattress watching her with love.

"Kalista how do you want to do this?" She beamed at him lustfully. *Mine.* She leaned into him pushing his knees apart with her own. As she leaned into him Barakan began to shake further. Whispering…

"Kalista." She stroked his face and ran her fingers over his lips before her hard nipples resting against him she laid her lips once again on his. His heavy erection sandwiched between them, she could feel his heat.

"This for starters." She kissed him but this time a little different feeling his smooth lips beneath hers fuelled her desire further. If he wasn't about to burst she was. She'd been so controlled till now. Kalista carefully moved her lips on his forcing them open and with a sigh licked at him, running her tongue over his lips encouraging him to try to do the same. Hardly a movement but he did he moved his lips always kept still frozen in time till now; then terrified he allowed his tongue to leave its haven between his teeth and touch hers. That was it Kalista groaned loudly her control fighting against her need. She loved his touch his earthy taste not unpleasant. She battled his to force her tongue into his mouth. Barakan pulled away. *Teeth.* But he had achieved it kissed her without drawing blood. She amazed him. He snarled low.

"Lay on the bed." *Finally.* Kalista complied just what she wanted from him. Stepping back from him she crawled onto the bed on all fours besides him. Her backside wiggling at him as she did so.

"Aaaa." He was lost. Barakan turned to her. One last time. "Kalista are you sure?"

"Yes… please Rak… I need you. I have never been surer of anything." He grunted and getting on all fours hovered over her. His beast shouting inside him. *I can have her take her. She's there waiting for you...* ***But*** *be slow careful make her scream. I want to hear her scream for more.* Even he now was showing scruples. It struck Barakan that neither of them were as bad as he'd always felt... Tenderness was theirs too. Barakan took a tight hold of the blankets either side of her and wrapped his claws taut in them. Blankets could easily be replace. He looked like he had massive mittens on. Kalista moved below him. Desperate for him to touch her; hissing at him. "Rak." He was taking too long. She was burning up.

"Sch little one... don't be so impatient; I'm trying." The rest of his words were lost in his mouth as he stared at her splayed beneath him. "My God Kalista." Barakan finally leaned down to her pushing her head with his muzzle to give him access to her neck. Breathing so heavily now his hot breath running down Kalista's neck and over the rest of her. Everything she was leapt and pinched like an animalistic earthly current running through whole body everything was wound so tight.

"Kalista my darling. You are my gravity." Her words were nothing now but noise. With more care than he had ever displayed Barakan allowed his tongue to touch her skin; running it down her neck.. Kalista moaned loudly; drawing more from him Barakan ran his tongue up and down her neck again before tracing a line down her clavicle and sitting in the dip of her throat. She smelt so good; he breathed her in? Knowing his next step was down. He too groaned. Taking his weight on his arms; his hands pushed into the mattress; tense wrapped in the blanket, they grabbed and twisted at the restraints. He moved his mouth and drew his tongue towards her heaving breasts. Unable to stop the automatic reaction to her he allowed his front teeth to show just a little sliding them over her healthy flesh.

"Barakan!" He knew she was enjoying what he did. It encouraged him he pulled his tongue around her areola finally flicking it against her nipple. Kalista arched her back forcing more of her at him. Barakan tried something else aiming not to loose control but it was so hard; drawing one pebbled nipple into his mouth gentle sucking. Drawing a gasp from her so loud it was like his a growl. Then the second nipple took the same treatment. Kalista panted, her breath came in short sharp gasps. Moving himself again. Barakan followed a line down with his tongue over the bottom heavy globes of her breasts. Not moving his tongue. Knowing he got pleasure from giving her pleasure. Her stomach pulled and rolled under his touch his tongue delved into her tummy button. He growled…

"Kalista!" Her female scent so strong now. He had to know before he delved deeper this was what she wanted. Man and beast alike were struggling neither wanted to hurt his little flower. “Are you?” He didn’t get to finish his sentence. Kalista grabbed at his head entwining her fingers into his fur; hanging on. His erection had never felt so painful. But he would give her all she needed.

“B a r a k a n.” Moving down he hovered above the core of her desire and his too he realised how very much he wanted to give her pleasure. Moving his heavy frame he pulled his hands further down. The grip they already had so taut; he found the blanket entangled around his claws came with them but right at this moment he did not care. He breathed on her taking her smell of desire to him. The strongest it had been; her desire would match his and he knew it. Pushing her legs further Barakan settled his shoulders between her soft limbs. The sight which now met his eyes was something so unique to them it burned into his memory. Desire; for him. As she saw him now, not anything to do with before. *My God Kalista you are my Angel.* He was so afraid of her; her desire, of everything that it meant. But right now fear was fast loosing to desire. He groaned so loudly his whole body vibrated moving through her legs. She shook.

“Rak.” She wasn’t the only one shaking. He delicately stroked her luscious folds of flesh with his tongue. She moaned again and again; needing more from him. Then with a sudden urgency which was taking him too. Barakan drew his tongue over her tightened bundle of nerves; Kalista squealed. That was what she wanted; he lapped at her again, then again and again, he was being swept away by her. His hands and claws just kept loosening and tightening shredding at both the blankets and mattress. Repeating her name… "Kalista." Kalista began to writhe beneath him her cries not quiet but raucous; this was pleasure she had never experienced; tears ran down her face. Her whole body began to stiffen and tighten; her hands dropped from his head as she tried to keep herself from rising from the bed. She was sure she was about to take off and explode. Kalista knew something was about to happen but not what. She was alone in this with him; her beast lover. Then as if out of nowhere Barakan took it on himself to give her all she needed and carefully sucking he pulled that tiny little bud into his mouth resting his teeth on her; gentle pulling. Kalista just stiffened her legs straightening alongside him; tightening against his shoulders. Out of nowhere her orgasm just happened; Kalista went with it; holding her breath as it came flooding from her. Everything left she was just a quivering mess. Slowly Barakan released his hold on her, watching as her hot wet body shivered. He groaned words at her..

"My darling. Are you." He looked up from between her legs to see her head tilted looking down at him; tears streaming. Immediately panic filled him. He tried to move but tied up so much in the blankets it was difficult. He snarled but Kalista smiled at him.. speaking hoarsely. He too was a sight to see nestled between her legs. And whatever he had caused wasn't entirely sated.

"Roll over."

"Kalista have I hurt you?"

"No just roll over would you."

"I would if i could." He pushed at his hands. Kalista chuckled at him: pulling her legs away she leant over him to help. Her glorious breasts dancing about in front of him. It was more than body and soul could take; wrapping his arms mittened blanketed hands and all around he pulled Kalista to him and set about licking her all over again. Kalista wiggled in his grip.

"Rak. Stop I want to touch you." He pulled away as she whispered in his ear. "Your turn." Pulling her with him he lay down at the bottom of the bed.

"Kiss me." Barakan had never expected to say those words again. She easily complied. Knowing that strange taste mixing with his earthiness was her. He licked at her face; tasting her salty tears. "You cried?"

"Yes my lover there are other tears than ones of

sorrow you know." His heart just kept expanding she was filling every bit of him. "I told you there was always a way; and." She whispered so low only he would hear. "I haven't finished with you yet." Barakan raised an eyebrow. *Hmm.*

Kalista stopped kissing him and pushed him back against the bed; his hands tied and trapped. She grinned at him as she slowly slid down his body deliberately grinding herself on his burning pained erection; he could feel how wet she had become, he knew how easy it would be to just impale her little frame. *No...* That wouldn't be happening.. Kalista took his throbbing erection between her hands she stroked, long and slow. Listening to his moans of pleasure now it was such a turn on. She toyed with his thighs; running her fingers over and around all he was. She ran her hands down to the soles of his feet and back up again. He felt her hair tangling in all he was. She moved and it stuck to both him and her face. An erotic sight. Barakan began to snarl his hips moving; this tonight for him wouldn't be long in ending as beast had never touched a woman so. He threw his head back and howled as Kalista once again put her lips on him. She sucked him into her mouth harder than before; then with a desire to hear him howl she dragged her teeth over him. With a tightened grip she began to pump her little fist stretching him till the skin would go no further as her lips followed suit and took as much of him as was physically possible. She was sure she could feel the blood pumping beneath her fingers his heart beat definitely pounded through her as did the vibrations from his growls and snarls. *I will never let you go my Rak.* The one and only being to make her feel safe and loved was him; man and beast alike . He belonged to her. Barakan could stand it no longer he could smell her desire still on him her taste lingering. *I have given her pleasure.* And now she was returning it. He stretched his hands out as she pulled and sucked until his body tightened and leapt from the precipice she held him on, the blanket finally giving way and it was torn it two; as in a howl he tried to stifle so it wouldn't hurt her ears he came. Hard. His whole body almost rising from the bed, unable to stop himself as his legs like hers tightened into spasm and pushed her from him.

Kalista managed to move with him and not get kicked from the bed.

Both lay panting; Barakan having trouble putting everything all his thoughts back in place. He wanted to love her; keep her always but take her fully too. And that he knew was an impossibility… *yet?* He had managed the impossible so far. But to walk now alongside her in life was all he could think of being alone so very long. He wanted her furiously; and if he couldn't he didn't want to go on any longer as he was. Thoughts drifted into his being which had been there from the moment he had met her just they been whispering and sniggering at him pulling first one way then the other but now after all she had achieved for him. *For me she has done this all for me. Should I?* He knew maybe the time was here to… He stopped the thoughts as Kalista crawled over him. *Yes yes yes. Fuck the curse!* He watched her as she pulled her face to his.

“Hello.” She smiled.

“Hello!” He answered her. Before smirking back at her. “You are… Stunningly wicked Kalista.” She laughed back at him.

“That good hey?” He pulled her to him encasing her in his heavy frame.

“You have no idea my sweet.” She shuddered as his breath once again ran down her neck; her body filled with goosebumps. She reached up to tickle his chest and began to play with his nipple running her little fingers over and around him pulling another growl from him. Barakan slammed his hand down over hers nails and all. Remnants of the blanket hanging from them.

“Stop. Sleep. There is only so much I can take from you in one night my sweet.” Kalista chuckled knowing she had him; she would be able to explore this thing further in the morning. For now she basked in him; and he her. She snuggled her head into the crook of his neck.

The only words left for her.

Rak I have waited years for you; I love you." She shut her eyes and fell into uninterrupted sleep. Barakan listened to her steady rhythm of breath. He pushed his muzzle into her hair. *Oh my God Kalista. I love you too. How had this happened? Why had it happened?* He had no idea. *But...* There had to be a but this could not just be it for her she deserved so much more. He couldn't just replace his own beast for the one she had only ever known. *No. Is there something to be done?* Thoughts feeling and emotions in turmoil; Barakan finally fell asleep. Fitful uneven sleep. Nightmares not that more like plans and ideas. Occasionally he found himself just hanging on to her staring. She was his little miracle. *Can I affect another?* There was only one way to find out. *Should I?*

# Chapter thirteen

Kalista woke alone again but that didn't surprise her. She stretched and untangled herself from the messy bed. The blankets not really that anymore. The top one anyway that was split into two large pieces and both of those had holes and looked like the moths had been at it. A large smile crossed her lips.

"Rak. I'm awake." She knew he would be listening for her. Swinging her legs from the bed; she put her feet to the floor. No idea what time it was not that Kalista cared or that it mattered. Time was their own and no one else's. She looked at her body; something this morning felt different. Better. She had enjoyed him so much. Stepping over to the plata on the desk she picked at the bread and meat; hungrier than she expected. The bread was a bit dry but the cold meat was still delicious. *As are you my sweet?* Thoughts of what Barakan had done to and for her made her quiver. *I would have more of that.* "Bathe." Even though Kalista new she would be alone; she still told him exactly where she was headed. Hoping maybe he would come to her. And with that in mind and grinning Kalista left their quarters and headed towards the bathing pool naked. Climbing directly into the water, she ran her hands down her body cleaning. Getting to know her body but in a differently perfected way to what she had already known. Her nipples hardened under her own fingers… she groaned.

"Rak.." There was no mistaking the subtly sultry tone in her voice.

But unfortunately she was disappointed his shadow didn't appear. *Hmm ...* Grumbling Kalista finished her chores; tried to brush her extremely knotty hair; his claws and her shifting and rolling it about had caused a real mess. It was just tangled; it took some doing to tease all the knots free but she finally did it. Smiling the thoughts of what they had achieved together making her shudder, quickly dressed she set about attempting to find him. The slightest amount of feared doubt creeping in.

Barakan knew she was up; he heard her and her speaking to him. He was used to this now but not unlike her this morning felt different there was something in the air which crisp and clear and kept poking at him. His thoughts drifted. *Could things ever be different for me?* He'd been looking for something which he knew existed. A wild flower; he'd never known the name but it was a certain colour, beautiful and he wanted to give to her. Like men would. Now having found it he was returning but not rushing his emotions spinning so tight he didn't know what he wanted apart from her, and she was so deliciously delicate and could so easily break. His fears once again raising their head. Then he heard her again. Clearer.

"I know you can hear me Rak. Where are you I would walk to you…" *My love.* Howling loudly he let her know he heard. Listening Kalista heard him deciphering which direction he was. She thought she knew. "I will walk down the left path. Find me my love." Putting one booted foot in front of the other she made her way down the path; pleased it was this way she could manage this one, the other would be more of a climb. That would have been more difficult. Barakan listened and knew where she was heading. Striding towards her he made his way back to her.

Kalista heard his grumbled breath before she saw him. Then he appeared between the trees. All sweaty and breathing heavily. She frowned at him.

"Where have you been? Your all."

"Sweaty I know. I was finding you something."

"Was you?" Her curiosity more than peaked.

"Yes I wanted to give you this." He held up in his fisted claws and there was a flower roots and all. He would have her grow it not just watch it wither to die. Kalista knew what his gesture was and smiled; beaming at him. His look so innocent.

"That is beautiful." *And very unexpected. So sweet.* She saw the gorgeous blue flower. *Maybe it was some sort of wild orchid.* "And thank you Rak. I love it." He was forced to answer her his words would not halt.

"As I do you." Everything in her glowed she felt herself warming with desire as he stood between the trees; she wanted him, and more. *So much more.* She stood looking at him her eyes full of lust. Barakan sniffed at the air. Her desire singing to him once again. He stuttered.

"Kalista!" Kalista knew what he sensed in her she saw it in him too as his erection began to grow. He groaned as if to move and hide it.

"Rak." Her sweet voice pulled his eyes back to her as lifting her hands to the bindings at her bodice she pulled easily undoing them. Her feet already pulling at her boots to slip them off. Not an easy task but she managed. His innocent gesture had just pushed all the right buttons.

"Kalista what?" She slipped her arms in one quick movement from its sleeves. Before allowing the dress to fall to the floor; she stood again before him naked. "What are you doing Kalista?" Kalista took a step towards him. Her eyes shining bright. But her words were raspy.

"What does it look like."

"Here?"

"Why not?"

"I…" Her name rolled of his tongue as she so sensually walked towards him. Everything about her shouting for his touch. She knew this time what she was doing and what she wanted. He did not.

"Put my plant down Barakan." He did as she told him; he was getting used to her orders. Especially when she looked so delicious. He found himself actually salivating.

"Kalista. You are being…"

"What?"

"Brazen!" She laughed at him.

"And you are not." She eyed his massive erection.

"Kalista it was only last night." This was all new ground for him; he had never not in his wildest dreams thought that any of this would have been possible for him and for her now to walk into the forest naked to him. She was a stunning vision. "Last night." He was worried that it would all become too much.

"Oh Rak will you stop fussing I didn't know

there was a limit on this." She gestured to herself.

"There isn't but."

"No buts. Sit on the floor. I promise I will be good." He snarled at her; squinting his eyes at her.

"Doesn't that depend on what you mean by good." She winked; chewing her bottom lip seductively as she reached him.

"Sit down and you will find out." He too smiled and did as she asked. Sat again between the trees. Kalista moved to stand straddled over him. Barakan's eyes nearly popped out his head. She was stood before him almost splayed for his ministrations. He groaned unable to resist.

"Come closer." He groaned…Easily she did. The core of his desire glistening at him. "K a l i s t a. You are wet."

"Yes… Touch me Rak." His invite. Lifting his hands to her he drew a single digit and allowed the claw to stroke her thighs. Getting braver himself. All very new territory.

"You are beautiful little one."

"Rak." She shuddered; he leaned into her and drew his tongue first up one thigh then down the other before with a sort of grasp on her thighs forced her to turn, her round shapely behind before him. He allowed his muzzle to drag over her; making her behind flinch as his teeth just caught her. He did it again. Whispering. “I won’t hurt you Kalista.” She hissed back at him.

“I know.” He licked her. Sending a shudder which chased up her spine and down her front settling in her groin. His teeth began to chew gentle against her. *If I were man still i would bury me face in you. God woman.* Barakan snarled. The noise affecting her too her lust just pooled. Barakan could smell what was happening to her again he spun her; Kalista nearly lost her footing as she stepped back over his legs . But Barakans strong powerful hands held her steady till she regained her footing. Without marking her. He’d mastered his claws a little.

“Rak.”He knew now what she wanted from him.

He; allowing his tongue to leave his mouth flicked it at

her hard nub nestled between her folds of flesh. Kalista squealed at his first touch. Then he did it again and again lashing her. Her arms flayed; standing she didn’t know what to do with them as the urgency for him to do more grew. She grabbed at his head holding him in place as he lavished attention on her. She screamed.

“Rak.” He pulled away from Kalista to watch her she was shaking from head toe.

"Kalista. Do you realise what you have done to me." Her eyes hazy lowered to see him. *Was this going to be a good or a bad thing?* "Between us we are a couple."

*My God was he saying what she thought?* She broke and began to sob. "Kalista what is it? Have I upset you?"

"No, no, no… Never. God I love you Rak. Please don't you ever leave me."

"I couldn't not now." Kalista dropped down to her knees over him faster than he had expected. Straddling him. His eyes blossomed with lust and fear both in equal measure. She did keep doing this; causing his emotions to battle one another.

"Kalista you should move." But for her foreplay was finished.

"No." He snarled loudly at her. *Oh my God she wasn't going to push him further. She couldn't; she mustn't. The rest has to be enough.* But Kalista had other plans it wasn't; she was on fire, and driven by her need to be loved wholly by him and just him. *There was always a way.* Just kept spinning around her mind. She shoved her hands at Barakans chest and digging her fingers into his very flesh held herself tight there as she answered again.

"No." Barakan stared stunned as she gyrated grinding herself on him. He could feel her wet flesh against him. Barakan fighting hard against all his instinct to just impale her. Yet he knew this time he was going to lose.

"K a l i s t a ! No!." But too late; laying her mouth on his she licked his lips as moving her hips she slid up and down against his full length. Enticing him further. His hands now wanted to grab at her. He could feel her soft wet heat against the head of his erection then with ease she slid down against him. Her intentions all too real. She moved onto him; fully feeling him just tipping into her. As she lifted herself a second time Barakan was frozen in time. He dare not move; could not, his hands flayed. But his body had other plans his erection had a whole need of its own. As Kalista moved her hips; she was so very wet and easily slid onto him, further and in a swift motion which took both their breaths he entered her. Kalista caught her breath and held it. Nothing could prepare her for what was to happen next. Kalista was lost to the pleasure she knew could be hers; he felt good, so different. Nothing was as she had thought, she could feel his heat even within herself. Her past no longer marred what she was expecting this was life pulsating flesh and blood filling her and it was tremendous. It only took seconds for her to lean into and onto him harder. She nipped at his face. Her feeling of so much fullness only lasted seconds before her body adjusted to him.

"Rak. You will not hurt me. You love me." He knew he did both the man and the beast loved her and wanted all of her for always… but. *But! Aaaaa.* She moved on him and he seemed to expand further in her. He growled loudly and it's vibration easily filled them both as Kalista pulled herself upwards then dropped back down on him. Picking her own rhythm. Both burning with passion. Barakan found his hips and thighs began to move with her; no matter what his sense told him. He was lost to her. But there was something more about this that neither of them realised. Neither had figured on.

"Kalista." All Barakan could squeeze from his lips was her name. She had him dumbstruck. He felt her fire; she felt so very good and she was moving on him making love to him. Only him; and enjoying it. He couldn't help but watch as she moved on him her soft flesh engulfing him; so erotic. *Gods woman. You are making love to me.* His whole being just exploded and there was nothing bar her. How he managed it will never make sense but his whole being just wanted this and her. Love filled all he was and like lightning he had her flipped and spreadeagled beneath him. His hips not, moving away from her one bit. He nuzzled her neck. As his hands slid either side of her head. Resting on the ground taking his weight.

"You could regret this."

“Never.” Becoming the controller Barakan finally gave into her. His hips began to move. As he too no longer fighting the pleasure gave into it. “Rak!” Kalista yelled . As he controlled all she was and his movements became more. His hands clenching hard needing taming. Barakan deliberately dug them into the ground his nails sinking into the grass and soil as he felt her tightening against him, he was so much bigger than her. But she moved and mewed at him finding more pleasure than he expected. There was no pain for her. It was sensual and good.

“Kalista.” Barakan thrust grinding himself into her. “You.” Kalista threw her head back baring her neck to him riding the pleasure building. Barakan lowered his head and licked her neck. She groaned and grabbing at his face with her hands managed a word.

“Yes.” Allowing his tongue to trace her lips. He thrust again harder. “Yes.” He snarled into her neck.

“You are mine.”

“Always.” Came back his reply and that was it he was lost and he thrust again the pleasure raging through him now as he knew so would his orgasm and it would not be like anything either had experienced before now. His hips began to move faster and faster as Kalista rode all he offered. Kalista’s face began to shine in the light as a sheen of sweat began to rise through her very flesh. A single bead of sweat travelling between her breasts. Barakan felt his own flesh burning with sweat. As his thrusts became even too much for him he pounded into her as if… their very lives depended on it. *But they do…*

Barakan forced his claws deeper. And felt the tension building his guts beginning to tie themselves up in knots. Man and beast both needed this. He snarled as watching Kalista beneath him she stopped breathing and held her breath. He growled at her. It was hurried but fulfilling; he had never expected to do this. Not in any lifetime. He snarled.

"Come for me." It was for him and only him. Kalista could hear but not see him her eyesight was no longer hers. Breathing in she held it as, she ran headlong into her orgasm; and something in her Just imploded. Her whole body stiffened then started to shake violently. As Barakan didn't stop he was watching her come undone beneath him and his love for her just exploded as did his own orgasm; he could not stop it she consumed him. Again and again he didn't think it would end. His chest heaved and breath was hard to catch; he tried desperately to get control but there was none to be had. And as he watched her through his own eyes loving her; the beast raised it head too and he let out an almighty howl hurting Kalista's ears and too fast everything shifted and changed and something in Barakan swore and it wasn't the Rak that Kalista knew. Something other than her consumed him. What had been good turned soar. There was to be no basking in her love this time. He whispered to her both man and beast wanting her to know they both fought; fighting for her. For her life and love. And the pleasure turned into something dark.

"I love you Kalista." He tried to pull away from her but couldn't he had no control; she was pinned beneath him by him. He couldn't move the struggle had begun. His eyes flamed red and his growled voice was one she didn't know. Her excitement and passion soon turned to something else something she'd never wanted to feel with him. Fear.

"Rak." Her voice trembled she didn't understand. "W what is." She stuttered. "Happening?" *My God my darling!* Her heart jumped into her mouth and she suddenly felt very sick. Barakan fought hard for control harder than he had ever fought in his whole life not then and definitely not now.

"I will not give in." He spoke aloud his face contorting in pain and the sweat just pouring from him. His lips raised over his teeth and his hands kneaded at the soil trying to get to her adorable flesh but it wasn't them. It wasn't him. A realisation of it all; of everything hit Barakan. Knowledge he'd been lacking all along and it was her Kalista his sweet love who had opened his eyes.

His erection did not dissipate but raged for more. Yet it didn't; nothing in him wanted this not the man he had been or the beast he was. He; they were not the killer. They loved her alike. Love. The beast Within him raged to let her go. It howled ear piercingly.

"I love you..." Barakan could hardly speak but his persistence paid of he forced the words between his teeth. This was her the sadistic witch she was controlling him as she must have before; he never understood just being beast. He could feel her so could the beast. She was getting off on this and wanted to join them in impaling Kalista till her little body gave in and he ripped her apart. It was never him. She had always been driving him he was just the vessel who she needed. He'd always been consumed by his own pain he had never took the time; between Victoor's and her they had taken everything he ever was and the beast too. Barakan as a whole; hated them. They would not do it anymore Victoor's was stopped now for her. Barakan could not just walk away this time leaving Kalista nothing more than a pile of bones. *Never. Kalista you have to run. I* . Barakan knew he needed to get off her and make her run. As very fast as she could. His lips curled high his so sharp teeth which had held on and given pleasure to her most intimate parts were just weapons. He drooled badly. Kalista was stuck; she was watching him change before her very eyes this was not her Rak. She froze. Anticipation of her own death. Tears steamed down her face now she was more than broken; a massive wave of sadness and confusion mixed in with the fear filling her.

"Rak?" She tried to reach him.

"Kalista." He tried to move finally managing a little movement and pulled away. "The bitch; the witch. The curse!" *What?* Understanding hit her. "Please…" He threw his body from her. Landing with a thud besides her… But it enabled Kalista to scramble away. "Go! Leave run. Now!" He seemed to gag he was in so much pain. He rolled on the floor. "Kalista go!" He began to rise to all fours. The witch less than pleased; they were fighting her. *What was the use if he doesn't do as I say!* Looking as if he was about to pounce; Barakan was a terrifying sight. Kalista managed to get to her feet but panicked she stepped towards him not away, now Barakan begged. "Kalista go now before she makes me kill you. It is all her. Go now run please. Please…" His head dropped to glare at the floor as his whole body strained; seeming to go into spasm. **"Go."** His bristles didn't just rustle but seemed to bang against one another as they moved and he filled with anger. He moved a single pace doubling in size. The smell he was emitting rotten. Kalista knew he wasn't her Rak. It dawned on her he was right she needed to move. Forcing herself to turn away from him Kalista shaking and sobbing took to her heels. Naked she began to move quickly away from him. Between sobs she just gaged.

"Rak… Rak I love please come back to me." But knew now even if he did it would be different. This was the curse and they hadn't beaten it. Moving through the forest the same way she had come. There was only one place Kalista could go; home, his cavern to hope and pray he didn't just hunt her there. But she also knew if he wanted to she would already be dead.

"Ouch." A branch whipped across her face slicing into her cheek. Her feet slipping on the damp morning ground. She struggled to stay upright and keep going. Then her bottom took the same treatment. She ran through brambles.

"Oh my God Barakan." She screamed and sobbed.

Barakan knew where she was headed the witch whispering… *Go get her. RIP the bitch to pieces. She is a whore.* But Barakan resisted. *You cannot resist me for long. I will have her. The beast will have her... She is mine.* He howled again the strain resonating through him. But the beast would not he fought alongside the man he had been. He smelt Kalista's blood knowing she was hurt and that only made things worse but he still heard her gambolling noisily through the forest. He could see her naked body as it ran away from him. Her discarded dress still laying where she had dropped it. He lunged at it; laying his muzzle against it breathing her in. *Is this me or the witch?* He found out as he couldn't stop his claws from shredding it in one move. But he didn't go after her he would not. "No. I will not." He snarled loudly. And finally turning he ran in the opposite direction.

"I will not. We will not kill her." But the witch demanded more. There was nothing Barakan could do he knew he was lost. He bounded through the forest there was only one course of action left open to him. Unless he was to kill her. And that he just wouldn't do; he as a whole both the man and the beast in him would rather die than do that. She was his heart. *I have a heart and I will not lose it.*

# Chapter fourteen

Kalista exhausted and hurt scrambled her way backup the path to the cavern; almost on all fours herself Everything hurt again including her soul. Tears just kept coming there would be no stopping them. She prayed and prayed hard. But would God listen? Barakan was one of the damned. On reaching the cave entrance she collapsed and everything was spinning; the bile in her throat burning as she threw up; violently...

"Rak…Rak." She just kept sobbing. Kalista had no idea how long she laid there. But eventually too exhausted to keep crying she tried to move her whole body just shaking. She was cold; tired and extremely sore. Pushing herself up from the floor on very wobbly legs. Her chest still shaking as Kalista tried to get a grip of herself. Her feet the most bloodied. They would swell and walking would be hard. But Kalista knew she had to get sorted. Practicality and instinct taking over. She managed to get herself inside and grabbing some soothing cream from her quarters; alongside a dry piece of bread it may help settle her stomach; made her way to the hot springs. Her own voice echoing through the empty cave as she walked it didn't feel so homely now. It was too silent. She hated it but this was where she needed to be; to wait for his return then between them they could see what was to be done. *Come back to me Rak.* But then what would they do? It; what they had; had turned yet another corner into the unknown, again. Life could be a bitch. *Damn that witch.* But Kalista knew she was already damned and had took Barakan with her. It took some time for Kalista to bathe and soothe her own wounds some weren't much more than scratches but others they were deeper; the forest could be a most inhospitable place. On her sore feet she made her way back to her. *No ours.* Quarters. And picked up her other dress but didn't put it on she just laid it ready, and sat on the bed waiting; thinking. *What now? Rak?* Tears once again threatening to stream. "No I won't give in no." Pulling the split blanket from the bed she wrapped herself up in it then climbing onto the top of the mattress and huddled up. Thinking; she had done it, had made love to him her good hearted Rak, and he had actually found release within her. She should have been less blatantly reckless. Kalista chastised herself. *But it's not your fault. He restrained and hasn't hurt me.* So in that she was right but the witch obviously still had him. "Barakan!" She wept. Not as violently as before but she just couldn't stop the tears. Until tiredness and strain took her into sleep. Fitful uncomfortable sleep where things were never as they should be.

Barakan went as far and as fast as he could. Fighting hard against the blood lust the Witch was trying to enforce in him. But she didn't win he did; once he was further away from Kalista it changed and quietened just a little her anger turned inwards on him because he didn't do what she'd expected. There was no way on this earth that he would kill her. *God she'd made love to me. Full on proper love.* It had been astounding and he'd loved it as much as he knew he loved her. But that was what had done it triggered the witches curse. He knew now."Bitch." There were things he needed to consider; knowing she would soon get bored and tire then that was the time for him. But there was no way he go anywhere near Kalista not even to explain and that hurt. His heart started to fracture; thinking that could be the very last time he ever set eyes on her, but what a time. She had made love to him. If he was to die finally what could be a better time than knowing he was loved. But …

"Kalista." Barakan put a little thought into it and there were things he could do for her. Giving her the flower for a start. That was how this day had started and that was how it was going to end. Turning around and forcing himself to combat all that the witch had tried to in-still in him; he quickly made his way back. But not to her. Roberts first if this wasn't to end then she would need him and Barakan knew exactly what he wanted her to have. She needed to be kept safe; always.

Kalista rolled and moved about the bed dreaming but different nightmares to before. It had all changed so much. She loved and was loved which right now meant so much to her. It didn't matter he had been forced to become. Barakan was no more beast than Victoor's… Her eyes opened and she listened silence. She knew he wasn't there. Crawling from the bed she pulled the dress to her and put it on.

"Barakan if you can hear me I love you." It was then that she noticed the flower sat atop her desk just plonked there. "Rak." She shouted but got nothing back. Standing she quickly stepped to the desk; staring down at her flower. He must have come back whilst she slept. A single sob escaped her it was then that she noticed the note. Neatly folded cream paper. Clenching and unclenching her fingers she just stared at it for several minutes. Not daring to open it. But the she knew she had to he had left it for a reason for her.

"Come on Kalista you should read it. Off course you should! It may not all be bad." But swallowing something told her it was; or he would have stayed to talk to her. "Rak." With shaky fingers she reached out for it but didn't open it straight away she returns first to sit in their bed. His strong male smell still lingering there it enveloped her. Breathing heavily trying not to be afraid Kalista fingered the letter nervously before opening it. She saw his writing he had tried so hard to make it neat. A single tear ran down her face as she read the first words.

My love; my life. I have had enough of being just this I want so much more. I want you always. But today ; she took a hold of me, although what we did was so real for me and delectable. You are the sexiest beautiful little female. And all mine. Never forget that. But for now till this is sorted I cannot be around you. She nearly took us both and I will not let that happen again. I will give you all my heart for all time know that but now; there is something I have to do first. I'm saying first because I do not intend to give you or what we could have wether I be man or beast up easily. I will fight to my very last breath. She needs to die.

Kalista held her breath as she read those words… *She needs to die!* "Barakan. No I will take whatever of you I can have. Please don't. **No."** Struggling she carried on reading; her eyes hazy from tears. Again.

Roberts will be waiting for you in the small clearing at the bottom of the cavern path. He will help you. Be safe always my darling and know above all else that you are loved. I love you with all I am man and beast alike we as one will die to keep you safe.

That was it Kalista gave in to the grief now; and sobbed again. *How dare!* How dare he do this without consulting her. She didn't have to go as far as she had earlier. Just holding him would have been enough he didn't have to go to his death just because of her. "My God Barakan I love you so much don't do this not for me . We can go back to how it was before. I'm sorry so sorry please." She begged him but it was to no avail. He heard and it broke his heart to know she was hurting but the pride which filled him to know that she loved him too gave him even more reason to keep going.

"The Witch has to die." And she had created him cursed him to be this. He was no longer just man with no ability to kill her. Now he was different and he'd managed as man to kill the brother. "I will kill her." He was more than adamant; the thought of his own demise was only plagued because of the thoughts of leaving her. Nothing to do with his own mortality. He'd lived too long as it was.

He charged forward only one single thing now in his mind. Killing the Witch.

Kalista must have sat there maybe another hour or two before this wave of sobbing and bewildered thoughts slowed. “Come on girl; this is no good.” She had to do something. Out the corner of her eye she saw the flower. “And you should be planted of your not to die.” It was beginning to wilt a little it had been put the ground for so long. Placing the letter carefully on the desk Kalista picked up the flower and went to the caverns entrance.

Poking to see where she could put it. At the left hand side there was more ground and soil than rocks. *There.*

“Ok; blue. Let’s get you back where you belong.” Putting carefully down Kalista knelt to the ground and started to scrabble about with her bare hands to dig a hole. It wasn’t an entirely easy job but she did it. The once she had thoroughly drenched the hole she tenderly put the roots down and covered them with the fresh dark soil she had managed to dig up. It was precious to her and needed proper care. It seemed to immediately to look better. Pleased with her present and with the fact that she had replanted it. Kalista wondered what should be her next move? Just to sit and wait. How many hours had gone by? When would it be night? She looked at the sky. Should she go down to the clearing now?

“No.” She knew that whatever time it was she didn’t have time to get there and back if Roberts wasn’t there; soon night would draw in on her and she wouldn’t be safe alone, not without him. Going back into the cavern she set about lighting all the torches and candles she had it would be a dark and lonely night alone. Then a little food. She needed to eat. Her stomach was growling like he did.

“Rak”

There was nothing else for her to do today.

Barakan was glad she’d stayed put Roberts would wait for her all night if necessary; he had the where with-all to keep himself safe all night. Barakan did feel okay about that; he had made sure they were paid well for this and to add to it the young Roberts actually liked her. Wife or not. Which would mean she would be safe wether he, Barakan was jealous or not it was her safety which was upper most.

He continued on. The stench of the witch getting stronger and stronger. She was exactly where he had expected. Still hanging round his lands. She knew this was going to happen he was sure about that too. So would be waiting for him. Which way it was going to end was anybodies guess.

Barakan followed his nose till he came to a sliding halt… knowing this was the first time he’d seen her since.. Barakan stopped the thoughts it was not time for his own fears. *I will do this.* No doubt about wether he could. Just a knowledge that he needed to; to save Kalista he had to.

“So there you are my mighty beast! What’s with the scruples?” She sneered showing none to good teeth even his were better. “You should be killing that pretty little pet of yours.” *God almighty she’s like death on legs.* His thoughts were plagued by her wishes but he didn’t care he was listening less and less and he could see that pissed her off. He didn’t want a half-life with Kalista. It was an all or nothing sort of thing for him now; even if this was who he was now man and beast combined he wanted all of her not just part. He was sick of leading a half-life. She was his everything.

“She is not my pet.”

“Oh look he has found his voice I would have imagined you to only growl by now.” Barakan did growl letting her know he was still beast too. He wasn’t total tame and that part of him; the tame gentle giant had no part in what was happening now. He needed the beast. She seemed to almost glide towards him. And he could see why.

She was a mess; age seemed to be showing in one which was supposed to be ageless, and too much time spent in bad magic was taking its toll. It was eating at her; adding to the rottenness which was already her. *Do you know?* Barakan couldn’t help but wonder if she knew how bad she looked and how weak. *Is is this all fake?* He did know he shouldn’t be fooled a second time; the cost of the first time had been so very high. Too high he wouldn't lose this time and risk Kalista too. *No.* Her long hair was thin and wispy nothing like Kalista's beautiful thick healthy dark hair. But she wasn't rotten to the core. The witch was; there would be no redemption for her. Her eyes sunken into her face which looked almost clear. Skinny to the point of being only flesh and bone and everything about her rotten stinking and yellow. She could be a corpse walking.

"I can do more than growl."

"Ooo I do hope so. Or all, this would be pointless." The witch tried to use magic but somehow Barakan still resisted. *Hmm* She was less than pleased. "You still think you can ignore me and what I want. No you will not be doing that." The witch drew a little spell through her fingers and attempted to force Batakan to kneel before her. Barakan felt his knees buckling and shaking beneath him. No matter what he did he couldn't stop them bending. The witch laughed. Raucous awful sound like a creature in death.

"I will be your puppet no longer." He forced them to take his weight. The air around them altered and became silent darkness.

"That's what you think." Having shown him what power she still held especially over him; she waved her hands about in front of her and changed her appearance. Kalista stood before him. Yet not

Barakan he could tell; the stink belayed who she was. It was of death; not his sweet sensual flower. *How do you know what she looks like?* "See I know what you want… it is this. I can be this for you. Then you can come to me." Suddenly she changed again and was naked but still it did not fool him she was not Kalista!

"I think before we go any further I will take a little of what you offered her. Good and hard should do." Urgh he recoiled.

"I don't think so."

"You telling me **no!"**

"I'm going to do more than tell you no." His whole body vibrated with building anger; he had managed to quell but now he allowed it to take over. *She thinks to use and abuse me again. I don't think so.* He dropping to all fours began to circle her. She spun watching where he was going.

"You cannot deny me. You are **mine.** From the moment you stuck that adorable cock in me." Barakan seethed at her words. He remembered but didn't want to. *This is going to end. No more.* Even the beast she'd created recoiled at her words. Sickening beast as much as man.

"Not any more." The saliva dropped from his teeth as he barred them at her.

"See I'm turning you on; you are like me you enjoy the pain and blood. I will have some more of yours." She again twisted her awfully looking bony fingers; where they still just that; fingers? Creating lust… Or so she thought. Barakan felt it. She was trying to stir him into needing. This was the curse. He tossed decisions around in his mind; wondering if he should allow it take him and in the process do to her what she had made him inflict in others; but **no.** She would enjoy that too much.

"Come to me I will fuck you senseless…" *Oh my God disgusting.* He knew what he wanted; to rip her voice from her throat and stop her disgust words. She aimed the spell again at him and momentarily it affected him. He felt his blood surging to where it was supposed to be. But this was more than unnatural. Again he fought against it. *My body is mine own not yours.* She hissed at him as he completed the circle around her. He did not care about the darkness and the air he did not need them; he needed all his focus now to be on her. He stepped a foot nearer. Knowing he could just leap at her but the idea was for him to at least try and get out of this alive. She still had magic but the more she was using on him and the more he fought it; she would eventually tire; that would be so much better for him. He just needed to keep her engaged a little longer. She spat at him.

"You cannot fight me you are my creation. Do not forget that. If I want to watch you rutting like an animal. I will." Barakan let out a terrifying howl. One she hadn't been expecting; he knew it was hurting her ears. The Witch pushed her hands against her ears. Cursing loudly. "Bastard." Barakan saw. But she too was angry now. Her hair flaying about like snakes around her head she created more magic and tried whipped at him. With them. "Bastard." She caught him; Barakan flinched; it had drawn down across his chest. Then again down his face.

"Argh. Bitch." He should have known better. He was angry at himself now. But then everything round him changed again and the air was like hell full of red hot smoke. And without warning she leapt at him. Pulling at him with her nailed hands; they felt like tiny knifes piercing his flesh. Full of her very life's venom. He snarled and snapped at her. But she seemed to be just that bit too quick.

Kalista awoke with the sun rising. Immediately knowing she was still alone. Was quickly dressed and ready to go Roberts had to know something; or why would Barakan tell her to go down to him? Curiosity raging now alongside a determination to find him. The fears she'd felt changing to something else. He was out there somewhere and she would find him! Kalista quickly ate; knowing she needed to. There was no point making herself ill. Then checking her flower it was important to her that it survived. *And you too Rak...* Her fear was still there just being pushed down where it belonged. Kalista tried to fill herself with hope. *He is out there and alive.*

"You are good my sweet little gift. Stay that way. Live. Ooo Kalista it is a plant." But having being alone all night even talking to the flower felt good. He Barakan beast or not had changed her life for the better; she wasn't going to give up on him easily. Setting of down the path at a fast pace; Kalista ran over and over what she was going to say to Roberts.

Kalista found her way to the clearing fairly easily. It wasn't hard though just straight down. And there he was. Charles she remembered his name immediately. Before he had even stood from his seated position. She rattled off questions.

"Charles where has he gone? You do know don't you? Please I have to know! What has he told you? What is he intending?"

"Wow. Stop." Charles put his hand up. "Slow down."

Then another movement; Charles wasn't alone. Kalista's head snapped over to see who else was there. An older man was trying to get up for the floor where he had been sat; on a blanket. He looked weary but something in his eyes as she stared at him saw something else too an excitement which was infectious.

"Who?"

"This Kalista is my father." Kalista just stared. *Why the both of them? What have they to say?* Here legs wobbled. She felt a little sickened but fought it. *No. It can't be bad news I'm not going anywhere I will not leave.* So many doubts and thoughts charged through her. She felt so alone; standing there with the others. Even more so than the night she had just spent alone.

"Why are you both here?" Charles rolled his eyes.

"Because we have differing views on what is to happen.." Kalista moved a step closer listening intently.

"What is to happen! Why?" Now the older man moved forward.

"My lady I am Andrew Roberts. My Great Grandfather was the original man belonging to the hall." Her eyes widened as she looked at the rough ungainly hand being held out to her. Gingerly she took it.

"Hello."

"And you are Kalista."

"Yes."

"Barakan's friend." But the way he said it implied so much more. Kalista tilted her head her eyebrows furrowing. *What do you know?*

"Yes." *What to say?* Kalista decided only the truth would do. "His sacrifice that he saved. Is that what you wanted to hear?"

"My lady I am not here to hear anything but." He pulled a face. "That will do." Kalista looked wide eyes. *What are you two up too?*

"What do you know?" Andrew shrugged his shoulders. "Nothing much I hope for more."

"Hmm." Kalista was undecided about those words. "Have you been told that the women taken from my village to be sacrificed…. Mostly… were not killed by him." Charles looked astounded at her words but not so much Andrew.

"Who then?"

"Victoor's my guardian." Now both seemed to stare open mouthed. Andrews mind racing. He was joining so many dots.

"And he sacrificed you?" Charles voice oozed disgust yet he didn't doubt her words not one bit. "Yes. If I had been killed it would have meant his problem; me would be dead… and his secret with me so he could carry on."

"You knew?"

"No."

"So what?"

"Because he did it to me too but I managed to keep going and survived it all. He needed me gone as I had begun to tell."

"Okay." It made more sense. "But he still lives… surely."

"Not for long. And Rak persuaded them. No more Sacrifice's." *Does it make sense to you?* She couldn't tell from either faces. After some minutes Andrew was the first to speak again.

"He persuaded or told?"

"Told them. No more."

"But what about the curse?"

"I was hoping you had the answers to that. It was all good until yesterday; then…" Kalista looked into the bright sky. Her eyes tearing. "It changed. I don't understand but the Witch; the curse he was possessed." It was the only way she could describe it but the thought of him being tortured like that hurt so much.

"But he still didn't hurt you Kalista?"

"No. he wouldn't **never.** He made me leave."

“Are you sure about that?” Charles butt in. He wasn’t as confident around Barakan as his father.

“Charles!” It didn’t matter that they were both grown men Andrew still chastised his son. “Get rid of the attitude. Kalista cares about him can’t you see it God man sometimes you can be so dense.” Andrews having grumbled at Charles turned back to her. “Kalista. My grandfather never thought he was a killer; my father was let’s say dubious; we can become what we are given.” Kalista nodded wanting to finish telling them about Victoor’s.

“Victoor’s he has been doing this all his life. He didn’t think Barakan.” She gave him his full name now he deserved it. “Existed; he used it as a way of killing the women.”

“All of them?” Kalista just nodded. “Terrible.”

“He is, even the ones when Barakan came down from the mountain would have died anyway. Victoor’s drugged them deliberately to keep them from saying what had already been done to them, he just left them to die. He would torture.” Both men saw so much welling in her eyes. *He tortured you! Yet Barakan did not.* “Barakan knew nothing. The curse took his sense, then. But Victoor’s will be dead soon; I’m not here to talk about him I just wanted you to know. Rak is not all he is said to be.”

“I never thought he was.” Andrew’s words were

honest. Kalista smiled at him pleased. "And you care about him?"

"Yes." Simple plain and more than clear.

"Father that doesn't mean anything can come of it." Kalista raised her eyebrows at him; and couldn't stop her none too tactful words.

"You sure about that?" Andrew couldn't help but smirk at his son.

"You deserved that." Charles just shook his head. "Father if she sells everything; she can start afresh it will bring her nothing but misery."

"Sell? What are you saying?" Charles carried on. "He has left us to execute his wishes."

"**What?** On what? What are you talking about?" Her voice pitched at them both.

"Charles you are about as subtle as a brick." Andrew shook his head. "Kalista my lady; Barakan has left us with instructions to execute his lands and the house everything is for you. We are able to execute his wishes if you want us to. But." She grabbed onto the word but almost as if it were a thing.

"But? What Andrew please tell me."

"This is where Charles and I differ he thinks you should come down the mountain with us now and begin again. Leaving him and everything that comes with him to be forgotten and wither to die. I saw him Kalista I saw what was in his heart because of you; no matter how the next 24 hours turns out he will die without you."

"Turns out? **Andrew** what? Do you know Rak's intentions."

"No but there can only be one solution. I have always thought it."

"What?" The lack of immediate information was annoying her. "Get on with it."

"He's gone after the Witch. It can be the only answer."

"He's what? Oh my God…She could kill him!"

"Or he could kill her."

"Ye but even that could end up in his demise none of us know what will happen this is all about her and the curse. Why did he have to do this?"

"because he loves you." Kalista shook she felt so angry at them at him.

"That's no good to me. He should be here with me not going after her."

"But he could have hurt you."

"He didn't."

"But he could have that is all he is considering. He would give his life for you that we both can see."

Andrew gestured towards Charles.

"But I don't want him to." Andrew moved a step closer to Kalista.

"There may be another way. But you are right we do not know what will happen but either way I think he would be better if you were with him."

"Dad I told you about this; what is she going to do? Nothing! She cannot fight a witch."

"No but her presence may help him. And we all win if he kills the Witch; she has hurt too many people already."

"I can't see it."

"No Kalista can hear that. But I still say this was meant to be."

"What?" Now Kalista listened harder. "What is meant? Why?"

"According to my grandfather who only heard what his grandfather said none of this is gospel Kalista; but they believed that Barakan was never a killer a lover maybe but not a killer, and that sooner or later he would get a different type of punishment. He would fall for someone and everything would change for him. He would love and when he did he would finally see the light making him see what he had done but also what he should do. Destroy the Witch he cannot nor should go through eternity like this. I have always believed it. Charles not so much."

"Where has he gone?"

"After the Witch!"

"Ye but where?"

"I was hoping you would know that" She thought.

"I do." Now Charles mumbled on.

"You are dreaming both of you."

"He's gone home."

"The manor?"

"Yes. He took me to show me and then something changed and he just grabbed me and brought me back here. Fast. It was only the other day."

"Then the witch attacked you through him."

"She tried."

"But didn't succeed Kalista that should tell us all three of us what we need to know." Kalista looked a little puzzled. But Andrew knew now exactly what he was saying. It pleased him. "Her hold on him is not that strong anymore Kalista. Yours is stronger…"

"Mine!"

"Yes yours. He needs you Kalista. You are his

life; he fights her because of you." That was it he had done enough to convince Kalista what Rak needed from her.

"Take me there."Charles looked on aghast.

"You can't…"

"I can and I will Charles you just shut up and go home. Go see to the family. We got this." Andrew looked at Kalista who had to admit she wasn't so sure he didn't look like he could make it that far never mind fast. But he knew.

"Don't be concerned about me Kalista. We didn't walk up here this time." Kalista realised there's was a rustling noise behind him in the trees she hadn't noticed before her concentration being only on the two men. "You do ride don't you?"

"Yes."

"Well that's good. Charles you can walk home and Kalista and I will take the horses." There was no room for argument in his tone, Charles nodded.

"But if you are not back by tomorrow I will come and find you both. And hope to find you still breathing not dead." Andrews shook his head at him.

"I apologise for him Kalista he has never been what you would call an optimist more of a pessimist."

# Chapter fifteen

"I don't care what he is nor you for that matter as long as one of you takes me to Rak; I cannot get there alone I do not know the way or I would already be on my way."

Andrew nodded. *That is how it should be... plenty of fight.*

Mounting the horses; they set of Andrew leading the way. Kalista urging her pony to keep up with him he obviously knew the way well. *But of course he had tended the property.*

Barakan felt the shit she was pumping into his body and it burnt; but he did not give into it. She would not do the same to him as before he would not give into her drugs,spells or her. She was a filthy Witch and this time he had the knowledge to back it up. He grabbed at her with his claws hanging on doing the same as her and pierced her skin easily with his. But something in the look on her face frightened him more than anything else. *You're enjoying that!* He retracted them as best he could hating the thought that he would bring her any kind of pleasure.

"Bitch..." He snarled heavily at her. Her snakes whipped at his face, and she laughed. He growled pushing her away from him. “Get of me you hag.”

“Never. You are my dog. I will have a lead on you before the end of the day. And then that…”

“Never.” Barakan yelled as he tried to fling her from him. His legs flaying managed to kick her in the back as she hung on. She didn’t like that and screamed. She pulled more power to her. Although Barakan was taking a pasting; he was allowing it. He wanted her to use all her power but the God damned snakes did keep tearing at his flesh as did her nails and the rotten venom was also taking its toll on him. He knew he had to begin to fight back better and not just wait for her to tire or he would be the one expiring. He threw her from him in one violent movement but she sprang straight back at him her chest in his face as if to suffocate him, with what once were breasts, he pierced her chest with his teeth but she liked it. Laughing at him she yelled.

“More more. Rip the flesh from my bones I will heal myself I love it more more more.”

“Urgh.” Barakan tried to spit the rotten filth from his mouth. *No, no, no.*

“You’re sick.”

“And you are not.” That hurt her words caused cut deep into his soul. In that single moment of doubt; the Witch took her chance and with all she was rolled him over and pinned him to the ground.

“I will have what belongs to me.” Her snakes wound round him as did the venom she had infused in him it sang to her own body from within his and the strength in her arms and legs was not comparable to before; if anything she hadn’t got weaker but stronger. He was pinned solidly.

“I will not!”

“What… Fuck me.” Her magic wound around her like smoke and into him. More than powerful and the venom in him wound its way back to her and he couldn’t help it but feel himself reacting to it. A sickness grew in his guts. She was holding him as steady as she could but he did fight he would not stay under her like this, he fought. But began to heave as naked she ground herself against him making the reaction even stronger. It wasn’t him but magic.

It was then in that second that it all changed and something in his soul screamed at him. He could sense her his heart chewed at him. *Kalista. No, n,o no. You can’t be.* But then he could smell her too; her subtle scent. The only thing he wanted to touch and be touched by not this terrible creature attempting to get her rocks off right now. He snarled so loud.

Kalista followed close behind Andrew but the house itself was empty the surrounding grounds too. Both had been at a loss as to where to try next when something had hit Kalista as if she’d been slapped in the face and immediately known what direction to go in. Or what her gut was telling her anyway. Without thinking she'd set of alone leaving Andrews standing dismounted he'd not been able to move quite fast enough to keep up with her. Something told her Barakan was being hurt.

"No, no, no." Kalista shouted into the air she would not hurt him again; the witch would not make him less than she already had. *Not again.* Urging her horse to move faster even though it seemed to shy away and want to turn and go back the other way; it was hard to control but Kalista kept a tight hold and made it keep going. Then she heard him her lover howling and snarling like never before. She wasn't sure if he was in pain or angry the noise was hard to decipher. But either way he needed her that was a certainty.

Barakan snarled and spat attempting to free himself from her grip but the more he fought the Witch the harder it became to get away; her grip just tightening. The hold around his chest compacting that tight breath was hard to control. But Kalista was here somewhere he had to move. He felt his ribs being crushed.

Kalista jumped from her horse it just wouldn't go the last few feet… Refusing to move; it stood snorting. She quickly rubbed its head as she started to run. The stench was dreadful she couldn't understand why. *My God.* She wasn't sure if some of that stink was him; Barakan, he did have a heady smell at the best of times; when happy; when angry. And right now he was more than angry. But at least she knew she'd found him without a second thought as to what she was going to do or find Kalista kept going… Reaching a large heavy bush full of thorns; Kalista knew if she went round it seemed to stretch out of sight she would lose precious time. Wrapping her hands on the skirts of her dress she pulled and pushed and made her way through. With absolutely no idea of what she was going to find on the other side.

What did shock her to the very core of her soul; freezing her in her own skin. She stood as still as death. *My God.* Her eyes still red and sore from the amount of crying she'd done in the last 24 hours just widened bulging. *What?*

She'd found him; Barakan and what? *What the?* Sense told Kalista it had to be the Witch but and the but was a massive one for her what she was looking at was herself. Straddling Barakan naked but that wasn't her figure that was nothing like her figure that was old stinking and twisted, the Witch. She felt sick to her stomach yet again. What was happening? Which one of them had instigated this? It could be anything… either of them. *No, no, no. Stop being an idiot Kalista. You know better.* She watched as the thing moved her hips trying to make Barakan enter her. She thrust moving her bum up and down. A horrible sight; Kalista saw Barakan groan at it and try to move away from her but she had him pinned that tight he couldn't move and looking at him now Kalista could see he was hurt; slices cut into his flesh everywhere. And he didn't look right at all his eyes glazed and running. He was in pain and this thing was taking him again. Against his will. Then with all her might not knowing what else to do Kalista just screamed.

Barakan heard her. *My God she has seen me! What does she think is happening?* He snarled… *NO.*

But that had done it Kalista had made her presence known. The Witch turned her empty black eyes on her. Droning at them both.

"Oo… So the pet has come. Hmmm." Barakan knew Kalista was in so much trouble now it physically hurt. He shouted and yelled; but it was getting him no where. Kalista heard the Witches words, but it didn't matter. She was hurting Barakan anything Kalista could do she knew she would.

"I am no ones pet." What else could she say?

"Hmm maybe you weren't but now… You look like you could be fun. I think you may become mine." Kalista began to heave at the words. *But what could she do that hasn't already been done?* Listening to her words watching the scene evolving before her, Kalista took a step towards them. The Witch allowed her true self to show she no longer needed the pet. Kalista gaged and lowered her eyes at the sight which was hanging before her. *Oh my God no.* And that thing was on her beloved Rak. Who at this present time was straining and desperately trying to move. His noises getting louder by the second. The witch altered her spells and twisting her fingers laid Barakan out where he was with nothing but spell she lifted her naked body from him: one lot of fingers twisting keeping him down like the dog he was and the other ones turned to her. Kalista but was surprised when she saw the foolish woman did not run.

"You should run."

"Why?" The Witch didn't know wether to laugh or curse. "Oh my… No wonder he wants you." The way she slurred her words made it sound sleazy and dirty but it wasn't. It was good and genuine. What he been born out of necessity had grown into so much more. Different but Kalista loved him. She didn't want to listen to the Witches baiting them but knew she had to. "Got some guts in there haven't you. But they won't do you much good now." She shot Barakan a sneering wink. "I think she could be **fun**… How's about if I take her first and grease her up ready for you. Dog." Barakan hated so much in that second but her words told him something she hadn't. *You don't know!* So for as much as she'd controlled him she didn't actually know what he had achieved with Kalista. *You don't know.* Which meant she hadn't seen through him; he'd controlled it and stopped her. *I stopped you.* He had to do it now. For himself for Kalista he would not stand by and watch her defiled and very possibly slaughtered. ***No.*** He had everything to give for her; his life for one. But he had no idea Kalista was thinking the very same things.

The Witch looked from one to another her energies building and showing in excitement; her eyes flashed and her body twitched, wanting. She was going to enjoy this day. Watching them both writhe with exquisite agony. Just her cup of tea.

Barakan needed to control his own furies. *You will not beat me this day! Control Barakan control...* Filling his chest as much as he could the hold she had on him still too tight to stretch his lungs to the fullest but it was enough. He managed to calm himself and think...

Kalista found her mind was going ten to the dozen. *Come on girl! Think? This is not the first time you have come face to face with evil.* And as far as she was concerned that was what she had faced sadistic evil that thrived on pain and this woman; Witch looked no different. *I survived once!* But Kalista did know that she, the Witch would be different she had no one to answer too for any death. Especially not hers or Barakans. *No that will not happen I won't allow it.*

"So." The Witch broke both's thoughts. She twisted her fingers quickly and Kalista found her body being pulled by invisible hands. There was no mercy in them, she was yanked and stretched. Her arms were being forced to widen; Kalista resisted at first but found the pull too strong. Barakan yelled…

"Kalista."

"Go on shout for her tell her what I will do to her then allow you to take the dregs I will watch you impale her and split her in two. Ride her like the dog you are." Bile rose into Barakan's throat. He hated all that he was all that she was the Witch. *Kalista my love.*

Kalista did not struggle she had learnt a long time ago compliance was the best form of survival. And right now although she would die for him she really really wanted to survive for him. *My love.* Her heart broke as he shouted her name so frenzied. She attempted to speak.

"Rak it is ok."

"Noooo!" It wasn't. Kalista's composure surprised the Witch her words even more so. Her eyes furrowed. *Was there something about this; these two that she wasn't aware off. Where were her screams?* She wanted screams, it was when they begged that she was at her best. The Witch still holding onto Barakan moved closer still to Kalista. Lifting her from the floor. Kalista found herself suspended in air. Barakans eyes bulging. His Kalista looked like she was being crucified. He knew she would not give in her strength would surpass even his. She would be killed. *Beg Kalista. Please live.* But he knew she wouldn't; he had to do something. His eyes watched them both intently; the ugliness of the Witch against his so beautifully pure Kalista.

"Well well you pretty. What makes you think it will be alright?" Kalista wasn't sure wether to answer her or not but. *Why not? What do I have to lose?*

"It won't I'm not daft… but what can you do that already hasn't been done?" The Witch frowned even more. And with a flick of her index finger. Split into Kalista's bodice.

"Plenty." Curiosity filling the Witch she wanted to know her story this little woman. Kalista's dress split by invisible knifes fell open and her breasts were displayed. Barakan began to move; again filling his lungs he was watching for his moment. He needed too move and soon. The Witch studied Kalista's flesh; as it came into view… *ah. So that is it.* She moved to stand below Kalista. Lifting her actual hand to Kalista's breast she ran a finger down from her throat following the scar she could see. Kalista's chest heaved as she couldn't manage to catch her breath as the sharpened nail ran along her. She swallowed back the bile rising. The Witch flicked at Kalista's nipple.

"That must have caused you some delicious pain. Did you scream?" Kalista was shocked by her question; and knew enough to understand.

"No."

"No." Kalista hadn't not that time. "Hmm not so sure I believe that."

"Believe what you like. It won't make a difference will it?"

"Suppose not." The Witch was more than interested in Kalista; Barakan could hear it in her voice. It encouraged him to be powerful. "These?" She poked at Kalista's scars. "Are they everywhere?"

"Yes." The witch licked her lips anticipating what she could do to Kalista. "And you felt every single delicious slice." She was almost ignoring Barakan.

"Yes."

"Well my little pet… Lets have a look at them." The Witch raised both her actual hands this time to Kalista's gaping bodice. Using them rather than magic. But first grabbed at both her breasts and squeezed hard; digging her venomous nails in, piercing Kalista's flesh. Kalista shut her eyes and winced but tried not to squeal. The Witch began to laugh.

"This could be so much fun breaking you." Her hands scrapped down Kalista's body grabbing at the rest her dress. "Let's see what is under here." Kalista's breasts began to bleed profusely the Witch had dug her nails in hard. Barakan smelt her blood. And watched as the Witch taking Kalista's dress in her hands stretched the material till it was that tight it would begin to split. Barakan knew that the Witch was engrossed with Kalista and he felt his own restraints lessening. He had to grab at the opportunity and stop her. *Now.* Before she did anymore damage to Kalista. His own injuries irrelevant. Breathing as much breath into his body as he could he silently filled every muscle he could and tried to expand and strain against her hold on him and as she tore at Kalista's skirt and it split. Barakan snarled the loudest howling one he had ever managed and tensing his whole body broke free of her magic. He bounded to his feet.

His own claws drawn.

The Witch tearing at Kalista's dress was intent on the view which was before her eyes and momentarily had loosened her grip on Barakan. She almost drooled her bad teeth and rottenness edging closer, Kalista; who could not watch any longer shut her eyes; grinding her own teeth to what she knew what was about to happen. But then suddenly it all changed and Barakan was on his feet, all fours and in one massive leap was on the witches back. Kalista found herself raised even further unable to do anything herself. Her chest bleeding it ran down her ribs and onto her skirts; flaying in the wind; it looked like she was some sort of bleeding ghostly apparition the whole thing now split down the middle. All she was on view. Not that Kalista cared she watched as again Barakan grappled with the Witch. She screamed

"B a r a k a n." As she watched the Witch reach up at him and grab either side of his head; piercing his flesh just missing his eyes. More of blood running down his skin. The witch screamed.

"You cannot kill me; you kill yourself." He snarled spitting at her.

"Do you think I care? It is empty life I will not endure any longer. Know this witch by the end of today we will both be dead." Kalista could hear his words; all of the pain she'd been forced to endure, it hurt more than anything physical.

"Barakan; no, please no." Kalista strained against the invisible ties that held her high. Barakan pulled at the Witches hair ripping the snakes from her head as they cut him again and again. He was gaining he could feel the difference in her already weakened frame. But her venom raged its way through him too. The Witch ripped at his face again as she wriggled from his grip. Turning on him. She looked like a demon possessed there was nothing female about her now. Lowering himself to all fours again Barakan stalked her; glancing momentarily at Kalista. *I will love you always.* He knew what he was about now before he weakened too much. His bristles rose and fell frantically. The Witch raised her finger again to try and hold him. But they were of no use now he stopped her; his decision had been made and he knew there was no more power in her which could continue to control him. He was in love with Kalista and would give up his life for her. Hers was so much more important than his. Kalista sobbed and yelled splayed out in air.

"No Barakan; she can have me, I will die for you. Please Rak. I love you." Her words were furious and frantic hardly making sense; and she kept going. Barakan's heart filled with pride for her. *You can have a normal life my love. Nothing else matters now.* He flung himself furiously at the Witch; whom he'd never called by name but now he would in death. He managed with difficulty to grab at her arms his large feet holding her legs and his clawed hands piercing her shoulders and his palms her arm. She screamed and spat and flayed bout as much as she could but without her magic holding him she was not a match for him.

"Bastard. You always were an idiot."

"Bitch! Go meet your lecherous perverted brother." The Witch felt his scorching breath against her flesh. "Bastard." She would not give up easily. Hanging over her; Barakan raised his lips barring vicious teeth, his saliva running from them. He could still hear Kalista in the background screaming. *You are my heart.* He couldn't stop repeating his love.. His love. She had become his very reason.

"Eudorous I would die for her as will you." Without hesitation Barakan snapped into the Witches neck. Grasping at her throat with his teeth before pulling his head back without relinquishing his grip. A sudden burning sensation took the Witch into surprised darkness. Blood sprayed immediately everywhere; thick smelly mud like blood. It stuck to Barakan's fur and dripped from his lips. Then as it slowed and stopped spraying it just ran along the ground away from both of them. But Barakan did not move or loosen his grip on her. *She is a Witch.* He had to be sure she was gone before he loosened his grip. Spitting what was left of her from his lips. He decided on a another course of action. Dropping his muzzle to her chest it would cave easily she wasn't much more than skin and bone. Opening his mouth against her chest he again bit down and pushing his teeth further into her chest he smashed his way through her ribs; what was left anyway, searching for her heart. Ripping it from her ribs. Shaking it between his teeth he felt it's beat then as he bit down harder he felt the vibration finally stop.

"Kalista!" Fast with his last energies he turned to see her begin to fall. Knowing if the Witch was dead her magic would fail. Kalista would fall. But he couldn't move quite fast enough. He watched as she fell. Dragging his huge frame as fast as he could Barakan just caught her head in his hands so she didn't crack it on the floor but the rest of her did with a thud.

"Aa." She hurt; Kalista winded couldn't move or talk at first. But her wide eyes red and sore just stared him. Her voice hoarse from screaming all she could manage was a whisper.

"Rak." He was laid out besides her; her head in his hands. He desperately kept his claws from catching her. He grumbled at her.

"My love." Kalista dragged her little bleeding body to him. She needed to be close.

"Rak. You did it! She is gone?"

"Yes. My darling we did." He allowed his head to drop to the floor. Something felt more than different; it felt wrong. But he refused to accept it right at this moment. He knew without the Witch alive his time on this earth had to be limited and he was hurt but it was the amount of venom she pumped in him that was causing the problem. Everything was on fire and the sickness it was causing was sweeping through him at too fast a pace. Kalista took the bottom of her ripped dress and wiped at his face trying to get rid of the awfulness which was covering him. The Witches blood; Kalista could not look at her empty wizened body, the crows and the beast of the forest could have her. The only person that mattered right now was Barakan.

"My love you shouldn't."

"Kalista Sch… I would not have a half life with you; I could not force that on you." Kalista's voice pitched up a tone.

"Since when has any of what we achieved been a half life? It was tender and special and oh my God." Barakan's breathing changed and it became raspy and he was wheezing. His lungs where collapsing. "Rak. Don't do this to me… You have made me whole you as you are my; God do you not know how much i love you." She began again to cry massive tears streaming down her face. They fell on his face one after another. Barakan didn't want the last thing he tasted to be her tears.

"Kalista. Sch. You shouldn't cry for me I have lived too long already this is not how I would have you live either. So be good and be quiet I am loved that is all that matters now. But I would take a kiss from you."

"Rak." She sobbed but without question bent her face to his and laid her lips on his. She could immediately feel his distress his breathing more than laboured. He was leaving her. """No no Rak don't you dare. **No** no no."

"Sch." Lifting his hand Barakan managed to wrap his digits; claws and all into her hair and holding her tight pushed her harder to his lips just allowing his tongue to sweep across her lips. His own special kiss just for her. "I promise you my love all will be good for you. You go live a good life and leave all this sickness behind. It is done." She cried and sobbed not hearing the footsteps coming up behind her. As Barakan had told him it had ended as expected. Kalista was ok she was alive looked a bit worse for wear but her body would heal not so much her mind. Andrew faltered tears filling his own eyes. This much genuine love he hadn't expected; it had been hard just staying in the shadows watching not that he had seen all that has transpired but he'd seen enough to know either one of them would have given up on life for the other. It was heart wrenching. But what was done was finished for the very best of reasons, love. And he had promised Barakan who seemed to know this was how it would end. He'd known all along that in killing the Witch would mean his demise; he had just been too irrevocably tied to her. In life but not in death and he had done it. Andrews prayed that it wasn't all the end for her too. This lovely little thing cradling the beast of a man; who had been reminded what his heart was for.

"My lady." He stuttered. "We." Barakan looked at Andrew with green eyes. Andrew was shocked he'd never seen his real eyes. "My lord." He felt he should say something. "You have achieved all you needed to." Kalista without turning to look at Andrew couldn't help but retort nastily.

"No. How could either of you think this was well done. He's he's …" She couldn't bring herself to say the words. Her breasts hanging into Barakan. He gentle tried to nuzzle her.

"Kalista you should not shout at Andrew he is going to help you"

"But I want you. Just you." Barakan struggled his chest was beginning to feel like a great weight was leaning on it beginning to crush the air from his very lungs. He needed her gone.

"Kalista; go with Andrew." She seemed to cling on to him even tighter of which Barakan found he was grateful off he knew it was the end his lungs were not moving they were shrinking in on him. "Kalista know I am yours always you must go with Andrew promise me." She could hear the change in his voice and the noises coming from the back of his throat realising he couldn't breath. "Promise!" She knew there was no time left to argue; laying her lips on his again she whimpered.

"I promise."

"And always know I loved you." He started to sweep his tongue again over her lips but it didn't finish. Barakan breathed out then nothing. He never again breathed in. He was gone. Kalista didn't move at first just held her lips against his willing him to breath. But he didn't. She did nothing didn't move didn't speak. Tears silently streamed down her face. But she didn't move. Andrew put his hand on her shoulder hanging on tight.

"My lady we have to go now." She shook her head unwilling to let him go. But Andrew knew it was important for them to go and fast. "My lady we need to go now. It has always been dark magic that filled them both you have saved him from it and his soul is now released but the dark magic will come to her. We **have** to go." Kalista didn't move as if she hadn't heard; Andrew couldn't allow her to ignore him. His thoughts now turned to Charles maybe he should have come he could just have lifted her from Barakan. Pulling his long coat from his shoulder Andrew covered her first dropping it around her shoulders. Before bending to take her arm and he pulled. "My lady, now!" She finally turned her face to him full of so much pain and silent screams.

She allowed Andrew to pull her to her feet. Finally relinquishing her hold on Barakan. But her feet didn't want to move.

"Rak... We can't just leave him." Andrew thought he understood.

"We won't my lady. Charles and his son will come and get him. We cannot carry him. You will have a grave. I will make sure of that he deserves one." Andrew meant that. He had always had a different opinion to Charles. But the nightmare had ended and Barakan had ended it. That had to be worthwhile. Kalista though her silence worried him.

The next few days and what happened where nothing but a blur to Kalista... She'd stayed with Andrew at first but had complained and sobbed; inconsolable, she wanted to go to the cavern she wanted to be near Rak. But eventually worried about her she had been sedated; she'd no idea what with, but didn't care. They waited until they believed she had calmed down. But Kalista didn't think that would ever happen. Everything was so cold and empty; there was even less now than before without him. But then Andrew had given her Barakan's letter... he'd given her his lands his home and monies. She knew where to find everything. It suddenly felt all important for Kalista to see him one last time. She'd not said goodbye. But then with

Andrew's statement had made her livid and they had one hell of a row; she'd asked to see his body… They had already buried him; or so they'd said. Unable to leave him… She had been present but too doped up she didn't remember. How could she forget? Something about his words felt false. *Do you lie to me?* But what else could she do now? It was so hard to understand she would just blank it out; and found it impossible to get her head around. But had to believe them there was no choice for her now. His grave was on his lands at the manor which was now hers. So her decision to go there was easy.

*"Rak."*

# Epilogue

It had been a long day Kalista still couldn't see a way through without him. Her heart and soul just felt so empty. Only a month had passed and she had tried to be brave. When all she wanted to do was lie on their bed; now just hers. Andrew and Charles has paid a large amount of men and women; the manor was quickly put into some sort of order, she had made her decision and stayed put much to Charles Chagrin but Andrew was with her all the way on this point. It had been a good home once and with some work could be again. Which they'd set about doing, they still worked on things daily and it had took almost a week to gather what were now her belongings from the cavern. Kalista has insisted that there had to be a way. She did not want new items she wanted what had been his belongings. All she wanted to do was surround herself with him. The sheets from the bed she had refused to let be laundered and the now laid across the bottom of the bed. She covered herself in them at night they still smelled of him and she desperately needed that closeness. But there were many frowns and raised eyebrows at her behaviour. But they didn't know what had transpired the only two who did were Andrew and Charles; and Charles was fast loosing patience that was very noticeable. Not so much

Andrew; he seemed to be wanting to say something but never quite getting there. Kalista saw him as a strange man. He had secrets too, but they didn't really affect her and she wasn't over concerned; until a month ago she didn't know him. Now they seemed to be her only friends. Her dreams were varied and sensual all she could find of Barakan was in there. The only nightmare which plagued her now was his demise… The Witch had taken all from her.

Or so she thought. Andrew kept his fingers crossed. Only time would tell. There was so much more that he could impart but didn't she wasn't ready to hear not yet. He didn't want to tip her over the edge. Hope wasn't always well accepted in the face of such dreadful facts. But she didn't know that grace was…

Kalista climbed out the bath; wrapped herself in the drying sheet and strolled over to her bed; flopping down on it. *It's not the same as the pool! Rak.* Her thoughts betrayed her feelings as much as the longing in her body. Something in her had been alighted and just would not subside. Then a noise a banging door made her listen harder. "Andrew?" She knew right now he would be paying the casual workers for the days shift and passing out orders for the next. Someone must have slammed a door. She ignored it.

*I will always love you.* Were all the thoughts

which had spun around his head. His breathing so very laboured and momentarily painful which felt like his breath was being squashed from him by knifes; but then it did stop and all was still. But then as if he had been suddenly shook violently he began to gag Barakan had found himself spewing up blood and all types of shit. Hanging his head low till it had subsided. Which seemed to take hours. He looked for her his adorable Kalista but she was nowhere. Her scent still lingered but she must have left immediately, which was what he had made sure Andrews knew. It was not every day one died. But he still loved her his memory of her still acute. Barakan didn't look at himself he just lay; there was no rush for him. She was gone; safe. That was all that mattered. The Witch was gone dead and now could no longer curse him. Nor control him. Slowly as the hours passed by he decided he ought to move. Dying had made him feel very different. It was then that he noticed...

It hadn't been an immediate change but gradual.. he waited and the days were just too long. He could not take it; this was one of the hardest times of his life. If he lost her now he would be dead.

Charging through the forest knowing exactly where he was heading not as quick as before but he still wasn't incapable his long strong limbs made light work of the miles and his eagerness to get to her helped.

Then the house came into view Looking so much better than he had seen it last. The sun going down behind it.

"Kalista." His eagerness took over and he began to run covering the distance easily forcing his legs to go faster the nearer he got. A few people still mulling about looked at him strangely. Not knowing who he was. Just a stranger to them. But he didn't give them time to stop and question him he just kept going. Throwing a sort of snarl their way. Making sure they did not try to interrupt his quest. Charging forward he pushed the heavy front door open and without any kind of forethought just stepped in; no hesitation. Andrew stood at the bottom of the wide staircase handing a portly looking man money; just stared at the stranger in the doorway, tall and broad not so well groomed but man. His shirt loose not tucked into the waistband of his trousers; hair long and covering his eyes. The skin on his face flushed; obviously he'd been running and a distance by the looks. The stranger flayed his hands frantically. Barakan snarled.

"Andrew where is she?" Andrew gobsmacked just stared. "Andrew?" Barakan didn't have time for explanation's. Andrew pointed up the stairs. *Wow. It is you.* Glee sweeping through him. His hope had paid off. Barakan mounted the stairs two and three at a time. Swinging the first door he came to open. *No... Kalista.* He breathed in waiting for a moment for her smell to tell him where. It did. Quickly he moved to her door. Then he shoved and the door opened banging heavily on its hinges as he stepped in. The beast in him still as rushed and tactless as ever. His eyes searching for her. *Kalista.*

He had found her. Laid out on the end of the bed just a drying sheet round her. Barakan stifled his growl. Kalista's head shot up. And she glared at him. *What the hell. Who?* Her shock showed.

"What the? Who are you?" She pulled the sheet tighter around herself as she stood up from the bed. This man was invading her space. But something about him made every hair she owned stand on end and her very being scream she squinted at him. *Who?* His long black hair hung over his face and eyes; obscuring everything. *If you brushed your hair once in a while people may see your face. Black hair!* But she could see he was sweaty had obviously been running and what she could see of his face was flushed. Something made her take a step closer. Barakan couldn't stop his body reacting his skin felt like it was on fire his erection jumping to immediate arousal. But she looked so thin; her eyes sunken into their sockets sore still. *You have cried today! You still cry.* It made his heart sing to know she still grieved yet he'd wanted more from her; more strength. Both just stared held in an impossibility. Or so she believed; finally Barakan broke the silence.

"Kalista." *My God he knows my name.* But still the penny didn't drop. Kalista scowled. A look Barakan knew.

"Who are you? What are you doing in my rooms? I will shout for my men."

"You can shout all you like but it won't do **you** any good." He smiled showing so many healthy white teeth. Yet there was something about him that was familiar. Kalista gasped. *Who?* None of this was making sense. *Who?* What was going to happen now? *Rak Rak I need you; I.* Then she watched as the stranger lifted a hand to his hair and running his fingers into it brushed it evenly away from his face and she saw his eyes. Her legs turned to jelly and she felt suddenly so very dizzy. Her eyes twitched, She swayed; knowledge banging into her. Hard.

"R…" She couldn't speak his name. Just in case all this was make believe and just her mind playing tricks. Delusions. "God I'm delusional." She grabbed at the bed post with one hand whilst trying to keep a hold of the sheet with the other.

"You don't believe that." Barakan flashed his eyes at her. Mostly beautiful green but there; there was the red too. She saw and this time slumped against the bed almost falling. But he was there next to her grabbing to stop her falling; his strong hands wound around her waist. She felt so very good. Kalista couldn't breath she just held onto the bed post still marked and carved where his claws had dug in she looked from them to this man and his hands. *No claws.* Her sheet began to slip. But Kalista couldn't do anything to stop it. She moved up his healthy frame with her eyes finally coming to rest on his. He held her look; beautiful eyes that she knew. Shakily she tried to speak.

"I. I." Was all she could manage; She really was struggling to get her head around this. "You can't be…"

"Who says?"

"I buried you." Barakan raised his eyebrows in amusement.

"Nope… Don't know who you buried but it wasn't me."

"But they told me."

"Andrew?" Barakan understood; the old guy could be conniving.

"I don't understand. I saw you… oh my God." Tears began to well again.

"Maybe Kalista you above all should know that things are not always as they seem. Looks to me like you have spent too much time crying." She shut her eyes trying to regain the control she was loosing.

"I. Barakan." She managed to say his name. "Is it you?" Barakan let out a quiet low growl which had Kalista holding her breath; pulling his shirt open and grabbing at her small hand he held it against his chest. Kalista could feel a heart beat thumping away healthily. Barakan lowered his head to whisper in her ear. His hot earthy breath whistling across her face.

"Look at me little one." Slowly with much effort afraid that none of this was real Kalista lifted her eyelids. She saw him the man. The same eyes from the painting; but ones she'd known, and the rest of him, her eyes drifted to her own hand resting on his chest; his finely toned muscles flinching. A line of soft black hair tracing around his nipples and then a finer line down she lowered her eyes. *Clothes!* Barakan leaned into her and slowly with tender care licked her neck running it down her throat. Growling. "It is me Kalista. I promised I could never leave you." A sob escaped her. And finally the floodgates opened and acknowledgment.

"Rak."

"Yes little one it is me. I'm here." Nuzzling into her neck he kissed it. Finally he could kiss her. "Kalista. I have missed you so much. I could not have left you not even in death. I love you. But I could not say.. it could have ended so differently."

"Rak." Her words hardly audible between the sobs. *It is you.* Barakan traced a line across her face and to her lips. Halting himself; this was a first, kissing her. But the beast still there grumbled. *Get on with it man.* Barakan smiled.. Both man and beast loved her and she loved them as a whole, it had been her love, her love that had saved them. Something the Witch nor the curse had banked on… Love. As first with his tongue he drew it across her lips. Kalista shook and groaned.

"Rak… Kiss me." He licked at her again. Reminding himself.

"Oh I intend to little one. All over." His lips touched hers so tender and gentle. Kalista moaned melting under his touch. Lips lips lips. *He has lips.* She moved hers on his. Gingerly at first but then she knew it was him and he was still the same. Outwardly his appearance may be different but he was still in there man and beast. Her kiss intensified as did his and Barakan groaned her name.

"Kalista." His hands tried to find her but couldn't the drying sheet trapped between them. It hadn't slipped far just cosseted her nipples. Grabbing it in his powerful hands Barakan pulled it free and threw it from them. She was naked. Coming up for air Kalista looked at him ogling all she was. Not that she cared. *This is different.* She smiled.

"What?" Barakans chest heaved as he breathed

so heavy.

“This is different.”

“What is?”

“Me being naked and you wearing clothes.” He grinned as sweeping her into his strong arms threw her on the bed.

“I can soon remedy that.” Kalista watched as he slid his shirt from his torso and quickly stepped out his breeches his huge erection pointing directly at her. Licking her lips seductively Kalista recognised all he was.

“This is for real Rak not some cruel rouse?”

“No it is real; I am real and about to show you how real.” He had waited too long to taste her the beast wasn’t bothered about foreplay. But there was no need both loved and Kalista was burning for him. He could smell her want and he had always wanted her from the minute he had set eyes on her. He crawled up and over her dragging his body against hers as he did; touch was no problem now. He wrapped his hands into her wet hair. *I am going to touch her.*

“I will never leave you again my love.” Barakan lowered his face to hers and began to kiss her as Kalista began to gyrate; lavishing attention on her lips. He allowed his tongue to explore her pushing it between her lips; her groan vibrating through his mouth, he found hers and teased it. Leaning into her just enough to feel the heat she emitted; stunning. He knew he couldn't wait much longer she wasn't the only one wet.

"God I want you." She eyed him back; an almost unreadable look. Her lips swollen and pouting from his attention.

"And I have always wanted you both man and beast." This pleased the beast in him Barakans eyes flashed red… staying that way. Kalista pulled at his long hair as it fell across his shoulders needing him to stop talking. "But what I want is to touch all of you till you scream my sweet." She coughed. Feeling he meant it. His hands untangled from her hair were already cupping her healthy breasts. He fondled and touched kneading his fingers into her. Then he dropped his head to them and began to lick her something she knew. Sucking first one nipple into his mouth and drawing his teeth over her then the other. She moaned loudly her gyrating building. Barakan knew her desire but he wanted much more from tonight; he wanted it all. There was something first though. Sitting up from her his face full of loving lust.

"Roll over." She tilted her head at him; he growled a little repeating himself. "Roll over." She did. Barakan groaned loudly. Not caring who heard.

Laying himself over her he started at her shoulders licking and kissing her; his hands following touching every bit of her that he knew. He felt his erection and the beast complaining but he would have this. *It is the first time I have touched her without knowing I would hurt her. I am going to enjoy her.* And he was and giving her enjoyment. Barakan could hear her mewing into the mattress. Kneeling over her he reached her lovely supple behind. He laid his hands on her and before she realised what he was about had grabbed both her ankles and pulled her abruptly to the end of the bed. “Stand.” She did; Barakan kneeling behind her nipped into her behind; she yelped. “Kalista.” Now she wasn’t the only one mewing. He buried his face in her she squealed again louder. As his tongue found the core of her desire; he kissed licked and nibbled at her till they were both in a frenzy. “Kalista.” Laying his large hands on the small of her back he pushed; bending her torso back onto the bed.

“God woman. I love you.” He drew his hands over her fiery folds and carefully with his fingers. *Fingers.* Watched as he toyed with her little bundle of nerves. Kalista had never experienced this. She wanted him to quench the ache he was creating. *Fingers.* Which made her shake with need.

“Rak!” She buried her face into the blankets; trying to stifle her noise... Then as Barakan watched he pushed his digit to find the desire he wanted, sliding it into her, he was engulfed. He watched as she tensed; drawing his finger from her before returning it followed closely by a second. He groaned too as she moaned into the mattress. His fingers claiming her. Her hips began to move against him. Barakan could see that her orgasm was building within her; his own sex pulsating for her. He leaned into her and again nipped at her behind pulling more noise from her. Barakan stood looking at her splayed before him. He could just imagine sliding into her.

"Kalista sit up." Panting heavily Kalista did as he bid and sat on the end of the bed. Her whole body shaking; her face flushed not unlike his. As she watched Barakan take a hold of himself and run his fingers along its length as she watched mesmerised by his sensuality. He was proving his fingers were so much more once again. Her own desire flaring Kalista leaned forward and stretching her arm out put her hand over his; squeezing. Barakan moved forward and pushing her knees apart with his legs got closer. She knew what he wanted. Grasping him tighter she pushed his hand away. She was lost in desire. He glistened at her wet too. Barakan felt her hot wet lips immediately sucking him in hard. His legs began to shake; she knew exactly now what he enjoyed. Her tongue flicked at him as she drew him in and out. She could taste his saltiness. Lavishing more attention on him. He thrust unable to control himself he wanted her… He snarled

"Stop. I cannot… I." Bending to her he kissed her hard. "Lay down." Inching herself back up their bed her chest heaving with every heavy drawn breath lips glistening at him. She waited. Kalista was safe; he was safe. It was all done. Barakan climbed on the bed beside her it dipped under his weight as he crawled up her body. Panting himself. In a sultry hoarse voice he watched her reaction as he spoke.

"Hang on." She licked her lips and purred at him.

"I already was." Barakan leaned into her sliding his own sex against hers running it's hot silky length through hers. So hot and wet. Taking a hold of himself he guided the tip to where it needed to be watching enthralled by all she was; as he carefully entered her. Kalista gasped… Barakan thrust again; needing to see. He watched as she took him into her body. *Oh my* ... His thoughts were lost in pleasure. He pushed again giving into her as she ground against him. She had him. Man and beast alike couldn't stop now. Grabbing at her hair Barakan pinned her to the bed; as his thrusts grew he lowered his lips to hers.

"My God woman I love you. I will never be able to get enough of you."

"Good." She bit into his bottom lip and pulled

enticing him further.

"You will make me lose control. He is still there." She knew exactly what he meant and wanted them both; all or nothing.

"That is my aim Rak. All or nothing…" *My words*. "Rak Love me…" He began to move his hips with more force… As Kalista groaned at him her own orgasm rising.

"Harder." Fiercely Barakan kissed her devouring all she was as he pounded into her lost in her love. Both man and beast shared the sensuality of her and they would love her always.

With a force that neither could have known existed they exploded into orgasm which fiercely burned in both pushing them from the cliff where they had been waiting anxiously. They fell into it together… Kalista screaming his name.

"Rak." As Barakan threw his head back and the beast showed he was still there and howled loudly. His whole body stiffening as if paralysed. He had claimed her for his. For now and always. He was home.

The End.

# *List of other books by the author*

**The Magic Blood Inheritance.**

To Pledge a Prophecy. Book 1

To Reveal the Prophecy. Book 2.

To Fulfil the Prophecy. Book 3.

**The Chronicles of Araceli.**

Listen. Book 1.

Promises and Lies. Book 2.

Don't Break Me. Book 3.

Misfortune Broken. Book 4.,

**Stand-alone.**

Veiled Destiny.

Printed in Poland
by Amazon Fulfillment
Poland Sp. z o.o., Wrocław

61597867R00197